Bittersweet Creek

Books by Sally Kilpatrick

The Happy Hour Choir

Bittersweet Creek

Better Get to Livin'
(coming soon!)

Published by Kensington Publishing Corporation

Bittersweet Creek

Sally Kilpatrick

KENSINGTON BOOKS
www.kensingtonbooks.com

KENSINGTON BOOKS are published by

Kensington Publishing Corp.
119 West 40th Street
New York, NY 10018

Copyright © 2015 by Sally Kilpatrick

All Kensington titles, imprints, and distributed lines are available at special quantity discounts for bulk purchases for sales promotion, premiums, fund-raising, educational, or institutional use.

Special book excerpts or customized printings can also be created to fit specific needs. For details, write or phone the office of the Kensington Sales Manager: Kensington Publishing Corp., 119 West 40th Street, New York, NY 10018. Attn. Sales Department. Phone: 1-800-221-2647.

Kensington and the K logo Reg. U.S. Pat. & TM Off.

eISBN-13: 978-1-61773-571-4
eISBN-10: 1-61773-571-X
First Kensington Electronic Edition: November 2015

ISBN-13: 978-1-61773-570-7
ISBN-10: 1-61773-570-1
First Kensington Trade Paperback Printing: November 2015

10 9 8 7 6 5 4 3 2 1

Printed in the United States of America

THE SATTERFIELDS

Benjamin Satterfield (1825–1874)
    1848—Married Sarah (1830–1861)
        Louisa (1860–1917)
    1863—Married Alma (1840–1923)
        Benjamin, Jr. (1864–1932)
        Sallie (1866–1966)
        Otis (1867–1874)
        Ruth (1870–1961)
        John Thomas (1871–1953)

Benjamin Satterfield, Jr (1864–1932)
    1886—Married Rose (1870–1962)
        Daisy (1886–1899)
        Benjamin III (1888–1944)
        Homer (1892–1940)
        Wisteria (1893–1961)
        Floyd (1894–1918)
        Myron (1900–1987)
        Lily (1902–1918)

Benjamin Satterfield III (1888–1944)
    1910—Married Opal (1896–1911)
        Benjamin, IV (1911)
    1913—Married Octavia (1890–1947)
        Robert (1915–1985)
        Calvin (1916–1918)
        Lucille (1919–1986)
        Geneva (1922)
        George (1925–2001) and Herbert (1925–1980)

Robert (1915–1985)
    1939—Married Lela (1925–2005)
        Joy (1940–)
        Glenda (1942–)
        Carol Ruth (1943)
        Nancy (1946–2003)

Sandra (1949–)
Bonita (1950–)
Hank (1953–)

Hank (1953–present)
1983—Married Rosemary (1964–1997)
Romy (1985–present)

THE McELROYS

Shaymus Magilroy (1830–1899)
1859—Married Janie (1845–1942) and divorced her in 1866
James (1860–1874)
Luke (1861–1918)
1867—Married Ruby (1850–1873)
Robert (1868–1918)
Jeb (1870–1932)
Stonewall Jackson (1872–1885)
1874—Married Sarah (1848–1912)
Euler (1874–1918)

Luke (1861–1918)
1880—Married Sarah (1866–1884)
Leroy (1881–1894)
Ruth (1882–1947)
Esther (1883–1984)
John (1894)
1886—Married Virginia (1860–1918)
South America (1888–1909)
Christopher Columbus (1890–1977)
George Washington (1893–1945)
John Adam (1896–1982)
Cuba (1898–1990)
California (1900–1948)
Dakota (1902–1918)
Grover (1905)

Christopher Columbus MacElroy (1890–1977)
1908—Married Eunice (1892–1911)
Jasper (1908-1909)
1912—Married Sarah (1895–1957)
Siller (1914–1918)
R. C. (1917–1963)
Houston (1919–1945)
Effie (1920–1922)
Exie (1923–1975)
A. T. (1925–1928)

R. C. McElroy (1917–1963)
1935—Married Martha (1913–1950)
Stillborn baby (1935)
Martha (1936–2010)
Mary (1937–1978)
Matthew (1938–1992)
Mark (1940–1990)
Luke (1942)
John (1943–)
Magdalene (1945–)

Matthew McElroy (1938–1992)
1955—Married Louise (1938–2001)
Curtis (1955–)
Charles (1957–)
Carol (1958–)
Cheryl (1960–1967)
Callie (1962–)
R. C. (1964–)

Curtis McElroy (1955–present)
1979—Married Janice (1960–1980)
1985—Married Debbie (1966–present)
Julian (1985–present)

Bittersweet Creek

Julian

I was minding my own business, trying to figure out how many shifts I'd have to take at the dealership to keep the farm afloat, when I saw the Porsche barreling straight for me. Shiny silver, it mesmerized me to the point where I didn't realize the driver wasn't going to stop despite the fact that I was clearly in the middle of the crosswalk.

And then, asphalt.

Well, Julian, if you're going to be run over by a car, it might as well be expensive.

"Oh, my God, I am so, so sorry."

That voice sounded familiar.

"Don't ever apologize, dear. It might be a legal liability."

That voice didn't.

"Julian?"

I shot to my feet, hardly registering the stiffness or the jolt of pain that ran down my right leg, the one I'd injured playing high school baseball. Today was the day I'd finally run into Romy. Or the day she had finally run into me.

I couldn't tell if it was the sun or a possible head injury that made a sort of halo shine off her dark, glossy hair. I kept blinking, thinking I'd see her in an old concert tee and cutoffs, but, no, she was wearing designer jeans and a form-hugging shirt scooped low enough for me to see the tops of her breasts. She raked straightened hair behind her ear with meticulously manicured fingernails.

It was like looking at Romy's evil twin sister.

"Romy, darling, don't you think you should move out of the middle of the road? It would appear he's unharmed." A dark-haired man leaned against the passenger door like he owned the damn car, which he probably did.

She registered the honking horns and the two lines of blocked traffic about the same time I did. She'd thrown me into the opposite lane and we stood there, blocking traffic going one way while the Porsche blocked traffic coming from the other direction.

"If you're sure you're okay, I'd better move," she murmured as she turned.

Something about seeing her walk away so casually caused a lump to form in my throat. "Aren't you going to introduce me?"

Cars honked. Someone speculated long and loud on our ancestry.

"Richard, this is"—she hesitated—"Julian, an old friend. Julian, this is my boyfriend, Richard."

Boyfriend. I knew I didn't like him for some reason.

Sirens wailed as the Yessum County Sheriff skidded into the intersection. "For the love of God, Julian, get out of the middle of the road!"

Len Rogers loved that bullhorn. I had a suggested location for it.

"Do you need for me to call an ambulance?" Len spoke slowly, enunciating each word.

"Hell, no."

"Good. Both of you. Over there. In front of the café."

Romy jerked the Porsche into one of the spaces along the curb on Main Street. I crossed the street, willing my injured leg not to limp. We congregated under the awning of the jewelry store beside the café, and the boyfriend decided to speak.

"Officer, I'm not sure what the proper procedure is, but we will cooperate to the best—"

"Oh, Richard, it's Len. I went to school with him." Romy sighed.

Len adopted his Barney Fife stance, puffing up to show his importance despite Romy's casual dismissal. He reached into his back pocket to take out his notepad, then licked the tip of one finger before he flipped through carbons to get to the first clean page. "Now what happened?"

"I didn't realize there was a new traffic light, and I accidentally ran it."

"Rosemary, you don't—"

She turned on her boyfriend with a raised eyebrow. "I made a mistake. I'm admitting it."

Len looked me up and down once more, no doubt trying to assess if I needed a doctor. "What about you, McElroy?"

"I got the 'walk' sign, started walking."

Len nodded, then went back to his notepad, biting his tongue as he wrote. Next he drew out a ticket book. He hastily scribbled a ticket and ripped it off with a flourish. "This one's yours for running a red light."

He scribbled again before ripping one out for me. "And this here ticket's for jaywalking."

Blood pumped behind my ears. "That's a load of horseshit."

"Hush up and go on down to the courthouse and pay that five dollars. You were a good three feet out of the crosswalk. If you don't knock it off, we'll add obstruction of justice."

"Okay, now that—" Richard started to speak, but Romy clamped down on his upper arm to silence him.

"Is that it, Len? I'm really sorry for the fuss," she said.

He smiled and tipped his hat. "That's enough. Thank you." He took two steps away before turning on his heel and coming right back.

"No, that is not enough. Now, look here, you two." He pointed his billy club first at me and then at Romy. "Things have been right peaceful since *you* went off to Vanderbilt, and I will have no shenanigans in my town. You got that?"

Romy and I looked at each other. I drank in the face I hadn't seen in almost ten years. It was a little more angular and slathered in expensive makeup, but she was still Romy and still beautiful.

"I'm sorry, officer, but what are you talking about?" Richard asked, bringing me back to the present.

"These two are troublemakers. Come from a whole long line of 'em. Satterfields and McElroys. I thought we'd got past the worst of it when they got together in high school, then this one"—he pointed to Romy—"up and ran off to Nashville."

He pointed the club at me. "And this one went on a few benders, but I've just about got him straightened out."

Romy's mossy-green eyes darted to me, her eyebrows bunched with concern.

"Got together in high school?" Richard echoed.

So, Romy hasn't told her new boy toy everything.

She turned to him. "Julian was the guy I was engaged to." She leveled those eyes back on me, daring me to contradict her.

That's part of the story.

"And I don't care why you're back or what happened between the two of you." Len leveled his billy club at Richard for the first time. "I don't even care who *you* are. If you cause any trouble around here, I will throw the book at you. Each and every one of you."

"Surely—" Richard began, but Len had already started ambling back to his cruiser with his exaggerated John Wayne walk.

"Well, good to see you again, Romy." I went to tip my hat only to realize it was still in the middle of Main Street getting run over repeatedly. That figured.

"Julian," she muttered.

"Nice to meet you, Julian, even if it wasn't in the best of circumstances," Richard said with a bland smile as he extended his hand.

His grip was surprisingly strong, causing me to study his face once more. He seemed familiar, but I couldn't quite place where I'd seen him before.

I kinda wanted to punch the smug smile off his face, but I didn't have cause. It looked like he was taking good care of her, and I'd given up any such claims long ago. If this was the man she wanted, who was I to stand in her way? I glanced at the Porsche as she slid into the driver's seat and Richard closed the door behind him. I sure as hell could never get her a car like that.

She jerked into traffic, and I bit back a smile. She still couldn't drive a stick for nothing. The vanity plate said PARIS1, and I frowned. That's where I'd seen him before. He was one of the Parises of Nashville, and they were lawyers and politicians all of them. Romy was dating one of the richest men in Tennessee.

And there were a lot of things she wasn't telling him.

Romy

"So that's the infamous Julian who broke your heart, eh?"

I didn't care for Richard's tone of voice, and I couldn't believe I'd been stupid enough not to see the new traffic light. First, I'd been distracted by the charred shell of what had been the Merle Norman store. Then, I'd fumbled with the clutch and the brakes on Richard's car. I still couldn't really drive a manual, but Richard had insisted I drive since I knew the way home.

Home. My heart clenched as I looked at the rows of cotton blurring together on either side of the car. His ridiculous sports car purred down the country road that led out of town to the farm where I'd grown up. Home meant fields and pastures, winding country roads.

And Julian.

Of all the idiots on all the roads in all the world, why did Julian have to walk in front of the car I was driving? I wasn't ready to see him. Logically, I knew I'd never make it through the entire summer without running into him, but I had hoped to prolong the inevitable for as long as possible. So much for that.

Seeing him lying on the ground had been a gut punch. First, I was afraid I'd hurt him. Then, I was hoping I'd hurt him because he'd definitely hurt me. But then those long eyelashes had fluttered and he'd trained those confused baby blues on me. Same wavy blond hair, same thin white scar on his chin—and same lost feeling when I saw him.

"Hello, earth to Rosemary!" Richard chuckled. "You okay over there?"

I summoned a smile for him. "Yeah, I'm just rattled, I guess."

"Almost running over someone or seeing Julian?"

"Both." The truth came out before I could stop it. I glanced over to Richard. He had the profile of a Greek god with a straight nose, strong chin, and firm lips. I'd once lost an entire twenty minutes of Western Civ comparing his profile with that of my textbook photo of Bernini's *Apollo and Daphne*. When Richard asked me out after class, I took it as a sign. No man had ever distracted me from class—not even Julian.

"I wish I'd punched him," Richard said.

But punching wasn't his style. Like the Greeks, he placed a high premium on philosophy, logic, and reason. He tended to use words and the law as his weapons of choice.

And that's why you should tell him about your predicament.

I should, but I wasn't going to. Satterfields cleaned up their own messes. Besides, what Richard didn't know wouldn't hurt him. He was dropping me off at home then traveling back to Nashville. With just the slightest bit of cooperation from Julian, I could have everything taken care of before Richard came back for my birthday.

"Your silence implies you don't want me to punch him. Interesting." His brown eyes bored through me as I guided the car up the hill, trying to give it enough gas to keep it from slipping out of gear.

"No, it's not that." Truly, Julian getting beat up by Richard was a satisfying, if unlikely, image. "He's just not worth your time."

Richard liked that answer and went back to studying the area where I'd grown up. My eyes traveled over to Wanamaker's store and I brought them right back to the road, not wanting to remember the last time I was there. But what did Richard see when he looked at that country store? Or the row of mailboxes on the corner from where an ancestor had decided he wanted his mail to go through one post office instead of another? Should I point out the houses of relatives and friends or the spot where the one-room schoolhouse had been? I couldn't find the words to tell him my mundane stories. What did he think about a place like this when he'd grown up in a mansion in suburban Nashville?

From the minute I pulled into the driveway, he stared in awe at the old farmhouse I called home. "Are you sure you can't stay for a minute? Come in and see my father? Get a drink of water? Maybe a bio break?"

He chuckled. He liked how I had picked up his more polite expression "bio break." There was a time I might've shouted, "But dontcha need to pee?"

"You know I'm running late, and Dad will kill me if I'm not there on time and in a tux." His hand traveled to my cheek, and his dark eyes turned serious. "I'll come back for your birthday when I can stay longer. Between that inexplicable jam just before the river and your sheriff's little production, I have to go now."

I leaned into his palm. He was right. "Are you sure? I don't want you to get tired and end up in an accident."

He kissed me gently. "For you, I will be a model driver. Pop the trunk, and I'll get out your suitcases."

Gentleman that he was, Richard carried my luggage to the porch and then gave me a better kiss to remember him by.

"Be careful." I hugged a banister on the porch and felt the peeling paint crackle beneath my fingers.

"No, you be careful," he countered as he hung on the driver's side door.

"Just a little farmwork," I said with a shrug. "I've done most of it before."

He arched an eyebrow as he often did when cross-examining a witness. "Call me if you need anything. I'm sure there's some-one we could hire to help you with all of this."

It was cute how he waved his hand around. He clearly had no

idea what to do with this foreign place where I'd grown up. Of course, even after all this time, I had only the most rudimentary knowledge of his multi-fork world. I shook my head as he settled into the roadster, but he popped out almost immediately. "And don't turn into Elly May on me, either!"

He eased into the driver's seat then popped out again. "Now, Daisy Duke on the other hand . . ."

"Richard, git on out of here and go to Nashville!" I laughed as I said it then clamped a hand over my mouth as my country-accented words echoed back. I'd worked hard to get rid of my accent. Ten seconds on my own front porch, and it was already seeping out. I'd never hear the end of it if I went back to the inner-city high school where I worked and attempted to teach English with an accent like that. Those hungry sharks would smell blood then eat me alive.

He started the car, blowing me a kiss as he eased down the driveway.

Be careful? How hard could it be?

Julian

I wanted a beer, but I wasn't going to find one of those in Ellery.

Instead I hobbled over to Calais Café for a cup of coffee. I had too much work to do to get rip-roaring drunk even if I made a habit of getting soused, which I no longer did.

As usual, the café was full so I could either wait for a seat or see if there was someone I knew. There Ben sat, half-hidden behind his laptop. A couple of the girls from the tiny local college sneaked glances at him, tittering. Of course it would have been a modern-day *Guess Who's Coming to Dinner?* if they ever brought Ben home to Daddy.

"Saw you almost got flattened out there," Ben said without even looking up.

"That's a neat trick, considering you were sitting here doing whatever it is you do."

"Lawyering. Squealing brakes and expletives have a way of making a man look up." He snapped his laptop closed and moved it to the side. "How you holding up, cowboy?"

"Do you have to call me that?"

"Weren't you just wearing a cowboy hat?"

"Yeah."

"Do you own cows and ride horses?"

"Yeah."

"Then you're a cowboy. Otherwise you would have swallowed your pride, followed Romy to Nashville, told her what a sorry, miserable son of a bitch you are, married her, made pretty babies, and saved us all from your misery."

"Shut up, asshole."

"So that's the best you've got when faced with the truth. I rest my case."

"Yeah, yeah. Why did I come in here to listen to your legalese again?" I leaned back as the waitress poured my coffee and took my order.

"Probably to lick your fresh wounds after being run over by the love of your life. I keep telling you there are other fish in the sea."

"Ellery's more of a pond," I said.

"Well, then maybe you need to swim downstream to the Gulf, find some fish gone wild by the sea." Ben picked up his mug and took a sip.

"Like you have?"

Ben frowned with his mug suspended in midair. I knew why Ben didn't leave. He still blamed himself for putting the grandmother who raised him in a nursing home. She only agreed on the condition she wouldn't have to leave the town where she'd grown up. So Ben had made it through law school and bought one of the pretty old houses on Crook Avenue. His grandmother's dementia prevented her from being proud of how her grandson had made something of himself, but he could be near her. Being in a small town didn't give him a lot of dating options, tittering experimental college students aside.

I kicked myself. "That was low, Ben. Sorry."

"I'm going to strike that from the record." He sat up straighter and grinned because he knew it annoyed me when he spoke like a television lawyer. "I think we can better conduct this conversation tonight at The Fountain. Maybe Beulah could help you forget all about this morning."

I'd heard Beulah could make a man forget about a lot of things if she was willing, but I wasn't. "No, thanks."

"Jay, you have watched every movie in Redbox and at least half of what Netflix streams. You need to get out and live a little because I'm getting tired of having everything we do remind you of a movie."

I had been about to tell him that sitting in a diner booth talking about nothing kinda reminded me of the end of *Chasing Amy*, but I didn't want to prove him right. "It's karaoke night, isn't it?"

Ben grinned. He'd never met a Sinatra song he didn't like. Of course, I knew another karaoke devotee, a certain petite woman with curly black hair and enigmatic green eyes. "You've got me. I want to sing Marvin Gaye and stir up the masses."

"Yeah, I'll go. But this time I'm not singing 'Ebony and Ivory.'"

"Ha! That's what you always say."

I drank deeply from my coffee. If Ben noticed I hadn't been to The Fountain in six months, he wasn't mentioning it. He'd been there the night I busted up the only tavern in a ten-mile radius. Fortunately, Bill, the proprietor of the establishment, was a forgiving sort. Well, that and I'd started paying him back for the damage I'd done.

Might be good to have a beer, though. Just to see who'd show up.

Romy

The front door was locked. I started to knock loudly, but I could see Daddy reading the paper in the kitchen, ignoring me. He had to know I was outside.

Walking around to the back of the farmhouse, I trailed my fingers along the rough pebbled surface of the green shingle siding Granddaddy Satterfield had chosen. He had loved that stuff because it meant he never had to paint again. Granny had thought it the ugliest thing she'd ever seen, but she'd secretly loved it, too, because it gave her something to complain about until the very day she died.

Mercutio, the guard cat, sat on the back step, tail switching. He meowed at the sight of me and started kneading the edge of the concrete stairs, what my granny used to call "making biscuits." I reached down to pat the scruffy gray Persian with the scrunched-up face. "You know you're not supposed to go into the house. Daddy *claims* he's allergic to you."

He mewed piteously and purred as he leaned his head into my hand. My fingers came away wet and warm. His ear was missing a chunk and still bleeding. "Did you get into a fight again?"

I relented and let the cat in as far as the closed-in back porch, bile rising in my throat. Damned McElroy dogs. For as long as I could remember, we Satterfields had owned cats: barn cats, pet cats, and many an adopted throwaway like Mercutio. The McElroys, on the other hand, always had dogs, usually mean ones. I poured out some food for the cat then looked at his ear a little closer. Not as bad as I had first thought, but it still wasn't pretty.

And Len had told *me* to stay out of trouble. Maybe he needed to go talk to the McElroys and tell them to do a better job of tying up their dogs.

I heaved my shoulder into the heavy door that led from the back porch to the kitchen, prepared to tell Daddy about poor Mercutio, but he addressed me first. "Couldn't even make it twenty-four hours, could you?"

My eyes darted to the cordless phone on the table beside his wheelchair where he sat hiding behind the *Ellery Gazette*. He looked like a weird papier-mâché project with only a Memphis Redbirds hat showing above the paper and his full-length leg cast jutting from underneath.

"I got distracted by how the Merle Norman building had burned, didn't see the light, and accidentally ran over Julian."

He folded the paper with as much rustle as he could and my own eyes stared back at me, green Satterfield eyes that squinted with scrutiny. "When you drive, you aren't supposed to be looking at buildings. You're supposed to be looking at the road."

It was hard to look away when the world snatched another piece of your mother, but he wouldn't know that. He wasn't there in the Merle Norman that smelled of mulberries on the day my mother held my hand while they pierced my ears. It was one of the last things we'd done together, and now the place was gone forever.

Shaking away my melancholy, I got a glass from the cabinet and went to the sink. Knowing he was right didn't lessen the sting. Just once, would it hurt him to say, "Good job. Next time hit the McElroy boy straight on—that'll teach him to look where he's going"?

You could tell him how you feel.

Yeah, right.

My head pounded. It was too much. It was all just too much.

My kingdom for a skinny venti Caramel Macchiato. Or better yet an appletini.

Well, Starbucks wasn't happening anytime soon out here in the boonies. And good luck finding anything alcoholic in this dry county—especially something other than a contraband beer.

Resigned, I took a gulp of water and looked through the window to the flat patch of land Daddy'd once told me he'd give me for a wedding present. A house would be pretty on that sloping hill. Of course, it would have been much smaller than Richard's mansion, and the cows were the only ones with a gated community out here. He kept telling me his cavernous house needed a woman's touch, and he had just the woman in mind.

"Rosemary." My father said the word softly, almost like he used to say it to my mother, for whom I was named.

I turned to face him because I couldn't not turn around, not when he spoke like that. "What, Daddy?"

"Just be more careful."

I nodded, not sure if he was talking about traffic laws or staying out of Julian's way. I could promise him I would be more careful on the first. As to the second, I was going to have to speak with Julian McElroy whether either one of us liked it or not. And it'd probably be best not to ask him for a divorce on the same day I ran him over.

Julian

Mama leaned out the back door as I was getting out of the truck. "Baby, you want some tea cakes? I'm about to take them out of the oven."

Baby, my ass. I surveyed the flagstone path between the mildewed, weed-choked trailer where I'd grown up and my house, the older clapboard one that used to belong to my mamaw. I'd never planned to live so close, but I'd missed the boat on college and needed somewhere to live. Besides, someone had to look out for Mama since she wasn't in the habit of watching out for herself. And she did make some damn fine tea cakes.

The minute I shut the truck door Curtis's pit bulls started barking. He kept them tied to an old oak tree and did everything under the sun to make them mean. We'd always had dogs, usually mutts that roamed free. This time, though, Curtis had spent a great deal of money he didn't have to buy the meanest dogs he could find. His greatest pleasure in life was "training" them, and he had delusions of taking them to Memphis and making a ton of money at dog fighting.

Something whimpered to the side of me, and I looked down at the beagle someone had thrown out down in the dip of the road. She only emerged from under the porch when I was outside, scraping the ground with her belly and begging for attention. Ignoring the others, I reached down to scratch between her ears before stepping into my parents' house. Mama was already fussing around the oven and bending over to get the tea cakes. As she turned around, I saw the hump at the top of her back. Mama was getting old. Too old to hobble around in the orthopedic boot she still wore from where Curtis had broken her foot a month before.

"Mama, I think you ought to get your foot looked at. Shouldn't it be getting better by now?" I asked as I stepped over to the sink to wash the dog off my hands.

She waved away my concerns and fished through the kitchen drawer for a spatula. "No, no, it's done this before. I know it looks a little purple now, but it's going to be fine. I guess it's lucky the insurance paid for this boot last time."

Mama and I didn't share the same definition of lucky.

Curtis was too smart for me to catch him in the act, but I knew he was responsible. Mama might blame ripped spots in the carpet or molehills in the yard or even her own clumsiness, but I knew better. What I didn't know was how to stop him.

Mama'd left him many times before, but he always played nice to win her back. Once when I was in kindergarten, I made the mistake of telling my teacher a little too much about our family dynamics. She called a social worker, who called the police. That didn't end well for any of us once Curtis got back from the police station. Later in high school, I asked Mama point-blank if she wanted me to make him leave, but she told me no.

Many's the time I wished I'd kicked his sorry ass out first and asked her permission later, but Curtis was a sneaky sonuvabitch. He'd rigged everything so all of the expenses and income from the farm came through his bank account. If I got rid of him, I wouldn't be able to run the farm. And he knew it.

Mama slid me a chipped plate with three steaming tea cakes, then bustled about the fridge looking for sweet tea. I let her carry on. Sometimes if I let her fuss over me enough, she'd hum the way she used to when I was a little boy.

The back door slammed shut. She started, and I tensed up. Today was turning out to be one helluva day.

"Well, well, look what the cat dragged in."

I knew he was drunk before I turned around. I could smell him, and I could tell by the way he slurred his words he was dangerous drunk. He could head to the recliner and fall asleep, or he could snap and start yelling at the first person he saw.

He wouldn't hit me, but he might decide to see if Mama needed another boot to match the first one. I had an assload of things I needed to do before meeting Ben, but I wasn't moving from my chair. Not until I saw what Curtis was up to.

It took him two tries to slap a meaty hand on my shoulder. He wasn't completely blind yet, but he was closer. I turned my head enough to see the ragged, grease-stained fingernails that needed to be cut. "Why don't you have a seat, Curtis?"

He scowled. He didn't like it when I called him by his first name, but he wasn't going to make anything of it. He'd ceased being anything more to me than a sperm donor on a certain night in May ten years ago, and I didn't give a rat's ass how he felt about it. My birth certificate might claim him as father, but that didn't mean I had to.

"Those hot, Debbie?" He pinched her behind harder than necessary, and her eyes widened. She scuttled off to get cookies and tea for him, too. She knew we were in the danger zone.

"Heard you got ran over in town today."

"Almost did."

He crammed an entire tea cake in his mouth, either not noticing or not caring it had to be hot enough to scald all the skin from the roof of his mouth. "I was thinking we could sue the Satterfield girl. You could even make enough to buy some of those damned rescue horses you're always fooling around with."

"I'm not suing anyone."

"Hell, son, did you know that each year over a thousand pedestrians get hit by cars in the state of Tennessee alone? I learned that from the TV the other day. And your uncle Charlie's a right fine ambulance chaser. We could make a pretty penny and put that Satterfield bastard out of business. Little bitch deserves it after she sneaked off in the middle—"

Suddenly, I had my father by the collar, his swollen drunken face just inches from mine. I didn't remember laying a hand on him, but it was a good reminder that hot McElroy blood flowed through my veins, too. "I'm not suing anyone. And you don't talk that way about Romy."

For a second I saw a flicker of fear pass through his squinting eyes. *Good.* I pushed him into a chair. He laughed. "This one's still sweet on the girl next door. Even after she left him cold. Debbie, what do you make of that?"

"She's not worth his time. Too big for her britches," my normally timid mother spat. This was the one safe topic for her, where she could air her opinions without worrying about making my father mad. "You don't leave someone you're about to marry. That ain't right."

Mama would've exploded if she'd known Romy left *after* we got married.

Curtis pulled her into his lap and planted a wet one on her. Apparently, he'd progressed through remorse and headed straight into lovey-dovey drunk. I sure as hell didn't want to see that. "Don't mind me. I'll see myself out."

I slipped out the back door, ticked off they both had to spew their vinegar on Romy.

She wasn't the one to blame—I was.

Romy

The next day, I got up entirely too late thanks to a full school year of burning the candle at both ends. Daddy only had instant coffee, and the sun was already high above me by the time my mental fog lifted enough for me to tromp to the garden to pick the green beans he'd asked me to get.

Good thing I'd ordered a Keurig coffeemaker last night. Paid an arm, a leg, and two toes to get it next day, too. It might not be as fancy as whatever contraption Richard had, but it was better than stirring coffee crystals into hot water.

I'd grown up working in the garden, often picking up potatoes in the heat of July, but my city years had made me soft. I picked only halfway down one row before the world started spinning. I couldn't catch my breath in the humidity, and something about the plants caused my hands to itch like the dickens. To top it all off, my fancy nails kept me from deftly picking the green beans as I must have done at least a thousand times in the past.

"I'm going to have to try this again tomorrow," I told no one in particular as I grabbed a half-full bucket and went to the shade of the barn. At least I'd been smart enough to bring a bottle of water with me. And to think, if I'd stayed in Nashville, I would've been lounging by the pool at Richard's subdivision and reading the fluffiest book I could find.

Instead of reading poolside I needed to check on the cows. Cussing under my breath, I walked beyond the garden to where the main pasture began. When I found a low spot in the fence, I straddled the ancient outer barbed-wire, then gingerly lifted my leg over the newer inner strand of electric wire. And promptly snagged my other leg on the electric one.

Jolting out of reality and back, I tasted metal and inspected the snag in my favorite jeans in a daze. Only I would get caught in the electric fence. Damned metallic taste stayed with me, too, as I picked my way around briars and cow patties until I found Daddy's small herd huddled under the shade tree by the pond.

I counted one bull, nine cows, and all six calves. Every last one of them was a full-blooded Angus, solid black. Fuzzy ears facing forward and tails relentlessly switching, they counted one ridiculously out-of-place city girl in their pasture—not that it bothered any of them as they chewed their cud, occasionally slinging their heads back to get rid of the flies. The cows knew an impostor when they saw one.

Tromping back to the barn, I lost my balance and placed one tennis shoe in the corner of a fairly fresh cow pie.

So that was going in the trash.

And I was getting some boots.

As I rounded the barn to perform my last appointed task, I couldn't help but wonder if there wasn't someone better suited to this job. I couldn't pick even one row of beans, I'd lost my ability to properly navigate the pasture, and I didn't know anything about cows with prolapsed uteri.

Maggie May, oh she of the prolapsed uterus, mooed at me from the corner as if to say, "Still good."

"Go on, turn around and let me make sure your stitches are holding up," I said. As if the cow could understand me or would do what I asked even if she could. Then the squat black Angus snorted and did a one-eighty so I could see that all was well beneath her tail.

"Well, thanks for cooperating, Miss Maggie," I said.

She flung cow snot over her shoulder and in my general direction.

"You missed," I said before walking back to the house. Using the concrete step to pry off my ruined shoes, I kicked them to the side. "Alas, poor Adidas! I knew them, Horatio."

On the other side of the door, the cat mewed, which made me jump.

"Wrong play, Mercutio," I muttered to myself as I entered the back porch and discovered I had another task to go: doctor the cat's ear. Mercutio howled and wiggled, but I washed his ear with soap and water. By the time I finished, we were both out of breath and sopping wet.

"See if I help you out again," I said before stepping into the kitchen.

"Who you talking to?" Daddy asked.

Um, animals. Why am I talking to all of the animals? I'm like a weird Dr. Dolittle.

"Just the cat, Daddy." I looked at the instant coffee and willed the Keurig to get there faster, then reached for a water glass instead.

"Genie called," he said.

Of course she did. I had been hoping for a day or two of peace before I met with Genie Dix to go over reunion particulars. We had been classmates since kindergarten, though, so I should've known she was too type A to let me rest when there was still so much work to do. "What did she say?"

"Wants you to meet her at The Fountain tonight for that singing thing."

I could tell by his growl that Daddy wasn't too keen on the idea. "Karaoke?"

"That's it."

"I told her your car broke down back in Nashville, so you had to leave it in the shop. She said she'd pick you up at eight."

I sighed. My flabby suburban self was tired.

But they would have something alcoholic, probably beer.

I leaned on the table to stand up because my quads hurt worse after a few minutes of bean picking than the last time I tried Pilates. A shower was in order. Then maybe I could curl up somewhere with a novel that didn't involve mockingbirds, dead dogs, flowers, Algernon, or insanely long paragraphs about a boat ride into the heart of freaking darkness.

Daddy folded down his paper so he could give me his tilted-head look. "You gonna go finish picking those beans?"

Or I could drink some more water and dream the impossible dream out in the garden.

Later that afternoon I'd managed to pick the green beans and trudge back to the house. I went upstairs to get a change of clothes and everything I needed to shower, but as I hit the last step coming down I heard something I never thought I'd hear in the Satterfield home place:

A meow followed by "Yeah, who's a good boy?"

I blinked twice. Was that Daddy? Talking to the cat? I pushed through the door that separated the steps and the living room, bobbling clothes and toiletries. Sure enough, Daddy sat in the recliner and Mercutio lounged on his lap. "I thought indoor cats were for 'stupid city people.'"

Daddy's lips quirked. "Well, if I leave him outside those damned McElroy dogs are going to chew him up. Some idiot took out his claws."

He was referring to the same idiot who'd dumped the cat in the dip of the road between the McElroy farm and ours. Almost all of my childhood pets had come from that very spot, a dark place where people slowed down their cars just long enough to abandon unwanted dogs and cats. Last year while home for Thanksgiving, I'd rescued Mercutio from that very spot. Daddy, not being a fan of Shakespeare, insisted on calling him Freddy Mercury or a more generic "buddy" instead.

"So you decided to go, huh?"

"Well, you told her to come on over."

He frowned. "I thought you might call her back and tell her no."

As if I'm a mind reader. "Next time give me the option."

His eyes narrowed, but he continued to stroke the cat, reminding me of Bond's nemesis Blofeld. "I'm not sure it's a good idea."

"Daddy, I'm a big girl. It's karaoke night, and I've been there before."

"Still."

He didn't mention Julian directly. He wasn't going to say that name because he'd taken Julian's betrayal almost as hard as I had. Maybe harder. He'd had to get over his initial prejudice against the McElroys only to be proven right. I had been proven wrong and gained the prejudice as a consequence.

I huffed out a breath. "You don't think *he* will be there, do you?"

"Doubt it. Goat Cheese told me he swore off going that night he and the Gates boy raised a ruckus."

Interesting. Julian had once told me he was done with fights, but he'd been in at least one more.

"It never ceases to amaze me that you can call a grown man Goat Cheese and keep a straight face."

Mercutio turned around three times and nestled deeper into my father's lap.

"Well, I'm not the idiot who announced to the world I was going to make my millions raising goats and selling their cheese." To my father's mind, the world was full of idiots. Idiots who tried to raise goats for cheese. Idiots who declawed cats. Idiots who kept cats in the house. I supposed he'd just joined the ranks of the latter, but I wasn't going to point it out again—that would make me one of those "idiots who can't mind her own business."

I shrugged and headed in the direction of the bathroom, a sixties add-on to the back porch—thank goodness Granddaddy Satterfield hadn't been so concerned about the integrity of the home place to insist we keep the outhouse.

"Hey, you."

I turned around, not entirely certain if he was talking to the cat or to me. Rather than answer, I gave him the same look I gave my students when they were disrespectful.

"Dammit, don't look at me like that. When you do, you look like her," he scowled.

"Well, I do have a name."

He muttered something under his breath before continuing, "Well, Rosemary, I found something the other day I thought you might be interested in. It's on the old sewing table by the window. Your mother wanted you to have it."

"Thanks, Daddy," I said softly. I walked past the kitchen table to the little sewing table that had been Granny Satterfield's. There on the top was a manila folder with papers jutting out at all angles. On the front my mother's neat script proclaimed, *A History of the Satterfield-McElroy Feud.*

I shifted towels, clothes, and such to the right and let my left hand skim her handwriting reverently. I'd heard about this folder. Before she got sick, Mom would tell me old stories, things she'd dug up from the newspapers and things she'd heard from the old-timers. She'd always told me she was going to write a book about it when she got better.

About that . . .

I laid the folder on the table and told myself not to worry about whether Julian would show up. Say what you would about Goat Cheese, he was generally the best source of Yessum County gossip.

As I turned to go, I snagged my jeans on the corner of the folder. Papers spilled then floated to the ground. I collated the typed pages, grateful for Mom's foresight in putting page numbers even though her work looked more like a draft than the book she'd wanted to write. Next I gathered the newspaper clippings and slick microfiche paper that had scattered. Finally, I saw a lone stack of papers that had slid underneath one of the chairs: *Happenstance in Love: A Comparison of Romeo and Juliet and Much Ado About Nothing by Rosemary Satterfield.*

Since that handwritten assignment had brought Julian and me together, I could see Mom had really been doing her homework. I thought back to how she took me to the big library in Jefferson and taught me how to use the microfiche. It was one of her last good days, and she told me, "Now this is something your father won't be able to teach you, and the good Lord will take away my cosmic library card if I don't show you how to do this before you go to college."

She couldn't have known that scanned files on the Internet were working to make microfiche obsolete by the time I got to Vanderbilt. She also couldn't have known that I would later take Julian to the same library and show him how to pull up microfiche or that we would end up leaning too closely together while I did.

But I wasn't going to think about that day. As a librarian, Rosemary Satterfield wouldn't have approved of love among the microfiche—especially not if her daughter had been falling for the worst possible boy.

Julian

The last thing I had to do before showering was check on Beatrice. The palomino ambled tentatively around the little paddock I'd made for her, reaching down to snuff the ground for a bite of grass here and there. The wind changed directions, and she sniffed the air then walked toward me, no doubt because she could smell the apple I held in my outstretched hand.

I reached out to pet her long face, and she snorted then rooted around for the apple. She flicked her ears forward as she crunched. For her, this was a good day. No miracle had occurred to bring back her vision, and the same milky film covered her eyes, making her look like the horse of a demigod. I should've had Dr. Winterbourne put her down because she wasn't going to get better from being moon blind, but I wasn't much on killing things. She nuzzled my hand as though she knew what I was thinking, and I reached out to rub her old nose.

"And how are you doing today, Beatrice?"

She nickered, which I took to mean she could really use another apple. Instead I led her to the fresh water I'd put out. She sniffed and snorted then stamped her front feet with a swish of her tail as if to say, "Does this look like an apple to you?"

I rubbed down her neck, picking a few pieces of hay out of her mane. "I'm thinking tomorrow might be a good day to clean you up a bit."

She drank deeply from the water, ignoring the man who'd brought only one apple. Her ears pricked and she turned her head in the direction of my other three horses in the pasture beyond the paddock. She held her head high and neighed in the direction of the other horses. They, of course, ignored her.

"I'm sorry, old gal, but they're just plain mean to you when I let you in there." Again, guilt stabbed at me. I should've put her down long ago. I knew the pain that went along with the flare-ups, and the medicine to help her was expensive enough to break us. But I couldn't bear to get rid of the horse I'd intended as Romy's wedding gift.

She backed away from me, tentatively walking in the direction of the fence that separated her paddock from the larger pasture where the other horses roamed. She called to them from her side of the fence.

"You know, I could shoot that horse between the eyes and put her out of her misery."

I didn't even turn around. "Don't even think about it, Curtis."

"Seems to me, we didn't get to finish our chat."

"I don't have anything else to say to you."

I turned on my heel and left, but he followed me. "Well, maybe I've got some things to say to you."

As I walked by the tree, the pit bulls barked with all their might, straining against their chains to get to me. "Well, maybe I don't want to hear what you've got to say."

He tried to clap a hand on my shoulder but missed. His eyes squinted and blinked against the light. A moon blind horse and a mean-ass old man who was going blind, too. How sad was it that I'd consider putting Curtis down before the horse?

"You might. I've been thinking about how I'm going to have to start turning some things over to you."

This was a dream—it had to be. If I could get Curtis off my back . . .

I wheeled around to face him. "What's the catch? Why so ready to make a deal all of a sudden?"

"You might've noticed I can't see for shit. Doc says I'm going blind."

"I've noticed," I said.

"He said my eyesight would go quickly. Said I might ought to get some things in order. I'm gonna have to trust you to write the checks one day. Might as well start putting your name on things."

Yeah, and then you can run up debt in my *name and I'll be the one who has to pay it off.* "Why don't you put it in Mama's name?"

"That woman wouldn't know her ass from a hole in the ground," Curtis spat.

My fists clenched, ready to knock the smug grin off his face. But if I could get everything in my name then I wouldn't have to kowtow to him anymore.

"All right, I'll bite. What do you need me to do?"

"I'll get Charlie to draw up some papers, you know, power of attorney and all that. Then we can talk about getting your name put on the bank account along with mine." Curtis stopped short of Mamaw's front porch. He knew he wasn't welcome in the house I'd fixed up and claimed as my own.

"I'm bringing Ben."

Curtis cussed under his breath, but he knew I didn't trust Uncle Charlie any farther than I could throw him. And Uncle Charlie was about a biscuit shy of three hundred.

"Do what you need to do," Curtis muttered before tottering in the direction of the trailer. I noticed the weeds around the trailer were about waist-high.

Feeling generous, I went for the weed eater and got to work on those weeds creeping up around the trailer. I'd been avoiding them on principle, waiting to see if Curtis would ever get off his drunk, lazy ass and mow his own lawn and do his own weed eating. He wouldn't have done that even if he could see. At least he lived in a trailer, and there was the possibility of hauling it somewhere else someday. Hell, I was helping myself by cutting these weeds! Now we'd be able to find the trailer hitch.

Done with that task, I put the weed eater away and absently patted the beagle as I walked through the back door. For the first time in a long while I felt like celebrating. Nothing with Curtis was ever easy, but there was a whisper of hope I might get shed of him.

Romy

While I was waiting on Genie to pick me up, I thumbed through the folder of my mother's notes. She had, of course, arranged them chronologically. The first piece was a yellowed paper she'd typed using a typewriter with an "e" that marked ever so slightly above the other letters. I could almost feel her frustration at not being able to make that "e" straighten up and get in line with the rest. I smiled as I read:

> No one knows for sure where or when the feud between the Satterfields and the McElroys started. The 1850 census records show that the Satterfields had already moved into their current property on what is now Bittersweet Creek Road. I have traced the family back to a Satterthwaite who arrived in New Jersey in the late 1600s, but I can't definitively attach him to the family because that assumes a change in spelling to the current name. It's just a hunch. We do know that Benjamin Satterfield purchased the current farm from John Wilson in 1849. Legend has it that Wilson was a fellow veteran of the Mexican-American War and that the two became such good friends they wanted to be neighbors.

The McElroys show up on the 1860 census, but the spelling of the name at the time was Magilroy. Since no one in that household could read or write, it would take more research to determine their origins. The census does list a grandfather with Ireland as his place of birth, so it's possible the McElroys were recent arrivals. Other county records show Shaymus Magilroy bought the property from a William Wilson, the son of John Wilson.

No record exists of any problems between the Satterfields and the McElroys until 1861. If I were a betting woman, I'd guess Matthew Wilson wasn't happy his brother had sold half of the farm that would have someday been his. I doubt Benjamin Satterfield was happy about his new neighbors, either. It's a safe assumption neither farm has been happy about much of anything since.

Leave it to my mother to give the farms themselves personality. A car honked outside and I laid the folder down on the scratchy couch and gave Daddy a kiss on the cheek on my way out. He grunted his good-bye, still unhappy I was going but knowing I was old enough to do what I wanted to do.

I slid into the car and did a double take. Gone were the frumpy hand-me-down clothes, frizzy hair, and glasses. The class ugly duckling had morphed into a rather beautiful swan. She'd traded in broken glasses for contacts, and she wore a neatly pressed linen suit that had no business going to a roadside tavern. We did an awkward half hug before I buckled my seat belt. She had to be at least twenty pounds lighter, quite a feat since I kept finding them instead of losing them.

"Genie, you look absolutely stunning!"

"And you, Romy, are looking pretty damn good yourself."

It took me a minute to realize I must look similarly polished and sleek, thanks to a flat-iron addiction and last year's birthday gift from Richard: a makeover in the Nordstrom cosmetics department. I'd already chipped the pinkie nail on my left hand, but I pulled it underneath my fist with my thumb so she couldn't see it.

"So, how's life been treating you?"

She set out to tell me every detail of everything that had happened since we parted just after graduation, and I half listened and half watched familiar fields and houses blur by in the twilight. Somewhere in the middle of her story, we arrived at The Fountain. It hadn't changed much in the past ten years. The cinder-block building still sat across the road from County Line Methodist, the church the Satterfields had helped found long ago. I walked through the same rickety screen door of what had been an old country store. Old Coke signs still lined the walls. The counter remained, but Bill had put in a pool table to go with the jukebox that never worked. He'd also added some chairs and tables around a stage.

Genie only paused long enough for us to find a table and order a couple of beers. If she noticed how uncomfortable I was to be in another place that reminded me of Julian, she didn't say anything. She also had the grace not to laugh at me when I tried to order an appletini, then a pinot noir, only to be informed my choices were beer, beer, or, perhaps, beer.

Even then I sounded like a pretentious ass when I asked what was on tap and ended up with a bottled Bud Light. That's what I got for trying to be low-brow. Apparently, I'd forgotten how.

At least I didn't mind listening to Genie chatter, because she'd done well for herself as the first person in her family to go to college. Now she worked as an RN at the Jefferson Hospital, but she was convinced she was still missing out on Mr. Right.

"I hear you've met him."

I almost choked on my beer. "Excuse me?"

"I hear you're going out with Richard Paris."

"I am. I see news travels fast around here." I focused on the infamous Beulah Land playing piano onstage. She didn't look a bit older than when I'd left, still a redhead who liked to flaunt her cleavage. Like every other girl in town, I'd always been secretly jealous of Beulah, but we'd never traveled in the same circles. Satterfield children weren't allowed to rebel—not even as teenagers.

Genie waved her hand around the tavern. "Not much to do, you see. Besides, when you drive into town with a car like that then run over your ex-boyfriend, people tend to pay attention."

Heat blossomed in my cheeks. "Yeah. I'm not used to driving a car that fancy. It's Richard's."

Genie took a long pull from her neglected and sweating beer. "Jim Price has a pool going that says you ran over Julian on purpose."

"Price always has a pool going for something," I said with a shrug.

"He's also got a bet going about whether or not you and Julian will get back together. He's got his money on Paris."

"That's ridiculous. And none of his business, either! I'm just here for the summer." *Why in heaven's name would I break up with Richard?* I glanced around the dingy honky-tonk full of self-proclaimed rednecks. Of course, if Richard came back here and stuck around for too long, he might decide to break up with me.

It was Genie's turn to shrug. "Just what I heard. Say, how are things going with the class reunion funds, Treasurer Lady?"

"Everything's collected and we're past the deadline so my job is done."

"Unless you wanted to help with a few other odds and ends." Genie batted her eyelashes.

"Oh, no. I'm going to have my hands full."

"Please, please, please. It'll be like being in Beta Club all over again. You've already collected the money, and I've already done most of the heavy lifting, and—"

"Fine. I'll help." *What? Where had that come from? Friends. You desperately want to remember what it's like to have friends.*

She reached the short distance across the table and squeezed my hand. "I'm so glad to hear that." Leaning forward, she lowered her voice. "None of the other officers are doing anything. And they live right here!"

I understood only too well how group work went: One person did all the work and the others showed up in time to bask in the glory.

"I have a feeling I'm going to be really busy around the farm, but send me a list of things that need to get done, and I'll see what I can do."

Genie beamed at me and extended her beer bottle to clink with mine. "It'll be the best reunion Yessum County has ever seen."

I clinked my bottle against hers and opened my mouth to say her expectations might be a little high, but the cuckoo clock in the corner cut me off.

Beulah led the raucous crowd through the paces of "Dwelling in Beulah Land," and I felt an eerie merging of past and present. The lyrics rolled off my tongue against my will, my heart warming at the words of the familiar song.

"In ten minutes, we're doing some karaoke, y'all!" Beulah announced before hopping to the floor for her break. Bill nodded to the Gates brothers, and they joined him in the corner to take out a couple of speakers, a microphone, and the other karaoke equipment. Pete rammed a speaker into Greg's back. Greg used a creative litany of curse words, and the two brothers pushed past our table and outside for a fight.

"Ha! You ought to put the Gates brothers on the committee," I said.

"Can't. They never graduated," she said.

"I am willing to help each of them earn a GED if it means having someone to cuss creatively while lifting heavy objects."

But she wasn't listening to me. Instead, she stared at the door, and my heart started to thump insistently even before she spoke.

"Well, well. Look who's decided to show up this evening."

I sucked in a breath and followed Genie's gaze to the door. Julian wasn't supposed to be here. But there he was, just as I'd somehow known he would be: tall and tanned from working outdoors, full of honestly earned muscles. *And you are remembering him the way you used to see him. You are immune to his charms now,* I chided myself.

He sat down by Ben at the tiny ledge that ran against the far wall. I had to peer around our waitress when she appeared with another round of beers. His eyes met mine, but I looked away quickly.

"Still got the hots for McElroy, huh?"

"No." My burning cheeks said otherwise.

"Is that you, Julian McElroy? AND Romy Satterfield? It's been forever since the two of you sang. How 'bout you start us off with a little 'Islands in the Stream'?"

I had never hated Beulah Land before that moment.

My pulse pounded in my ears, and I shook my head no, but Beulah's mouth had curved into a little smile. She liked to stir the shit, as my father would say.

Some traitorous punks in the back started a low chant, "Is-lands, Is-lands, Is-lands . . ."

I looked at Julian. He'd stood at the sound of his name, but he remained rooted to the spot, his eyes now locked with mine.

Folks stomped their feet in time: "Is-lands, Is-lands, Is-lands . . ."

Julian looked ready to bolt. *Was he about to run? Again?* I stood and shouted my challenge across the room. "I'll do it."

"Fine," he spat as he walked in my direction. I let go of the breath I'd been holding.

The house erupted in cheers, applause, whistles, and catcalls, but I couldn't think of anything but the fact that Julian McElroy had taken a step in my direction for the first time in ten years.

Julian

Beulah Land could go to hell.

Damn her hide for dredging up memories of the first time Romy and I sang that song. We were each about seven, and both of us had wandered to the creek that bubbled between our farms. Our mamas would've had a fit if they'd known we'd wandered into the woods where the coyotes lurked.

They called the creek Bittersweet, but it was nothing but sweet back then. I liked to walk there and look over at the Satterfield land and wonder if they were really as bad as Curtis made them out to be. The fact that the creek was far enough away from the house so I couldn't hear my mother's cries when Curtis smacked her was another reason I hid out there.

One day I heard someone singing as I approached. A little girl with black pigtails hopped from one side of the creek to the other, singing about islands in the stream and asking how anyone could be wrong.

I knew that song. Mama listened to the local country radio station in the mornings while she got me ready for school. She also had every Kenny Rogers cassette ever made.

I sang about sailing away to another world and invited her to come with me. She stiffened at the sound of my voice, but then she gave me a wide grin and kept singing.

We didn't know about lovers or making love back then. That came later when Coach decided I needed some extra tutoring in English. Somehow, as we stumbled through Shakespeare, we began to see our relationship as a little island of sanity in that teeny creek. She was the one who figured out I couldn't read but I could listen. And that's how she fell in love with me.

I fell in love with her the moment I saw her jumping over that stream like some kind of woodland fairy in knee-patched Sears jeans. And up until the night she gave up on me I had always thought we really would find a way to sail away together.

Instead, Romy disappeared to Vanderbilt, and I hid out in Mamaw's abandoned house licking my wounds.

And now I'd agreed to sing our song like the damn fool I was.

Romy

Beulah handed each of us a microphone, and I willed myself to smile as I looked out into the audience. Thank God Richard wasn't there—this wasn't something I wanted him to see. I wanted to look at Julian, to see if he caught any irony in the words as he sang them, to see if I could figure out exactly what had happened on the night of our high school graduation.

Julian, however, was focused on the little blue monitor.

He didn't need the monitor. We used to sing this song all the time both as kids and back in high school when Bill had experimented with a "family night" and made anyone under twenty-one wear a fluorescent wristband to show they weren't old enough to drink. Julian had never once looked at the monitor back then.

He sang the first part about feeling a peace unknown, his voice reverberating through me. I had forgotten its honey timbre, the twang he'd picked up from years of listening to country music and nothing else. I snapped to and sang with him about the blindness of tender love. Then there was the part about dedication.

I stared through him. I had been blind. I had given the required dedication. Kenny and Dolly were so wrong about not needing conversation, though. What had Julian McElroy ever given up to me through words? He'd given me his body, but there had always been a part of him he'd held back. If I'd been anything other than young and stupid, I would have seen we were headed for trouble because there were so many questions he wouldn't answer.

My eyes were drawn to his when he sang to me about how I wouldn't cry and he would hurt me never.

Bullshit.

As we sang about starting and ending as one and interspersing "uh-huh"s with making love, I blushed. I couldn't help it. I threw myself into the lyrics, forcing myself not to shout *"how can we be wrong?"* because I knew we'd been wrong but I still didn't know the how or why.

I didn't need to know how. I only needed Julian's signature on the dotted line. The why wasn't important. My eyes landed on Genie, who studied us with her head tilted to one side like a zoologist studying primates. What did she think about Julian and me singing a song about making love?

Blessedly, the song came to a close. The Fountain patrons erupted in applause, either not noticing the undercurrents or reveling in them. Julian stepped off the stage then reached over to give me a hand.

"I need to talk to you," I blurted as I jumped down in front of him.

He put both hands on his hips and leaned back. "Go on, then."

"Outside would be better."

Julian cut a glance to Genie. "Thought you were here with her."

"She can wait for a minute." I gestured toward the door and Julian headed off while GiGi Taylor started singing the world's most off-key version of "Save a Horse, Ride a Cowboy."

I cleared my throat as I stepped over to where Genie sat. "I need to step outside and have a word with Julian. Do you mind waiting?"

"I can do that." Again she had the look of an anthropologist taking notes on human behavior. I began to wonder if she secretly worked as a spy for the Paris family. Would she report back to Richard? Tell him I was singing in bars with my ex?

Ridiculous. What did she care?

Heart still pounding, I walked across the bar and out the door before my confidence could leave me.

Julian

As a general rule, I wasn't much of a pacer, but being alone with Romy for the first time in ten years? That had to qualify as an extenuating circumstance. It ate me up to think of her with her city boyfriend—especially after we sang together, her voice humming through my body. But what could I do about it? I'd sealed my fate the night I hadn't shown up at Wanamaker's store.

Knowing Romy, that night she'd packed entirely too much for our honeymoon—especially since I'd planned to keep her out of her clothes as much as possible. I had a vision of teenage Romy, lugging that old red suitcase of her mama's as she walked up the road. We had agreed to meet at three in the morning, a time of night when no one should be passing. Her mama's suitcase was too old for wheels so Romy would have fumbled along the road, occasionally passing the suitcase from one hand to another as her arms got tired.

Once she got to the store, she probably sat down on the suitcase and hugged herself. She didn't let anyone but me know it, but Romy was still afraid of the dark or, at the very least, afraid of not being able to see where she was stepping. Considering the wrong I was about to do her, she should have been more scared of me.

The screen door to the tavern popped open, and she flew outside, jarring me back to the present. She had to have been born running because I'd never seen Romy Satterfield slow down for anything or anyone. I used to kid her she was a blur.

Then she stopped.

"You wanted me?" I asked.

Poor choice of words. Or wishful thinking.

She sucked in a big breath to help her carry on: "Julian, I need a divorce."

I opened my mouth to say yes, to say I'd known this day was coming. Instead my traitorous lips said, "No."

"What do you mean, no? Who do you think you are? You can't begin to think you could just leave me on the side of the road with no explanation and think I would still want to be married to you. I swear, Julian McElroy, I don't know what kind of demon cupid shot me with his arrow and made me think for one solitary moment I wanted to be married to you. Four years of college and almost six years of teaching and you have not so much as called or sent a note or said you were sorry. Now you want to tell me you aren't going to give me a divorce? That is the most ridiculous—"

"Just stop." Whatever it was that had been squeezing my heart for the past ten years loosened its grip, and I grinned. Romy Satterfield was the only person I knew who started using bigger words and more of them when she got mad. Most of us resorted to shorter words and repeating a lot of them.

"Just stop? Are you out of your mind? I can't believe I managed to screw my courage to the sticking place to ask you this question and that you, of all people, would tell me no after all that—"

"Why'd you have to go all *Sweet Home Alabama* on me? Why couldn't you ask me years ago?"

That shut her up. She studied the gravel for some time and we listened to the frogs sing. Finally, she looked up at me. "I couldn't bear to look at you."

Tears glistened at the corners of her eyes, and I had to look away from the hurt. I kicked at the gravel, making a rut in the ground. "So I guess you're really in love with this city boy. If you're willing to come out here and look at me."

She crossed her arms, angry again. "Yes, I love Richard. And he loves me."

Just do it, you dumb-ass. She's better off without you. Look at her.

My brain told my mouth to say, "Pass the pen," but "I'll think about it" came out instead. Now that she was finally home and standing in front of me, I couldn't let go. I knew I should. I knew I was being selfish, but I couldn't seem to give her the answer she wanted. Not for that guy. Oh, hell, not for any guy. Who was I kidding?

She flew at me, but I grabbed her wrists and pulled her near. I came close to kissing her, close enough that her breath got shallow just like it always used to. Back in the old days I would sometimes hold my lips just an inch from hers and wait for that hitch in her breath. And I *could* kiss her. She was, after all, my wife— at least on paper.

"Julian, please."

Please sign the papers? Or please kiss her? I didn't know which, but I was about kiss her when Genie appeared at the door.

"Julian, you're up." Genie assessed the situation, and her eyes narrowed. "Romy, are you okay?"

I let go of her wrists as if they'd scalded me.

"I'm fine. I was just coming back in."

Genie nodded, but opened the door wider instead of making a move to go back inside.

"This isn't over," Romy spat to me over her shoulder before walking back in.

God, I hope not.

No, it is *over. You are going to make it over. Remember what happened the last time you were at The Fountain?*

How could I forget? Those first few years after Romy left I was on a mission to piss off as many Baptists as I could. I drank, I smoked. I picked bar fights. I flirted like a sonuvabitch.

But one night in particular, Pete Gates started telling a story in the back corner. A group of men hung on his every breath as he described in vivid detail everything he had done to a girl and everything she had done to him. To hear him tell the story, other women were involved, even a well-endowed horse. I sidled over out of curiosity but spewed my beer when he suggested Romy Satterfield was the woman in question.

I should've known the whole thing was a lie, but I'd had a few beers too many and maybe some leftover pain pills. At the sound of her name, I scattered those men and started throwing Pete Gates around like a rag doll, beating him up enough to land him in the hospital. I totally trashed The Fountain, then promptly wrapped my truck around Lester Ledbetter's tree. If I'd hit a car or hit a tree on anyone's property other than ol' Goat Cheese's, I would've been in jail.

That night I looked at how the massive oak had crumpled the front end of the truck and how the truck had splintered the tree and came to the conclusion there was too much of Curtis in me to even think for one moment that I deserved to be with any woman, much less Romy. I'd poured the last of those pills down the drain and cut back on the beer. I'd apologized to both Pete and Bill, helping pay for hospital bills and busted-up tables and chairs. That didn't change who I was or what I could do.

Beulah leaned out the door this time. "C'mon, Julian, we don't have all day."

A quick glance told me what Ben had been up to while I was outside. He'd pulled up two chairs to the table where Romy and Genie sat and was now standing onstage with "Ebony and Ivory" cued up behind him.

Benjamin Little, Esquire, was a dead man. And no way would a jury of my peers convict me.

From Rosemary Satterfield's
History of the Satterfield-McElroy Feud

The first recorded instance of trouble between the Satterfields and the McElroys came in 1861. The *Ellery Gazette* mentions the arrests of two men for public drunkenness and that they had squabbled over a calf. The calf supposedly belonged to the Satterfields but had wandered over to the McElroy pasture. An argument broke out in the local saloon resulting in both men spending the night in the county lockup. The calf was never returned.

Problems with alcohol will crop up again and again in a history of the Satterfields and the McElroys. From this first altercation to moonshine stills and beyond, nothing good ever comes of mixing Satterfields and McElroys with drinking.

Romy

It was hard to say which was worse: having to share a table with Ben and Julian or listening to Ben and Julian's painful rendition of "Ebony and Ivory." Ben sang more like Frank Sinatra than Stevie Wonder, and Julian sounded far more like Brad Paisley than Paul McCartney. Even Beulah winced through the whole thing and offered a mulligan with piano accompaniment in a lower key, but Julian's vehement no ended the issue—thank goodness. A few of the rednecks in the back muttered because they still hadn't quite reconciled themselves to the fact that humanity could, indeed, live in perfect harmony like those keys on a piano.

Ben took the seat next to Genie, which left Julian sitting next to me. Fight or flight warred within me with a heavy emphasis on flight. Spite took the upper hand, though, and I raised my hand to signal for another beer. Damned if I was going to let Julian make me walk out of The Fountain. As bad as that song was, he was the one who needed to leave.

"So, Romy, what've you been up to?"

A casual observer would think Ben Little was making pleasant conversation. I knew he was up to something because he and Julian were thicker than thieves and had been since playing high school football together. By this point he knew about that morning's accident, and he knew I was seeing Richard Paris. He would've known who Richard was, too, because, well, everyone in the state of Tennessee knew who Richard was.

"Just getting settled in today," I said. "I'm going to be here for the summer to help Daddy out since he broke his leg a couple of weeks ago."

"I wonder how your father managed to get to the hospital after that happened," Ben said. "A man like that all alone out in the barn."

Julian choked on his beer. My eyes shot from Ben to Julian. "Did you help him out?"

"Happened to be mending the fence on that side when I heard him yell."

Hank Satterfield, stoic extraordinaire, had, of course, left out this part of the story. "Well, thank you, Julian. I'm glad you were there that day."

"You're welcome." He shifted in his seat—just enough for me to see there was still more to the story. When I looked at Ben, he was glaring at Julian, his lips in a thin line. But I could've told him that was all he was getting out of him. Julian McElroy could be the poster child for "hostile witness."

"Well, I was thinking we should sing a rendition of 'YMCA' before we go," said Genie. "I'll be the construction worker."

"No!" all three of us said together.

"I mean, I think it's about time for me to go home," I said.

Julian nodded toward the two empties in front of me. "Are you sure you should be driving?"

I opened my mouth to ask if he thought he was one to talk, but I saw he only had one beer bottle in front of him. The other empty was a water bottle. Interesting.

"I'll be fine." I stood up too quickly, knocking the chair behind me and interrupting Old Man MacGregor's off-key rendition of "You Never Even Called Me by My Name." I swayed a little in spite of myself and bent over to pick up my chair.

"You do remember that you rode with me, right?" Genie said.

The fact that I'd forgotten that crucial piece of information suggested I was, indeed, in no shape to drive home—not even in my imaginary car. Still, I would sit there all night before I'd let Julian drive me home. He muttered something about "stubborn women" under his breath.

The smart thing to do would have been to order water. Instead, I chugged my Bud Light and raised my hand for another.

"Well, if I'm not driving . . ."

Julian

It wasn't the first time I'd ever seen Romy get drunk. I liked her pleasantly tipsy when everything made her giggle—or I used to. Watching her tonight, a night when I knew there'd be no sex under a full moon nor any mosquito bites in places you didn't want to explain, was sheer torture.

To make matters worse, Genie and Ben were hitting it off as if just discovering each other instead of having gone to school together most of their lives. At one point I almost told them to get a room, but that would've meant leaving Romy with me. I shouldn't have been shocked when they said they were getting another beer but instead sneaked out while Romy was in the middle of singing "I Will Survive." I shouldn't have been, but I was.

They were trying to play matchmaker. Ben, of all people, should've known better. He knew why Romy and I couldn't be together. He had seen it with his own two eyes. Me and him were going to have ourselves a chat tomorrow, and he was not going to like it.

"I think it's time we took you home," I said as Romy stepped off the stage. She'd nailed the song despite being drunk, and she was flush with both victory and alcohol. Then she frowned.

"Where's Genie?"

"Said she needed a ride home herself." *Bullshit.* "So she let Ben drive her home."

Romy frowned, looking around the rapidly emptying tavern for another option.

That she would look to someone else in that crowd before looking to me felt kinda like someone had a crowbar under the rib over my heart and was trying to pry it off. I started to ask if I was really that bad, but I knew the answer. I deserved no less from her.

"C'mon. It's just a ride home." I grabbed her elbow.

She snatched it back from me.

"Hey, now. I don't bite."

Her arched eyebrow and the memory of at least one well-placed hickey contradicted me. "No. You do worse."

I reached for my hat only to remember I still hadn't replaced it and ran my hand through my hair instead. "Look. I'm not drunk. You are. These other assholes are. Please let me take you home."

She nodded, and we made our way to the door.

Riding home reminded me of too many other times she'd ridden home with me, times we'd taken a detour to Robert Smith's abandoned orchard. I still had a stack of old quilts in the back, but these days they gathered dirt and dust. I'd seen no reason to wash them and only used them to cushion the bed of the truck from whatever I was hauling.

"Why didn't you show up?"

She continued to lean against the door, as far from me as possible, gazing up at the moon. That imaginary crowbar stabbed the meaty part of my heart, the pain so intense I couldn't find my voice for a minute. "I had my reasons."

Her head jerked to me, and tears streamed down her cheeks. "You could've talked to me, you know. I know you always thought you needed to protect me, but you could've told me stuff. I told you everything."

And she had. She'd been completely honest with me, but it was easier to be honest when your secrets weren't so dark. There was nothing in the world she could've told me to ever make me stop loving her. Glancing at her tear-streaked face, I knew there'd never come a day I didn't love her. But loving someone meant doing what was best for them. Sometimes what was best for them wasn't all that good for you.

Sometimes, loving someone meant you had to let them go, send them off, even.

"I changed my mind."

I almost choked on the words because they weren't the truth, not exactly. They told what I did, but they didn't explain why. And I could never, ever tell her why. After I told her, she would never look me in the eye again, and I wouldn't have that. I'd rather her look at me with hate in her eyes than pity.

Romy broke into sobs, her face hidden in her hands, and a boulder of a lump formed in my throat. Was there anything I could do that wouldn't make her cry? I couldn't swallow. I couldn't think. I could hardly keep myself from stopping the truck and pulling her into my arms and telling her it was all a lie.

If only it would be as simple as telling her I'd been kidnapped by the Dread Pirate Roberts. She'd always liked *The Princess Bride*.

Ben was right. I had been watching too many movies—girlie movies at that.

But, dammit, real life wasn't a movie—at least not a happy movie. Real life didn't have a happy ending—not for anybody I knew. If anyone deserved a happy ending, it was Romy. She might not realize it, but I knew she'd never find that happy ending with me.

Romy

I collapsed on the front porch steps, but Julian just sat there with his headlights blinding me. It took me a few minutes to realize he was waiting for me to go inside. He wanted to make sure I made it into the house safely. I had to wave him on at least five times before he got the hint and started to back down the driveway.

I didn't want to go in and face Daddy. Sure, he was probably snoring in the living room chair while he pretended to watch the late-late show, but if he were awake, he'd see that I was drunk. He'd dress me down even though I knew from Granny Satterfield that he'd had a few benders in his youth, too.

Why won't he just tell me why?

I didn't think it was too much to ask. If a girl got jilted, didn't she deserve to know why?

In spite of myself I went back to the night in question, a night a lot like the present one. It was warm with just a hint of the cooler days of a spring just past. We'd graduated, finally made it through the minefield of high school. In the shadow of the football stadium, Julian leaned in to kiss me even while other students and families milled about the football field taking pictures and looking for the caps they'd flung into the air with careless jubilation.

"We're still on for tonight, right?" he asked with his forehead still touching mine.

"Daddy is going to kill me."

He frowned. "Are you sure then? Sure you want to do this? We can do it the right way, you know."

"This is the right way," I said. I was so young and stupid back then, so sure my father would say no and so sure I knew better than him.

"All right. If you're sure. I've got the truck washed and waxed. Oil's changed, and it's full of gas."

My heart swelled. What might be a checklist to some were actions of love from Julian. "I trust you."

"You shouldn't," he said with a wolfish grin as he reached for the hem of my white graduation gown and started lifting it along with the hem to my dress. I slapped his hand as he knew I would.

"Come on, now. I couldn't even concentrate on your speech for wondering what you could possibly be wearing under that gown. I couldn't see the outline of anything. Are you commando under there?"

"Wouldn't you like to know?" I countered.

"I aim to find out." This time he reached for the zipper at the collar. I smacked his hand.

"Later!"

He kissed my lips gently. "Don't blame a man for being excited about his wedding night."

"Then let's go now."

He frowned. "Your daddy would have the cops on us before we got to Nashville. We'll go tonight—but make sure to put out that letter where he can find it."

I tried not to think of how I later stumbled home before dawn and took my letter to Daddy off the kitchen table before hiding it in my suitcase and sneaking back up the stairs.

Instead I thought of how Julian had kissed me long and hard, almost as though he knew he wasn't going to show up later that night. At times over the years I'd thought of that kiss and wondered if he'd known in that moment what he planned to do, but I didn't think so. No, the kiss and the smile that followed had held promise, not betrayal.

Julian had known I didn't like going to his house because his dad scared me and his mom hated me, so I had been sure he would call me. I hardly got out of bed the next day, worried sick about him. When Daddy asked, I told him I was just tired from all the work of the last few weeks of high school, that I needed to sleep it off and I'd be fine.

But I wasn't fine, and I didn't sleep. Finally, after an entire day with no word from Julian, I called his house. I cringed when his mother answered the phone.

"May I speak to Julian, please?"

"No, you may not." Her crisp reply startled me. Even though she hated my guts, she'd never kept him from me before.

"This is important, so if—"

"He doesn't want to talk to you."

And she hung up on me.

My teenage world upended itself. I ran across the room to the trash can and hurled inside it, then had a momentary panic about what if condoms broke and I was now pregnant *and* without my husband of only a few hours. I gasped for air. I had to see him.

So I ran downstairs, ignoring Daddy's questions of where I thought I was going like a bat out of hell, and I jumped in my car to drive the short distance up the road. I tripped as I ran up the steps to the front door of the McElroy trailer. The acrid taste of vomit lingered in my mouth, but I couldn't be bothered with that. I rang the doorbell once, then twice, before I heard feet heading in the direction of the door.

Julian's mom didn't even undo the chain, instead peering at me with most of her body hidden behind the door, no doubt to conceal whatever damage Julian's dad had recently done. "I told you he doesn't want to speak to you."

"Please." My voice came out on a sob, and tears streaked down my cheeks.

For a minute I thought she was going to cave because I noticed her eyes were puffy and red, too. I thought she might open the door to me. Instead, she pulled herself up straighter with new resolve. "He's gone. I don't know where he is, and it's all your fault. Now go on off to college or whatever it is you *smart* people do."

He left without me?

She slammed the door shut with as much force as one could muster when it was held only a chain's length open. I pinched myself to make sure I wasn't in the midst of a horrific nightmare. It couldn't be happening. Julian had promised to love me and cherish me forever. I'd heard him say those words just three days before. I'd seen the love and admiration in his eyes, his confident cocky grin.

It made no damned sense.

And because it made no damned sense, I had no choice but to drive home and go back to bed where I could cry myself to sleep even though the sun hadn't even begun to set.

If Daddy thought something was wrong with me that summer, he kept it to himself. He didn't even say a word when I told him I wanted to go to Nashville a month early to see the sights and get settled in. He didn't question for a minute that I was staying in an apartment with a girl I'd only met once at the Volunteer Girls State program the summer before. Either he'd decided I was eighteen and could do as I pleased, or he knew enough about losing the love of your life to figure I was going to do some stupid things whether he liked it or not.

And I did some stupid stuff then, just as getting drunk at The Fountain and letting Julian drive me home now had been incredibly stupid. As I heard Daddy wrestle with the front door, I realized I'd been very, very stupid.

I expected him to bless me out, but instead he sighed deeply as I wiped away my tears with the back of my hand. "Come on in here before the skeeters eat you up."

I got up and walked into the house. I wanted a hug from my daddy. I wanted a fierce hug, as though it would somehow make up for tonight and what'd happened ten years ago. But he couldn't hug me very well from his wheelchair.

I was lucky. He'd get the cast off, and then I'd be able to get one of his crushing hugs, but that wheelchair reminded me he was old. Even when he got out of the cast, he needed to start taking it easy and not take any more chances with temperamental bulls who snapped legs like twigs. I'd already lost my mother, and I couldn't bear to lose him, too.

For the first time ever I wanted to stay home. Forever. It was a stupid pie-in-the-sky kind of wish, but I didn't want to miss another moment with my father. Of course, if I stayed, I'd be stuck next door to Julian and would run the risk of running into him every time I needed a carton of milk. Every time I saw him and he looked away, I'd hear those four words that had ripped my heart out all over again: *I changed my mind.*

"Julian? Again?"

I nodded.

"C'mon." He turned the wheelchair with a grunt and rolled to the kitchen. He nodded at the table, and I took a seat while I watched him rummage through the lower cabinets. By the time he emerged with the bottle of Jack he was panting from the exertion.

"Need some help?"

"Nah, get a Coke out of the fridge, though."

"You sure this is a good idea?" I asked as I reached for a couple of cans of Coke.

He raised an eyebrow. "Already drunk off your ass, aren't you?"

By the time I sat back down he had two coffee mugs—the only glasses he could reach—and he'd already poured a finger or three of Jack into each mug then passed them to me. He tilted each mug sideways before slowly pouring Coke on top.

"You're going to have to let that boy go," he said as he lifted his mug in a sad toast.

I clinked my mug against his. "I just want to know why. That's all, Daddy. Why?"

He drank for a while before setting his mug down hard enough to make his drink slosh. "I ask that question about your mother every damn day."

From Rosemary Satterfield's
History of the Satterfield-McElroy Feud

In the first of many lawsuits, Benjamin Satterfield took Shaymus Magilroy to court over the calf, but the case got abandoned in favor of more important things like the Civil War. As a transplant from up north, Benjamin Satterfield sided with the North. Shaymus Magilroy supported the South.

While the Satterfield sons fought in blue, half of the Magilroys fought in gray. The other half commandeered everything on the Satterfield farm and other neighboring farms that they could get their hands on. Eventually, the entire Satterfield clan moved up north to wait the war out. They came back in 1864 once the Union was in control. By returning early, they kept their land and property despite the best efforts of the carpetbaggers. But they'd lost everything. Their farmhouse and all of the outbuildings had been destroyed.

Ben Satterfield had a new Yankee wife, though, and it was her family's money that saved the place. That genteel finishing-school graduate, your great-great-grandma Alma, had to learn to work with her hands. And she also had to learn to deal with the slurs and snubs of almost everyone in Yessum County.

Meanwhile, the Magilroys barely held on to their smaller farm, being called into court more than once for being delinquent on their taxes. Then Shaymus Magilroy's wife called him into court for something unheard of in those days: a divorce.

Julian

The first rule of Fight Club really is that you do not talk about Fight Club. I didn't have a destructive alter ego, but I had been born into that special club. Curtis didn't talk about hitting, and Mama didn't talk about getting hit. In those early days when I showed up for school hardly able to walk from the tanning my hide had received, I didn't talk about Fight Club. And most of my teachers didn't, either, because they'd heard about Curtis McElroy and what he had done to my kindergarten teacher when she had the gall to break rules one and two by calling social services.

So, instead of talking, I'd taken to hitting. Only I couldn't stand the sound of fists pounding flesh, of teeth cracking, of the grunts and whimpers that came from being beat up. I worked hard one summer until I could buy a punching bag. First, I hung it from one of the rafters in the old barn. Later, when I inherited Mamaw's house, I strung it up on the back porch. I would beat that bag until I couldn't catch my breath, and I tried like hell to replace the memory of my mama's cries with the groans of the ceiling rafters as the bag swung back at me. The damn thing always swung back at me.

After dropping Romy off at her place, I needed to beat something. First, I punched at Curtis's imaginary face. He was the reason I was like this. His poisoned blood flowed through my veins.

Then I couldn't help but punch at the impossibly handsome face of Richard Paris. That lucky bastard had the only thing I'd ever wanted and enough money to make her truly happy. He probably didn't even know what kind of woman he had.

Pounding, pounding until dust came from the bag and my knuckles started to ache.

Why didn't you just sign the papers, you dumb-ass?

Deep inside, I'd hoped she would come back. Now I'd finally got my wish, but I couldn't answer her question. Time and distance had shown me all too well the hundreds of reasons I couldn't be the man she thought I was, nor the man she deserved, so I beat my fists against that punching bag some more.

You could've gone to her, you know.

I could've, but if I'd gone she would've followed me back. No matter what I told her, she would've followed me back, and Curtis would've made our lives a living hell. Besides, Romy had the smarts for Vandy. She belonged there.

You could've gone to her and stayed there.

Yeah, I should've, but I couldn't leave Mama. And I wasn't getting into Vanderbilt, that was for sure. I still remember the deep belly laugh from the high school counselor when I told him I wanted to go to Vanderbilt. He'd said, "Son, Vandy's the Harvard of the South. You think you can hang with that crowd?"

Of course, we McElroys don't like being laughed at, so I'd held on to that dream all the way up until the spring of my senior year when I broke my leg—playing baseball of all things—and ended any chance of a football scholarship. Romy told me that was no reason not to go to Vandy, but we both knew I didn't have that kind of money. I sure as hell didn't have the grades to get an academic scholarship, either.

That SOB Richard probably didn't have the grades, either. But I bet he had the money.

I pummeled the punching bag until my fists were on fire and my lungs burned. I was no stranger to pain. Sometimes I welcomed it. Any time I started thinking about what might have been, I went to my punching bag. I might picture a cheery farmhouse, a glowing Romy who was decorating a nursery or grading papers at a sunny kitchen table. Then I would punch until the exertion helped me remember who I was and the havoc I could wreak.

There was a time when I was young and stupid, a time when I thought I would somehow be able to outrun my temper. Maybe I'd call on the Collins part of me and find something meek to counteract what Curtis had given me.

But now I knew.

I knew I needed to sign Romy's papers and let her go.

My fists, now numb from pain, flew into the bag.

She deserved to grade papers or decorate nurseries in a mansion, not a tiny farmhouse. Heck, she deserved the ability to do or be whatever she wanted. As long as she was stuck with me, she wouldn't have a lot of options.

Sweat dripped down from my brow and stung my eyes as I launched everything I had into my own Fight Club.

She deserved everything that Richard bastard could give her and a million things he couldn't.

The beam holding the punching bag groaned, and one of the chain links gave way. The bag thudded to the floor followed by the clink of the chain.

You gotta sign those papers.

I wiped away the sweat and bent over to catch my breath. Tomorrow. I would go up there and sign the papers tomorrow. Then I would badger the hell out of Curtis until he made me power of attorney like he'd said he would. If I couldn't have Romy, I could at least have the old home place.

Romy

Holy hell, my mother was right about nothing good coming from Satterfields and drinking. Farming and hangovers don't go together at all.

Running behind from the previous night's festivities, I couldn't help but give the stink eye to the bedroom door that shielded Daddy from me. He snored as he always did: with a roar, a pause, and a gasping gulp of air. After all the work he'd done in his life, he deserved to sleep in at least one morning.

Thanks to still having only instant coffee in the house, I was running late again. To make matters worse, I'd forgotten to order the boots and thus had to stuff socks into the toes of Daddy's boots to have something to wear. I tripped over my feet all the way to the barn, then spent too much time staring at the practically empty barn and wondering how I was going to start filling it with hay for the winter. I could buy hay, but I was rapidly running out of funds and Goat Cheese had told Daddy there wasn't much hay to be bought that year.

I wondered how many other women stood looking at an empty barn and dreamed of putting a café in the corner complete with friendly barista. Shrugging off the impossible—health code violations galore in the old barn, no doubt—I turned to the garden instead. Making it to the end of both rows through sheer determination, I finished up the green beans. Then I cut some okra and picked tomatoes. The cows obliged me by standing close to the barn and being all present and accounted for—that left me with Maggie May.

I rounded the corner of the barn and climbed a slat up on the gate to look over into the little pen. Squat and black with fuzzy ears and enormous brown eyes, Maggie stood chewing her cud, oblivious to how lucky she was. That cow was living proof that Hank Satterfield was a soft touch because she was old and now had trouble calving, but he wouldn't get rid of her because she was the last calf my mother had named.

Inexplicably rejected by her mother when only a few days old, Maggie had been bottle-fed by my mother, who would come with bottle in hand each morning singing an off-key "Wake up, Maggie, I think I've got something to say to you." Now, why Rosemary Satterfield, staid librarian, had sung Rod Stewart to a baby calf, I'd never know, but the name stuck. And soft touch Hank couldn't bear to part with the old cow, who now snorted and anxiously paced the pen, her uterus obviously prolapsed despite the vet's earlier stitches to hold it in place.

Shit.

"I'm going to get Daddy and call Dr. Winterbourne, so you can stop your fussing."

My country accent bounced off the barn. Great. There was that West Tennessee lilt again, the one that would make me the laughingstock of my students, not to mention all of Richard's friends. Oh, good. More get-togethers where we played everybody's favorite party game: Let's ask Romy to speak so we can hear her accent. Maybe she can trot out those quaint weather expressions or explain to us once again that she did, indeed, grow up wearing shoes.

Damned cow should've already been ground chuck.

As if soft touch me could take her off, either. Since she'd been bottle-fed, Maggie was friendlier than the rest of Daddy's cows. She ambled over and sniffed my outstretched hand, then snorted cow slobber with tiny bits of grass all over me as if to say, "You're close, but you're not quite *my* Rosemary."

"I know I'm not," I muttered under my breath as I scratched her dirty forehead. "And she was your mama, too, wasn't she?"

Maggie did her sniff and snort at me again.

"You know what? That's more than enough cow slobber for one day." I wiped my hands on my shorts, knowing they were destined for a double wash with color-safe bleach anyway. "Besides, I'm not happy with you for what happened with Daddy."

She laid back her ears again and tossed her head back to lick a quivering fly-infested spot on her flank. I wasn't being fair to her. It wasn't her fault Beauregard, the old bull, had taken offense to having one of his sister wives culled from the herd. He'd been the one to kick Daddy into the old wooden gate and break his leg. Thanks to that, Old Beau was now on his way to being USDA Grade A. None of the cows seemed too sad to see him go, either.

This time Maggie butted my elbow hard enough to knock me back from the fence. "All right, I know the drill. I'm going to call the vet. You're an awful lot of trouble. You know that, right?"

I walked back to the house, Daddy's boots still slipping up and down on my heels. If I were a smart woman, I would've ordered some new boots along with that coffeemaker that should have already been there, since I'd paid an arm and a leg to get it faster. Whatever. I could stand anything for two months, now one month, three weeks, and some change.

I kicked off my boots and tromped through the house. "Daddy, time to call Dr. Winterbourne," I hollered. Then I passed through the kitchen, saw we had a visitor, and blushed to my very core.

Richard Paris did not need to see me in a ratty T-shirt, holey socks, and worn-out jean shorts with cow-slobber veneer. And yet there he was, smiling at me instead of frowning at my disheveled appearance.

"I think that can wait a minute," Daddy said calmly. "Richard, here, says he's got something to ask you."

The world threatened to upend itself as Richard, in his neatly pressed Brooks Brothers chinos, got down on one knee and took my hand, not knowing that five minutes ago it'd been covered in cow slobber.

No. Not here. Not now. Not when I haven't even talked Julian into signing the papers yet.

"Rosemary Jane Satterfield, would you do me the honor of being my bride?"

I can't! I'm already married!

"But, Richard, look at me." I gestured to my nasty work clothes, the farmhouse that suddenly looked shabby instead of homey.

He squeezed my hand and looked up at me with warm chocolate eyes. "I love you just the way you are. I've never seen you looking lovelier."

My breath caught. Tears stung my eyes. Then Daddy stifled a laugh into a coughing fit. "Yes, Richard. I will marry you."

Just as soon as I'm officially divorced. Not that you ever need to know about that.

He jumped to his feet and grabbed me into a bear hug before I could warn him about sweat, cow slobber, and the hundreds of tiny spiderwebs I'd walked through in the barn. He kissed me full on the mouth, and I felt an honest-to-goodness excitement about getting married! A real marriage with a minister and a white dress! We would stand up in a flower-filled County Line Methodist Church with bridesmaids and a flower girl. We might even convince Bill to let us have a little reception over at The Fountain, and—

"Oh, I'm so glad you said yes! I was going to wait until your birthday to propose, but one look at the ring and I couldn't wait. Then Mother casually mentioned that the cathedral had an unexpected cancellation around Christmastime. I'm sure you can put something together in six months with her help."

"Cathedral?" Hank and I said it together with the exact same country accent.

Richard's smile faded. "Yes, the cathedral. That's okay, I hope.

I mean you had to know my family would want a Catholic cere-
mony. There's even an opening in the August confirmation class.
How convenient is that?"

Not very, considering I have no intentions of converting.

I looked to Daddy without thinking. Wrinkled flesh hooded
his eyes, making him look like a cross between Tommy Lee
Jones and Droopy Dog.

"I thought it was traditional to have the wedding in the bride's
hometown." Even as I said the words, I knew better. No way
would the Paris family schlep their whole brood out to the boondocks for a small church wedding and a reception in a cinder-
block honky-tonk. When I looked back at Richard, his eyes were
on me, patiently waiting for me to come to that realization.

"Come on, Romy, it'll be a storybook wedding, one for the
ages."

Hank cleared his throat. "This is beginning to sound like a
bigger production than I can afford."

Richard turned toward my father with his best damage-control
smile. "No worries, Mr. Satterfield, I'm sure we can work something out."

He started to say something more, then realized Hank didn't
care for those words. He especially didn't care for the implication
that he needed help getting his only daughter properly hitched.
I suppressed a hysterical giggle. Little did anyone in the room
know she was *already* hitched.

I sank onto the world's scratchiest couch. I was going to hell
for this. I just knew it.

This *was* my hell for the sins of my youth.

"I'm going to call Mom and Dad and tell them the good
news!" Richard said as he took out his cell phone.

I summoned a smile for him, hoping he wasn't noticing a dis-
tinct undercurrent of despair.

"O-kay, I'll just have to step outside to get reception." He
leaned over to give me a quick kiss on the lips and stepped out
on the porch to make his phone call.

"Well, that went well."

"Daddy, don't."

"A cathedral, huh?" Mercutio appeared out of nowhere and jumped into Daddy's lap. He started scratching behind the cat's ears. "Thought you always wanted to get married at County Line."

"I did. I mean, I do. I'll talk to him."

"Well, you'll have some time. He asked if he could stay until your birthday."

I buried my head in my hands. I really was paying for the sins of my youth. And someone else's, too.

From Rosemary Satterfield's
History of the Satterfield-McElroy Feud

Things calmed down for a while in 1866 after Janie Magilroy divorced Shaymus, but he wouldn't let her take the kids. Both families concentrated on putting their lives back together after the Civil War. Shaymus found a new bride. Problems arose in 1873 when his new bride died unexpectedly after being thrown from a horse. Suddenly Shaymus had two strapping young boys from his first marriage and three more children under the age of five from his second marriage with no one else to help him raise them. He was certain that thirteen-year-old Louisa Satterfield was the answer to all of his problems.

In a story similar to the biblical tale of Dinah, he decided to take Louisa as his bride whether she liked it or not. Benjamin Satterfield had gone on a trip to Memphis and returned just in time to keep Alma from reclaiming her stepdaughter with a shotgun. Instead he, a neighbor, and a brother went up to the Magilroy farmhouse and took back his daughter by force.

At the end of the day, Benjamin had been shot fatally, as had thirteen-year-old James Magilroy. Shaymus had been shot, too, but he would live to serve his prison sentence for also shooting little Otis Satterfield, age six, who, in all of the confusion, had managed to tag along after his father to help free his favorite sister.

Nine months later, Louisa gave birth to a bouncing baby boy. She refused to list his last name as Magilroy. She named him after her little brother Otis instead. Otis Satterfield went on to be a Justice of the Peace, fitting since he was both a Satterfield and a Magilroy.

Julian

When I walked up to the Satterfield place, I immediately regretted the decision not to drive. Sure, it was a short distance, but there was the silver Porsche and there was Richard Paris pacing on the Satterfields' front porch. I stopped short.

Go on, coward, what do you have to fear from him?

As I got a little closer, I couldn't help but hear his conversation.

"Yes, Mother, of course she said yes!" He paced a bit, his other finger in his ear. "Well, I'm not sure the wedding will be in the cathedral after all."

He held the phone away from his ear, noticing me for the first time. Even I could hear his mother, and I was still a few feet from the porch. City Boy stepped aside to let me pass, and I knocked on the door, almost tripping over a box there against the wall.

Romy answered the door looking shell-shocked, and I couldn't look away from the rock on her left hand. I mean, Gibraltar wouldn't have measured up. A lump came up in my throat. It dwarfed the ring I'd given her: the worn band decorated with orange blossoms that had belonged to my mamaw.

"Mother. Calm down. Just keep the reservation for the cathedral. No, I'll talk with her. No, you don't need to—"

I picked up the large box by the door and entered the house, glad to leave that conversation behind. Romy swallowed hard. She looked more like she'd narrowly survived an *Independence Day* alien attack instead of becoming engaged to one of the richest men in Tennessee.

"I'm ready," I said, but she continued blinking as though looking through me.

"Ready for what?" Hank asked.

That got her attention.

"I have something of his I needed to return," Romy said hastily.

"You can bring it to him, then."

"But he has that box." She turned to me. "Mind taking that upstairs?"

As if Romy had ever once asked me to carry something for her before. I gave her a look, but said, "Not at all."

"Tell Richard I'll be right back," she said to Hank.

He pursed his lips and lowered his brows. Apparently, in his eyes, being closer to thirty than twenty didn't make it any more appropriate to take a man up to your bedroom alone.

I ducked as I reached the top. It was significantly warmer upstairs, and she had a couple of windows open to pull what little breeze there was across the house.

"AC doesn't work as well up here," she said apologetically. "Granny didn't like to use these rooms because she was afraid of fire, you know."

I waited in the area at the top of the stairs, the spot that was originally designed to be a sitting room. Romy disappeared into the first bedroom and returned with a manila file folder and a small box. I swallowed hard at the sight of it. "That's it?"

She nodded. "This is it."

There was a little end table beside a tiny couch. She moved the lamp and opened up the folder, then handed me the pen before pointing me to the X below her name. I handed her the box I'd picked up outside, and she made an almost orgasmic sound when she read the label.

My hand hovered over the paper and I had to ask, "What's that?"

"It's my Keurig," she said with reverence. "I'll have coffee again."

I shook my head and almost told her it was pretty sad when coffeemakers could cause her to make that sound. Before I could form the words, she reached to push back a strand of hair, and the sun caught the solitaire on her finger, flashing a kaleidoscope of color on the opposite wall.

Nope. No way I could top that show.

I scrawled my name in each and every place she pointed out, then pulled myself up straight. "That's it?"

"Well, except for this." She chewed on her bottom lip as she handed me the small box. I knew what was inside, but popped the lid open anyway. My mamaw's ring sat sternly against the velvet but looked as though it'd been recently cleaned. Irrationally, I wanted to tell her to keep it, but it had belonged to Mamaw and had never fit Romy's ring finger anyway.

I took the ring out of the box and crammed it in my pocket before setting the box down. No need for anyone downstairs to see me return with a ring-sized box. "All right then. For what it's worth, I'm sorry."

"Me, too."

We stared at each other for what seemed an eon. Richard's muffled voice echoed off the window above the porch. A dirt dobber whined in the window, batting against it while trying to reach the sunlight.

"This is good-bye, then," I said over the lump in my throat. "I'll do my best to stay out of your way."

She nodded, something glistening at the corners of her eyes. Breaking up with someone was always sad no matter what, right? I had this irrational urge to beg her to rip up the papers, to go all Julia Roberts in *Notting Hill*. I'm just a hick, standing in front of a girl—

Hell, I wasn't going to sissy out like that.

Instead, I kissed her softly on the cheek, telling my heart not to race at the familiar scent of her pear shampoo, a scent made all the better by the hint of sweat from an honest morning's work in the garden.

"Good luck, Rosemary Satterfield."

As I went down the stairs, practically crouching because the stairwell was so narrow and steep, I ran into Richard on his way up. We shimmied past each other as best we could.

"Congratulations," I said, leaving off the *jackass* that I wanted to add.

"Thank you," he said with a grin full of impossibly straight and professionally whitened teeth, a politician's smile—or a shark's.

I should've left it at that, but I couldn't resist adding, "Hurt her in any way, and I'll hunt you down and kick your ass."

Romy

"There's the future Mrs. Paris!" He was all straight white teeth and perfect hair with a slight curl. Dear God, I should've been swooning. Instead I was sick to my stomach.

"Richard, I—"

He pulled me close and kissed me gently before resting his chin on top of my head. "You have made me the happiest man on earth! Although I should've come up with a better proposal. Is it too late for a mulligan?"

Oh, I hope not.

I twisted off my ring and handed it back to Richard, whose face deepened into a dark frown. "I was just kidding, darling."

"Richard, there's something I have to tell you before I can accept your ring."

He ran a hand through his hair. "You're still in love with him, aren't you?"

"What? No." *Most certainly not. Never again.* "But there is something I have to tell you."

Richard put his hands on his hips and trained his chocolate eyes on me. "I'm listening."

My hand was halfway to my mouth before I realized I was about to do that disgusting thing where I chew on my hangnails. Seems like my accent wasn't the only bad habit I'd picked up since coming home. "Remember how I told you I was engaged to Julian?"

"Mm-hmm." Richard's eyes narrowed. He didn't like the direction this was going. For what it was worth, I wasn't too keen on it myself. Better to take a deep breath and get it over with.

"Julian and I secretly got married the day before graduation. Only he stood me up that night."

"Stood you up?" Richard's righteous indignation warmed my heart and coaxed a few extra beats out of it. "Wait. You married him?"

"Yes, but we never actually lived together. Besides, he just signed the papers. That's why he was here."

"I can't believe you would hide something like this from me. Wait. What kind of papers?"

"Divorce papers."

Richard ran his hand through his hair again and started pacing. "Romy—"

He couldn't finish the thought and went back to pacing. At first I couldn't tell how angry he was. Finally, he turned to me again. "Romy, I can't marry you if you're divorced. You have to get the marriage annulled."

Nausea hit the pit of my stomach with such force my cow-slobber hand clamped over my mouth. Dear God, I couldn't face Julian again. Not to tell him I needed an annulment. Not after I'd finally convinced him to sign the divorce papers. We were supposed to be done. Through. *Finito*.

"Come on, Richard, there has to be another way—"

He clamped his hands on my upper arms, realized his grip was too hard, and eased off. "No. Did you have sex with him?"

My face felt as though it might burn off. "Not on our wedding night."

Something died behind those warm chocolate eyes. "How many times?"

What did that matter? "I don't know. How many women have you slept with and how many times?"

He pinched the bridge of his nose. "Fair point."

I couldn't help but notice he wasn't answering the question. I told myself I wasn't about to feel guilty about having slept with Julian. I hadn't asked Richard if anyone had come before me, but his response told me someone had.

"Romy, I need to think this over."

"So this is it between us?" I could hardly force the words over the lump in my throat, and tears blurred my vision.

He grabbed both shoulders and looked me in the eye. "Of course not, you crazy woman!"

I should have been feeling relief. So why did it feel so much like sorrow instead?

"Look, I'm not happy you lied to me, but I know you haven't been with Julian because you only come home once every few years, and—" He stopped there, his eyes crazed. "Did you?"

"I swear to you, Richard, I hadn't even *seen* Julian until the other day."

Richard plopped down on the old love seat and buried his face in his hands. "I'm sorry. This is all so crazy. I would've never thought that you, of all people, would have kept such a secret from me."

"I was ashamed," I whispered.

He stood, and I could see him shifting into solutions mode. "If you didn't consummate the marriage, we can still work with this. I'll call my lawyers. Tell, tell . . . *him* that he's probably going to need a lawyer, too. As for these?" Richard picked up the papers and ripped them down the middle. "Never happened. I'm going for a drive."

I was still staring into space when the Porsche purred to life then sprayed gravel as Richard tore off down the road. I needed to cry, but I couldn't find the tears, just an overwhelming sadness. This was supposed to have been one of the happiest days of my life.

Instead, I'd disappointed him. Deeply. He said he still wanted to marry me, but I wouldn't blame him if he changed his mind. He might decide while driving around the sticks that he didn't want to have anything to do with me. Staying married—on paper, at least—to Julian was such a stupid thing to do for someone who was supposedly so smart. And to think I used to get mad at Granny when she told me I needed to get some common sense to go along with my book learning.

Placing the engagement ring on the table, I plopped onto the love seat. "Mom, I could really use you about now. You see what a mess I've made of all of this?"

She didn't answer me, of course. It's not even like I could feel her presence wrapped around me in some kind of maternal hug from the great beyond. Maybe that's why I was so deficient with the boys. I'd blamed it all on Julian for so long, but the truth of the matter was that I'd screwed up things with Richard royally. And all by myself. Would I have done any better if Mom had been there to talk me through periods and crushes and what to do when jilted by your high school sweetheart? Would I have done better talking about sex if I'd had someone to answer my awkward questions instead of reading about periods from that pamphlet that came with my introductory Always kit? And about sex from romance novels and my mom's dog-eared copy of *Everything You Always Wanted to Know About Sex, But Were Afraid to Ask*? The former was more entertaining but not always as informative.

Now if only there were a book called *How to Tell Your Ex-Husband You're Still Married After All and You Need an Annulment Instead of a Divorce*. That would be handy.

Julian

Somehow after signing divorce papers, I didn't want to be alone and I had some time to kill before going to the dealership for my other job. So I drove over to Ben's place to give him hell about stranding Romy with me the night before. He, of all people, should've known not to pull a stunt like that.

I pulled up beside the old Victorian house he called law office and home. Sonuvabitch owed me after making me sing "Ebony and Ivory," too. That's why I was surprised to see him edging out on the front porch to meet me. He had to know I was going to be less than happy with him.

"Got company or something?" I laughed as I took the two cracked steps up to the wide veranda.

Ben ran a hand over his super-short black hair and scratched a place at the back of his scalp. "Uh, actually . . ."

At his embarrassed expression my anger evaporated. "You didn't!" I slugged him hard on the arm.

He flashed a grin. "Yeah, I did." He punched me back. "But you don't say a word because I'm too much of a gentleman to kiss and tell."

I held both hands up in surrender and eased into the glider rocker that had belonged to his grandmother. "Well, I came here to kick your ass over last night, but—"

"You could try. I would mop the floor with your pasty ass."

"If I didn't need cheap legal advice so often, I'd prove you wrong. What the hell were you playing at leaving Romy to ride home with me? We've had that discussion before. Besides, City Boy proposed. I signed the papers. It's a done deal."

Ben frowned. "Aw, man, I was rooting for you two crazy kids, but I guess I can't stop you if you want to be a miserable son of a bitch the rest of your life."

"Your support is encouraging."

"Hey, Ben?" Genie appeared at the door wearing one of his dress shirts and nothing else. "Where's the coffee? Oh, hey, Julian."

Not so much as a blush from her, but I felt a twinge of something lost. I had to find a way to get over Romy and find someone to make me coffee. Or maybe I needed to get one of those coffee thingies like she got. Might be a full-service kind of machine, based on her sound effects.

"In the pantry by the fridge."

She disappeared and he turned on me. "Don't look at her like that."

Had I really been staring at Genie? "Wasn't really looking at her, more like looking past her."

"The hell you were," he muttered under his breath.

"The way she was looking at you, I'd say the show was just for you," I said.

His head snapped to me. "I thought you weren't looking!"

"Not that much, but I do have a pulse," I said. "So if Curtis were to draw up some papers transferring power of attorney to me, do you think you could look them over?"

"You want me to look over some papers?"

"Next oil change is on me?"

"Ha! If he brings the papers, then I will peruse them thoroughly and make sure he isn't taking you for all you're worth."

Genie appeared again, still not shy. "Hey, Julian, you want some coffee?"

"No, thank you," I said, making sure I kept my eyes on hers

because I could feel Ben's glare. She disappeared inside, and I got to my feet. "I gotta put in some hours at the dealership. In the meantime, don't do anything I wouldn't do."

Ben harrumphed. "I've already done a lot of things you haven't done in a *long* time, and I'm going to continue to do so because *I* am not an idiot."

I waved away his comments and climbed into my truck. Poor Genie wouldn't last long. None of Ben's women did. The first time he invited them to Sunday dinner at the nursing home where they had to watch him spoon-feed mush to his dementia-addled grandmother, they fled.

Then again, maybe she'd stay. Hadn't nurses seen it all?

When I pulled into my parking spot at the dealership the sunlight caught something on the seat beside me. I picked up the delicate gold hoop and sighed deeply. A hoop like this had once brought Romy and me back together.

I'd been carrying around Mamaw's ring for a while, letting it burn a hole in my pocket while I tried to get the courage to ask her to marry me. One day we'd been up in the barn, and I couldn't wait anymore. I got down on one knee and proposed. After what seemed like an hour, she said yes. We took a little celebratory roll in the hay then promptly got into an argument about the particulars.

"I'm not getting married at the Baptist church," she'd said.

"Well, I'm not getting married at your church."

"Why not?"

"Because I'm not." At that point it occurred to me I'd just screwed up royally. I had a gorgeous naked woman on a quilt in a hayloft. She'd agreed to marry me, and I was arguing about the how.

"Well, I'm certainly not agreeing to obey you, so I'm not getting married by a Baptist!" She started jerking clothes on, and that wasn't the direction I wanted things to go.

"Romy."

"Don't you 'Romy' me!"

She ran off, but that afternoon I found her earring, which gave me the perfect excuse to come see her and to make an alternate suggestion: the justice of the peace.

Now I stared past the gold hoop. It looked an awful lot like the same earring. But even Cinderella didn't lose the same shoe twice, so I put her earring in the ashtray and got to work.

Maybe this time I'd return the earring by mail.

From Rosemary Satterfield's
History of the Satterfield-McElroy Feud

While Shaymus was locked away, his first wife, Janie, moved in with his third wife, Sarah. I'd like to think they actually got along pretty well: Janie got to be with her son again, and Sarah got an extra pair of hands. Thanks to a well-timed conjugal visit, Sarah managed to have a child before Shaymus was shipped off to another prison, but she had a girl, so Luke, Janie's only remaining son, was set to take over the Magilroy place.

Benjamin Junior's son Myron once told me that he'd heard that Luke Magilroy and Sallie Satterfield had a little romance. He said his daddy sent her off to finishing school in New England the minute he found out. She ended up marrying a man not quite as rich as Rockefeller, but she never forgave her brother.

In 1886, Benjamin Junior married Rose Brown. Luke Magilroy married her twin sister, Virginia. For two decades peace reigned between the two families. Twice they came close to uniting the farms, but then Benjamin Junior's daughter, Wisteria, did something stupid: She fell in love with—and I'm not making this name up—Christopher Columbus MacElroy.*

*The 1900 census as well as Yessum County property records show that Magilroy became MacElroy about that time. By the next census they'd dropped the "a" and adopted the current spelling.

Romy

I was still sitting upstairs in a daze, feeling sorry for myself, when I heard the dogs. At first I thought it was Goat Cheese's old mutts. They liked to wander over from time to time.

No. Those dogs are snarling.

I scrambled down the stairs, slipping once and bouncing into the wall, hard. Daddy sat back in his chair snoring as I ran for the back door and the boots. How he could sleep through it all, I didn't know.

As I ran across the side yard from the house to the pen, I could hear Maggie lowing. I hit a trot, my boots rubbing up and down my heels. When I reached the fence out of breath, two pit bulls circled her. She had her head lowered, shaking it at them to warn them off.

I froze. I couldn't get in there with those snarling beasts. Maggie had red streaks down one flank where they'd jumped at her. She lolled wild eyes at me as she bellowed for help.

As she turned to kick at the interlopers, I saw either her uterus had prolapsed more or the dogs had somehow jumped high enough to bite at it. She was trying to have her calf and the dogs could smell both her blood and her fear.

I looked around me frantically for a weapon, but all I saw was an old ax handle leaning against the adjoining shed. I grabbed it and climbed over the gate rather than taking the time to undo the chain. One dog, a brindled one, lunged for Maggie's backside, but she rallied with a solid kick that sent him whimpering. The second dog, a yellow one, barked Maggie May into a corner. I approached the dogs, forcing myself to stay calm and stare them down. "No! No! Now, git!"

They paused, and the yellow one took a step backward. Just when I thought I'd convinced him I was alpha, he lunged.

He clamped down on my left arm. Pain burned through me as the dog tried to pull me down to the ground. I whopped him on the nose.

No response.

Even though my heart raced, icy adrenaline ran through my veins. At first, I'd jerked out of instinct, but I knew the dog would tear my arm apart if I tried to pull it back. Those few seconds seemed like an eternity as the yellow dog jumped at Maggie. Fury snapped behind my eyes. We weren't going to have to bottle-feed another calf because some McElroy dog took her mother.

I raised the ax handle to hit the dog on my arm even as Maggie kicked him. In the split second the dog let go, I drew back my arm and held out the ax handle instead.

The dog chomped down on the handle, and I looked for the yellow one. The world swayed around me, then everything went eerily still.

Both dogs froze, their ears pricking up. A rifle shot rang out, and they ran through a low spot in the fence and back to the McElroy side.

That's when I heard Daddy.

"Rosemary, are you all right?"

His voice was hoarse, muffled, and desperate even. I propped the post beside the gate with shaking fingers and leaned on my good arm to clamber over the gate. As I trotted in the direction of his voice, a lesser pain on my fingers registered and I looked down to where I'd broken three nails. One of them bled from being broken so far into the quick. "Daddy?"

"I'm over here."

He'd been in such a hurry his wheelchair had gone off the makeshift ramp over the front porch steps and capsized. He'd pulled himself to sitting position and dragged himself to the rifle that'd no doubt flown from his lap. My heart caught in my throat at the thought of all that could've gone wrong.

"Daddy, did you hurt yourself? Are you okay?"

"Baby, you're bleeding."

Dazed by the dizzying ache in my arm, I didn't answer him for a moment. "Dog bit me. But are you okay?"

"Dammit, Curtis's damned pit bulls got loose again, didn't they?" he panted from where he was still trying to right himself.

He choked back a sob of sorts. For the sake of his pride, I had no choice but to ignore it. "Let me help you back into the chair, and we'll get you into the house. You may want to call the vet, too. Looks like Maggie's worse."

"What about getting you to the doctor?" He grunted as I lifted him back into his chair.

"Don't you need to check on Maggie first?"

Hank's eyes narrowed. "You're a sight more important than a cow. Let's call Julian—"

"No!" I fumbled to get my cell phone out of my pocket and awkwardly dialed Richard. He might be mad at me, and rightfully so, but he'd still take me to the hospital, right?

The procession of rings followed by his chipper voice-mail message suggested otherwise.

"I'll drive myself," I said.

Daddy grabbed my good arm. "Hell, you can hardly dial a cell phone. I'm calling Julian, and that's that."

Shit. That's just what I need. Why couldn't we have neighbors other than the McElroys or old man Smith, who was ninety-seven if he was a day?

Five minutes later I'd managed to help him roll into the house using my good arm. He'd called Julian and was still muttering under his breath, "Damned cow is going to cost me a fortune." But he was looking at me with worry in his eyes.

"It's just a dog bite, Daddy," I said. He knew I'd suffered something similar the summer I worked for Dr. Winterbourne. That was back when I thought I wanted to be a veterinarian. The next school year, a fall chemistry class changed my mind.

"Well, you know what, Rosemary? You're all that I've got. And to think what those mean-ass dogs might have done—"

"They didn't, though. I'll get patched up. I've done worse— remember that time I fell out of the tree over there?"

"Yeah, I remember. You shaved ten years off my life."

Julian opened the door, concern hooding his eyes. He looked to Hank, and my father nodded. Something passed between the two men before my father looked away. I would've expected hatred or at least distrust. Instead, Daddy's nod had held more trust and approval than his halfhearted reply to Richard that he could have my hand. The two of them were in on something, and I was going to figure it out if it killed me.

Julian

I broke at least thirty laws getting Romy to the doctor's office in Ellery. Now that she wasn't in the thick of things, her eyes were glazing over from pain.

"When did you and Daddy get so chummy?"

Of all the things I expected her to ask, that was not one of them. "What do you mean?"

"Don't play dumb with me. You helped him when he broke his leg so now you're his go-to guy for Satterfield family emergencies? Something's up."

"Nothing's up," I said as I rolled through a stop sign that brought me into the town limits.

"Julian, the two of you hated each other back when we were dating."

"Well, I'm older and wiser."

I yanked the truck into park and got out before she could ask me any more questions. Truth be told, helping Hank out the day he broke his leg actually made us even, but I wasn't about to tell Romy about the time Hank had helped me.

I placed a hand around her waist to walk her into the doctor's office. As we walked, she stumbled out of her right boot. What the hell was she doing wearing Hank's boots?

"I think you need some smaller boots there, Romy."

"Kiss my ass, Julian."

Better to have her cuss me than question me.

The receptionist took one look at Romy's gray face and decided to send her on back to the Ellery Clinic's tiny "emergency room." We didn't have to wait long for Doc Malcolm, though he walked much slower than I remembered. Despite his shock of white hair and stooped posture, I felt like a kid again. All I needed was one of the lime suckers he kept in his pocket.

He turned to Romy first. "Well, well, Stinky, what have you got yourself into this time? Still falling out of trees?"

Romy blushed at the older doctor, a man who'd nursed both of us through colds, the chicken pox, strep throat, stitches, and just about every other ailment under the sun. "Dog bite."

Doc Malcolm tsked, then acknowledged me with a slap on the shoulder. "I always told her they'd have to chase off the boys with a stick when she got older. I must've forgotten to warn her about the dogs, eh, Julian?"

I smiled, swallowing hard. I appreciated his attempts to lighten the mood *Patch Adams*–style, but I wanted Romy to be out of pain as soon as possible. Still, he took his time washing his hands and gathering supplies. When he unwrapped the towel from her arm, he whistled. At the sight of the jagged gashes, some spot in my chest ached sharp and fierce because I couldn't take Romy's pain for her. Instead, I'd once again caused her pain—just indirectly. She gasped at his touch, and I instinctively moved to her good side and took her hand. She crushed my fingers but wouldn't look my way.

"Okay, Stinky. As bad as it looks, I'm more concerned about what's under the skin. We've got to clean this and make sure you don't have too much damage," Doc Malcolm said as he shuffled back to the counter. He looked at me. "What do we know about this dog, eh? Had its shots, I hope?"

"One of my father's dogs," I managed over the lump in my throat. "They've had all their shots." That was no thanks to Curtis. I'd been the one to load them up and take them for their shots.

"Well, that's good. We don't want to do the rabies treatment. I think we'll get a tetanus shot ready, though," Doc Malcolm continued as he put on his gloves then started washing the wound and feeling his way around her arm. Romy flinched the moment his fingers pressed against her forearm. By the time he felt his way to one of the gashes, she'd turned white and looked ready to pass out.

"Now, Stinky, you're making it worse when you jump like that each time I touch you. You look up at that McElroy boy instead. He isn't too bad to look at, now, is he?"

Romy

No, Julian wasn't bad to look at, especially not when his blue eyes harbored that kind of pain and guilt. I didn't mean to actually look up at him, but I had always been one to follow doctor's orders. To make matters worse, Julian's other hand reached toward my cheek with trembling fingers, but he drew it back as though singed.

Dr. Malcolm's merciless fingers felt around the wounds. He flushed the wound with something that stung enough to bring tears to my eyes. Julian thumbed the tears away, and my traitorous body itched to lean into him, quivering with the effort it took to keep that arm still while the doctor poked and prodded. Julian stepped closer, and I leaned into him in spite of myself. I needed someone to lean into.

"All right. I've got some good news and some bad news," Dr. Malcolm said. "The good news is that I don't *think* you've got permanent damage. The bad news is that I'm afraid to suture you up for fear of infection. Now, you'd be less likely to have scars if I do the sutures, but there's always the chance an infection would set in."

"What would you do?" I asked.

"I'd clean it up and hope for the best," the doctor said.

I swallowed and nodded for him to continue, then leaned back into Julian, trying not to think of how he smelled faintly of aftershave but mainly of cars and freshly cut hay.

"There we go," Dr. Malcolm said. "All bandaged up. Now for that shot, and I'm calling in some antibiotics, too—just in case."

Julian's hand squeezed mine while I got the shot, lingering for just a second before letting go. Dr. Malcolm turned on him, looking over the rims of his glasses, his bushy eyebrows arched. "Now about those dogs—"

Julian's lips made a thin line. "I'll handle it."

My heart skipped double. We might not still be together, but Julian had that steely-eyed look I'd seen before, the one that said, "You'd best not mess with my girl."

Dr. Malcolm caught that vibe because he turned to me. "And you, young lady, you are to rest and to take care of this wound per the instructions on this sheet—and they include elevation. Come see me in about three days to make sure it isn't infected. Take it easy, Stinky. That's an order."

I nodded and slid from the table, almost coming out of my boots again. I tamped down the irrational urge to kick them against the wall. *Damned boots.*

Julian put his arm around my waist to guide me out. For a minute I fell back into that old habit, enjoying the feel of his protective arm. Then I came to my senses and shrugged free: The last thing I needed was for Richard to drive by and get the wrong idea.

Julian started the truck. I wanted to ask him what he was going to do with the dogs, but I was afraid I wouldn't like the answer. He eased the truck into the street, but his knuckles were white.

"You know," I said softly, "the dogs didn't ask to be made mean."

He drove the next two blocks in silence but killed the motor once he'd parked behind the pharmacy, then trained his baby blues on me. "I know that."

"Maybe—maybe they could be rehabilitated. You know, maybe someone could teach them how to act differently so they wouldn't be so dangerous."

"Can't teach an old dog new tricks," Julian said with a humorless smile. "They'll be rotten until the day they die."

And we weren't talking about dogs anymore. Before I could say anything he got out of the truck and went around to my side to help me out.

"Thanks for taking me to the doctor."

"Least I could do," he said with a heavy sigh as he opened the pharmacy door for me.

I handed Mr. Giles my prescription and stepped back out of everyone's hearing range. "I don't suppose I could ask another favor of you, huh?"

"Shoot."

"I, uh, kinda need to get an annulment instead of a divorce. Richard tore up the papers."

Miss Georgette looked up from the Metamucil at the end of aisle five and frowned at Julian when he swore under his breath. "So we're still married. And he knows."

"Yes and yes."

"Just tell me what you want me to do, Romy."

"At this point? I don't know yet."

"Well, tell me when you figure it out." He sat down at the little desk that tested blood pressure but popped back up and guided me to the seat.

He looked ahead with a disgusted resignation I'd seen once before. When we were both freshmen, the football coach pulled me out of class one day. Apparently, he'd been informed I was the best English student in the school. So who better to help one of his star football players stay eligible? In his defense, he was new in town and didn't know about the Satterfields and the McElroys. He couldn't have known that Julian and I had drifted apart when my mom got sick.

I walked to the library, hall pass clutched in one hand. What would he say?

There he sat at one of the old wooden tables, leaned back in his chair with his arms crossed over his chest. No longer a boy, he didn't want to be there any more than I did. I pulled out the chair beside him and waited. Finally, he turned to look at me, and his eyes grew wide. Then he did something very curious: He blushed.

"*You're* going to be my tutor?"

"Maybe," I said. "Coach Davis said we'd take today as a trial period. If it works out, we'll study together in the afternoons." And the boosters were going to pay me for my trouble, but something told me Julian didn't need to know that.

Julian looked away. "You're not going to be able to help me any more than the other two."

My Satterfield stubbornness reared its ugly head. *Wanna bet?* "What makes you say that?"

"I can't read. No way I'm going to pass English if I can't read."

He can't read? The idea was so foreign to me that I couldn't find anything to say.

"See? Told you this wasn't going to work out," he said as he stood. "Now you know. Guess you were right to stop hanging out with the likes of me."

I put my hand on his arm, blushing to my very core. "I only stopped—" I had started to say playing, but we had been in junior high, too old for playing, when my mom was diagnosed. "I only stopped hanging out with you because Mom got sick. Then I didn't really want to hang out with anyone for a while."

His blue eyes softened, but he gently took his arm away. "Yeah, well, that don't change the fact that I can't read."

"Then I'll read to you."

And read to him I did. I even talked him into reading to me. That's when I figured out Julian had some kind of dyslexia, but everyone had assumed he was dumb or lazy. He'd taught himself to read some of the basics, but the old English of Shakespeare and the odd wording of poems were particularly challenging.

Guess that's why his poem about why I should go out with him persuaded me to give him a chance. Julian being Julian, he hadn't settled for a simple rhyme. No, we'd studied haikus and how difficult they were, so I found a note in my locker that said:

> *Black hair and green eyes*
> *Entice me. Your smile haunts me.*
> *Movies next Friday?*

As haikus went, it wasn't what the Japanese had in mind. That said, any time I thought of Julian counting out syllables on his fingers and no doubt looking through the dictionary for the word *entice*, I couldn't help but grin.

"What are you smiling about?"

His question brought me back to the present. "Nothing. Just something I remembered."

His blue eyes cut through me. Now a man, he was far removed from the cocky boy who'd two years later stuffed an entirely different kind of poem between the slats of my locker:

> *Roses are red, violets are blue*
> *I love your ass, and the rest of you, too!*

I'd slapped him on the arm for that one, but we'd both known I didn't mean it, not when I was just as crazy about him as he seemed to be about me.

Oh, Julian. What have the last ten years done to you?

"Miss Romy, you're ready." Mr. Giles motioned for me to come around to the lower spot at the counter and rattled off a ton of instructions I didn't have the wherewithal to comprehend.

As soon as I paid, Julian put a hand under my elbow and ushered me out of the pharmacy. "In a hurry, aren't we?"

"Yep."

That was the last word he said the entire trip, but I could tell by the set of his jaw he'd made up his mind about what he was going to do to those dogs.

From Rosemary Satterfield's
History of the Satterfield-McElroy Feud

Back in those days it wasn't as shocking for first cousins to wed. Young Wisteria Satterfield's love for her cousin Christopher Columbus "Lum" MacElroy was, however, unrequited. Your great-aunt Lucille told me stories about visiting her aunt Wisteria at the mental institute. She also told me that Wisteria was as sane as you or me—only about fifty times meaner.

But according to Benjamin III, Aunt Lucille's daddy, Wisteria had never been quite right in the head. She took a shine to Lum at a family picnic one Fourth of July and could never seem to understand why he didn't return her feelings. When he married another girl in the neighborhood, she couldn't stand it. One evening, when she knew Lum had gone hunting with one of her brothers, she sneaked up to the McElroy home place and set it on fire. Since she was caught, it was either jail or the insane asylum. To the asylum she went.

Eunice, Lum's wife, managed to make it out alive, but she lost the baby she was carrying and never quite recovered, eventually dying in 1911. That was the same year Benjamin III lost his wife and infant son in an eerily similar fire. At least six McElroys swore Lum was with them the entire time.

In an ironic twist of fate, Eunice McElroy is buried catty-cornered from Wisteria in the Ellery City Cemetery, even though Wisteria spent the rest of her life at Western State in Bolivar. Your father went with your granddaddy Satterfield to visit Aunt Wisteria once when he was little. He told me it was a crowded, nasty place. Your aunt Wisteria swore she'd had babies that had been stolen. At the time, your granddaddy thought she'd had too many shock treatments, but when all that stuff about Georgia Tann's black market babies came out, he had to wonder. There could be a Satterfield baby or two out there—maybe even one of Joan Crawford's kids.

Skirmishes continued throughout the years, but neither family wanted to have anything to do with arson—at least not for another fifty years.

Julian

I dropped Romy off and went to find Curtis. Forlorn, he sat on the back porch looking at the place under the old elm tree where his dogs should've been. I got out of the truck and studied the chains that had held the dogs, surprised by what I found.

"These aren't broken. Or loose. Or anything."

Curtis cleared his throat. "I guess I couldn't see the clasp on the chain and thought I had them tied up but didn't."

I pulled up to my full height. "You mean to tell me they got loose because you won't admit you can't *see?*"

"It's not my fault my damn eyes don't work," he roared. "And I can still see the big stuff!"

I glared at him—not that he could see it. "Now the dogs could be anywhere."

He waved some kind of dog whistle. "'Bout an hour ago I called them back with this, but they ran off when they saw I didn't have any kind of treat."

That sounded about right.

Curtis sighed heavily. "Goat Cheese called to tell me they're over in the church cemetery by The Fountain." He paused. "Could you go get them for me?"

It sounded as though Curtis had finally tried a slice of humble pie.

"I'm going to go get them, all right."

I turned for the house.

"Don't you kill my dogs!" Curtis hollered. "They cost me a lot of money."

His words bounced off my back. Once inside, I took my best rifle from the case, my hands shaking. I didn't want to kill those dogs. Romy was right. It wasn't their fault they were mean.

But they weren't going to chew up anything or anyone else. I grabbed the gun and some shells then almost ran into Curtis on my way out the door.

"Don't shoot my dogs, Julian." The quaver in his voice made me sick. He'd summoned more emotion for those two dogs than he'd ever managed for me, for Mama, or even for Mamaw.

"Out of the way, Curtis." I brushed past him.

With the gun in its rack and shells on the seat, I grimly drove toward the cemetery. I hadn't planned on having an *Old Yeller* moment, but that didn't mean I wouldn't.

Romy

Julian had been in such a hurry he didn't even walk me to the door. He practically had the truck in reverse before I hit the second step. I would've tried to talk him out of whatever he was headed to do, but it wouldn't have done any good. Something had hurt me, and he was going to take care of that something.

My gut churned for the dogs, but I couldn't seem to summon up too much pity considering my arm was on fire. If past experience were any indicator, the worst was yet to come. Uncle Liston had been bitten by a Doberman and ended up in the hospital when the wound became infected.

But no need to think about that now because nothing could be done to help it. I trudged up the stairs, noting the still empty driveway. Richard hadn't made it home. He hadn't returned any of my calls, either.

Do you blame him?

No, I didn't blame him. I banged on the door, but no one came to get me so I walked around back again. Sure enough, the back door was open. As many meth heads were running around, Daddy and I were going to have to talk about leaving doors open.

Once I'd taken my meds, I noticed the house was still eerily silent. The only sign of life, Mercutio, sat precariously on the breakfast room windowsill. His tail switched seemingly in time with the world's loudest wall clock.

I scratched between the cat's ears, and he purred. "Where's Daddy, Merc?"

He raised his head into my palm for a little love, but he didn't have the answers any more than I did. At that moment I looked out the window and saw Daddy in his wheelchair, poised outside Maggie's pen. He was so still, I bolted from the house, worried he'd wheeled himself out there only to have a heart attack from the exertion.

"Daddy? You okay?" I called as I trotted across the yard.

He didn't say anything until I stood right beside him. "It's the damnedest thing."

At first I thought he was talking about how Maggie had the calf while I was at the doctor. Nothing short of a miracle could explain how she managed to calve before we could call Dr. Winterbourne to take out the stitches. Then I followed Daddy's eyes. A spindly-legged calf trotted for Maggie, but she turned her back on the calf, moving away any time the calf tried to nurse. Only then did I realize why Hank was staring.

Son of a motherless goat.

The calf was mostly black, but she had a white face and white stocking feet, just like a Hereford.

We didn't have Herefords.

But the McElroys did.

"Well, shit fire and save the matches," I muttered.

For once, Hank didn't admonish me for having things in my mouth that he wouldn't hold in his hand. Instead, he added, "You got that right."

I watched cow and calf dance, and I could see how I missed the markings at first. The cow hadn't licked her calf down. As the calf wobbled behind her mother, dread formed a pretzel in my stomach. "Something's not right."

Hank grimaced. "She ain't taking to it like she ought."

"Do I need to get in there and try to help?"

Hank stared through my bandaged arm as though he could count my stitches. "I reckon not. Why don't you—"

"I'm not calling Julian."

We watched Maggie give her baby the cold shoulder, which, in cow terms, also included the occasional butt or kick. "I can't stand this. I'll be careful."

I climbed in and shooed the calf toward her mama with my right hand as I cradled my left arm to my chest. I even tried to distract Maggie long enough to let the calf nurse. More than once I tried to pick up the calf or to push her toward her mama, but Maggie wasn't having it.

"If you pick up that calf one more time I'm going to wear you out—I don't care how old you are!" Hank hollered. Startled, I stepped back from the calf and noticed blood oozing up through the bandage on my arm.

He was still going. "I knew we should have called—"

"Don't say it! I can't let this baby starve!"

He sighed deeply. He couldn't bear to see the calf suffer, either. "Shoo ol' Maggie into that little pen under the barn, and I'll call Dr. Winterbourne to patch her up. You go on down to Goat Cheese's house. He keeps colostrum in the freezer for times like these. We'll get something in the baby's stomach, then I'll send you to the Co-op for some of what they have."

With a grunt, he heaved his wheelchair out of the ruts on the other side of the gate and headed for the house. I opened the back gate, the one that led to a tiny area just in front of the chute we used to get the cows in the trailer, and shooed Maggie inside. Sentiment or no, Hank didn't take kindly to bad mothers. She, like Beauregard, was destined to wear USDA sooner rather than later.

And we would have to bottle-feed another calf whether I wanted to or not.

The calf, meanwhile, had lain down, drawing its skinny legs close. I crouched down to scratch her head, but her eyes were glazed over with hunger and what looked like dejection, although

I might have been projecting that part on the poor girl. "I know, baby," I said as I scratched her forehead. "Every living thing deserves a mama."

How much time had we lost while I was at the doctor? I stood quickly. "You hang in there," I told the calf before I climbed over the fence and went in search of Goat Cheese.

Julian

When I pulled into the County Line Methodist parking lot, I didn't see the dogs right away. Finally, I saw them nosing around the back of the cemetery.

All right, Julian. It's for the greater good.

I loaded the rifle and closed the truck door.

Dammit, Old Yeller *makes me mist up every damn time and I'm the one who has to do this?*

I picked my way around the gravestones to where the two dogs sniffed at a rabbit that was half eaten by fire ants. The dogs pawed and whined, but they were too late to snatch the rabbit from the ants. The yellow dog had the audacity to growl at me when I was two rows away. I raised the rifle, and looked through the scope to a spot between his eyes.

"Stop!"

I turned around to see Pete Gates running across the road from The Fountain. Knowing Pete, he wanted to shoot the dog himself.

I brought the rifle down and waited for him to reach me. When he did, he was out of breath. "What are you doing?"

"Taking care of these dogs," I said.

We looked over at the two, and the brindled one chose that moment to wag its tail.

"I'll take care of them," Pete said. "Curtis called me. Said I could have 'em if I could catch 'em."

Curtis really did love the dogs more than anything or anyone else.

Either that or he thought he could win them back playing poker.

"I *am* the closest thing to Animal Control around here," Pete added.

And so he was. Sorta. The official Animal Control had to serve three counties, so most people called Pete to help them with unwanted critters. He worked cheap and usually got there pretty quick. Still . . .

"Pete, Curtis has made them so mean they were after one of Hank Satterfield's cows. That one"—I pointed to the yellow one—"bit Romy so badly I had to take her to the doctor."

"Ah, I see," Pete said with a lopsided grin that made his nose seem even more crooked. I'd broken his nose the night he was spewing such hateful things about Romy. "They hurt your girl, and you can't let that stand."

"Pretty much."

"How long has ol' Curtis had them?" Pete stroked his stubbled chin while he studied the dogs in question.

"About six months, I think."

"Let me show you something." Pete approached the two dogs, slowly murmuring to them the entire time. When he was about four feet away, he held out his hand. First, the yellow one came up and smelled Pete's hand before backing away. Then the brindled one walked up, growling all the while. After smelling Pete's grease-stained hand he sat down and let Pete scratch the top of his wide head.

Pete looked at me over his shoulder. "Ain't none of us too far gone."

I wish I believed that.

"I know we ain't really pals, but why don't you let me do this for you, and you can forget I insulted your girl."

"And if you can't make them right you'll shoot them?"

He winced. "I'll take them to the pound. How about that?"

Not good enough. I raised my rifle, but the brindled one sat down and started hassling and wagging his tail like any other dog. I lowered my rifle. "So help me if either one of those dogs hurts another living thing, I won't hesitate to shoot them."

Pete scratched the crown of his head, and I noticed he had a tiny balding spot. "I don't know shit about people, but I can handle these dogs."

I nodded and walked back to the truck.

Ain't none of us too far gone, he'd said.

I'll believe it when I see it.

I looked over my shoulder to see Pete coaxing the dogs to follow him across the street to where his truck was parked outside The Fountain.

He even let the bastards get up in the cab with him before driving off to work his animal magic out at the Gates place.

Screw this. I'm getting a beer.

When I walked in, The Fountain was almost empty. Bill sat on a stool behind the old store counter, and Goat Cheese sat on a similar stool on the other side. A guy I didn't recognize sat at a table in the shadows. Goat Cheese hunched over the counter smoking a Camel. Only God knew how old he was for sure, but he was at least as old as Bill. They'd played football together at Yessum—I'd seen pictures at the Fieldhouse. Goat Cheese looked about thirty years older—probably thanks to all the Camels.

"Ho there, Julian," Bill said. "Come on over and pull up a seat. It'd be good to hear something other than this old windbag."

Goat Cheese sucked on his cigarette, making his wrinkled face look even more like a prune under his Yessum County Co-op cap. "How's your dad?"

"Same as always." I pulled up a stool, and Bill put a Budweiser in front of me.

"So, his eyesight isn't getting any better?" Goat Cheese asked.

He was fishing for information again. Since I didn't need anything from him, I wasn't in the mood for some sort of *Silence of the Lambs*-style quid pro quo.

"He'll be as blind as a bat by Christmas." I had no idea if that was true, but it'd give Goat Cheese something to spread around.

"Find those dogs?"

I took a gulp of beer. "Pete's got 'em. I was about to shoot them when he showed up. Put them in the cab of his truck and drove off."

Bill tugged on his suspenders, his belly straining against his shirt. "Well, maybe he'll make it home in one piece."

"Oh, I wouldn't worry about ol' Pete." Goat Cheese took a long drag on his cigarette, knowing full well both Bill and I wanted to know why we shouldn't worry.

"Why's that?" I finally said.

"He's a damned animal whisperer. Got a pet raccoon up in his trailer *and* a de-scented skunk. Took a mean ol' dog off Bill Bob's hands and has the thing eating out of the palm of his hand. Literally."

Better him than me. "You let me know if you see those dogs again," I said. "I'll shoot 'em before I let them bite someone else."

"Hey, McElroy," said Goat Cheese as I pushed my stool away from the counter, "Tell me, how many stitches did the Satterfield girl have to get?"

Damn, news traveled fast.

"Doc didn't advise stitches," I said. "He's more worried about infection setting in."

"Infection?" The man in the corner stood. Richard Damn Paris. Of course.

"Rosemary had to see a doctor? What did you do to her?"

Goat Cheese leaned back from the counter so he could see what was going to happen. He'd asked that question on purpose because he'd known who was in the corner.

"I didn't do anything to Romy. She got bit by a dog, and I took her to the doctor."

"She didn't call *me?*" His eyes fell.

I felt sorry for him in the split second before he punched me in the jaw.

I hit the floor, but I bounced up. Curtis had taught me it was easier to kick a man when he was down. As if by reflex, my fist flew toward Richard but stopped short. My reward for such restraint was to be knocked down again. The next thing I remembered was my fist connecting with his nose. He went down hard, and Bill stepped between us, his massive belly an effective barrier.

"That's enough, boys! I'm not going to have any of this mess in here. That's all I need is for Len to come in here and shut me down."

Richard stared me down, both hands over his nose with blood running between his fingers. "I don't know for the life of me what she ever saw in a redneck hick like you."

"Well, you're the reason we're still married."

The words came out of my mouth before I thought. Goat Cheese almost swallowed his cigarette, and Richard made a lunge for me. Bill easily stopped him since he still had both hands over his nose.

"Julian," Bill said gently. "This is strike two. Third one and you're out of here. For good."

I nodded and walked out the door, waiting until I was outside to work my jaw back into place. Sure enough, there was the silver Porsche parked underneath the tree beside the empty parsonage. If it'd been a snake it would've bitten me.

When I climbed into the truck, I slammed my hands against the wheel. News of Romy's and my secret marriage would canvas the whole town before nightfall.

So much for keeping that little secret from Hank.

Romy

Goat Cheese wasn't at his house when I got there, and his wife, Adelaide, had no recollection of having ever met me. Finally, I talked her into loaning me some of the colostrum stash her husband kept in the freezer by giving her my charm bracelet as collateral.

Despite how long it felt, it was only twenty minutes before I was back in the middle of the pen trying to get the calf to take the bottle. I heard the Porsche speed up the drive, but willed myself not to look away from the task at hand. The calf skittered away, and I cursed to the point where Daddy muttered something under his breath about the student surpassing the master.

"Mr. Satterfield, I need to find Rosemary!"

"There she is," my father deadpanned.

"Rosemary, we have to talk about this Julian character."

The calf backed away from me again, her wobbly legs collapsing under her. She needed to eat.

"Richard, I'm busy here!" I hissed under my breath.

"What the hell?"

"Shut up or leave." When I looked over my shoulder, Richard stared at me slack-jawed. No one spoke to a Paris that way—especially not a farm girl who'd been wallowing in manure and mud.

"But, Romy, you're bleeding."

In the second I looked down at my bandaged arm, the stubborn little calf latched on to the bottle. Tentative at first, she ended up taking me for a ride. I could commiserate with those mama cows whose babies would butt the udder so hard the cow's back feet would come off the ground.

"Romy, did you hear me? I said—"

Daddy and I both shushed him as the calf finished the first bottle.

"Make yourself useful and hand her that second bottle," my father murmured.

Holding the rapidly emptying bottle with my left hand, I stretched with my right for the second bottle that Richard held over the gate. I fell backward, breaking the calf's latch, but she stepped forward and eagerly took the second bottle. Now that the adrenaline had faded, my left arm ached like the devil. Still, I held the bottle steadily as the calf slurped and bucked, her tail swishing and her back feet stamping.

Finally, she let go.

I sagged into the gate as she danced around in a circle before bedding herself down with a sated moo. "We did it, Daddy."

"No, Romy, you did it. Proud of you, girl."

For those few moments, I forgot Richard was even there. I hadn't felt so proud since I was in sixth grade and Daddy had spent an afternoon teaching me how to catch fly balls.

"Rosemary, seriously. The blood is seeping through the bandage. I have half a mind to find your ex and beat him to a pulp for what he's done to you."

"Julian didn't do anything to me," I started, but then I saw Richard's swollen nose and a few traces of blood. "Good heavens, what happened to you?"

"Your *husband* punched me in the nose."

"What?" No one could punch out a flat "what" like Hank Satterfield.

"Daddy, it's a long story—"

"When did you haul off and marry that McElroy sonuvabitch?"

"A few days before graduation. You know, maybe I ought to take care of this arm, after all." My arm had progressed from ache to burn but I preferred it to anything else the two of them were discussing. I unchained the gate and squeezed through, forcing Hank to back his chair up to let me pass.

"Oh, you aren't changing the subject so easily. When exactly did you plan on telling me about this? And what are you doing agreeing to marry Richard here if you're already married to Julian?"

"It was a mistake, Daddy." I shot daggers at Richard. What in the hell was he thinking? "And I would already be divorced from Julian if Richard hadn't torn up the papers."

"You also could've not married him in the first place." Hank snorted.

"That ship's sailed."

Both men looked at me expectantly, so I did the only reasonable thing I could do: walk back to the house and hope they wouldn't follow me. Unfortunately, follow me they did, arguing all the way.

"Rosemary will need an annulment to marry me anyway," Richard said.

"And why is that?"

"I can't marry a divorced woman!"

"Are you saying my daughter isn't good enough for you?"

"Mr. Satterfield, I love Rosemary with all of my heart. Since she never consummated the first marriage, getting an annulment shouldn't present that big of a problem."

"Huh. Did she do any consummating before the marriage? That's what I'd like to know. Maybe you and I—"

I wheeled on the two of them, holding the palm of my good hand out but almost getting trampled by Daddy's wheelchair nevertheless. "What I did with Julian is none of either of your business. And it's in the past. So you can both get over yourselves. Now I'm going to take a shower. That way I don't have to listen to the two of you."

Taking satisfaction in letting the screen door slap behind me,

I grabbed some clean clothes from the stack on the dryer and locked myself in the bathroom. The faucet squealed, but the sound of running water soon drowned out everything else.

I peeled off my clothes in record time, but unwrapping the bandage took longer. Too long, since I knew only too well the limitations of the ancient hot-water heater. Beneath the gauze, my skin looked angry. The bleeding had stopped, but it seemed I was destined to have ugly scars after all.

From Rosemary Satterfield's
History of the Satterfield-McElroy Feud

Your daddy once told me that he'd grown up thinking all Satterfields had to have scars. His father and uncles would compare theirs, talking about where they came from, who administered them, and who got the worst end of the fight.

One of your granddaddy Satterfield's favorite stories was about the time he went back into the woods with his father (Ben III) and his uncle Myron to check on some property lines. Tucked away in one of the Satterfield hollows they found Christopher Columbus "Lum" MacElroy and his brother George Washington. They'd apparently decided to move their still to Satterfield land after their last brush with the sheriff.

Your great-granddaddy told the McElroys in no uncertain terms to get off his land. Lum and George Washington wanted to bottle what they had first. When your great-granddaddy, a teetotaling Methodist of the highest order, told them no, the McElroy men lunged for him. Uncle Myron pushed your granddaddy, who was only ten, out of the way. Your granddaddy watched all four of those grown men fight over a moonshine still.

Before he died, your granddaddy told me the story himself. He said fists were flying and the glint of knives blinded him. The McElroys won that battle because they weren't afraid to fight dirty. Lum and George Washington filled up their jugs and loaded up their wagon then took off, leaving Myron to bleed to death for all they cared.

Both of the Satterfield men recovered, but your granddaddy could still remember the pinched face of his mother as she sewed the two men up with her own needle and thread. He said his uncle Myron always walked with a limp from that day forward and that his daddy never rolled up his shirtsleeves again because he didn't want anyone to see the angry scars on his forearms.

The McElroys did not win the war, though. The Satterfield men went out and burned down the still, but your granddaddy often said he wondered if it was worth it considering what the McElroys burned next.

Julian

After The Fountain fiasco, I drove straight to the Co-op. I needed a new chain for my punching bag and a couple of salt blocks, but when I walked through the door I saw a whole display of steel-toed rubber work boots. Hoping Romy still wore the same size as that pair of cowboy boots I'd got her for her birthday back in high school, I grabbed a pair and put them on the counter along with everything else.

I dared the clerk to say a word about my weird purchases or my rapidly swelling face.

She didn't.

She did, however, look from the smaller boots to my hands and back up to my eyes before quirking an eyebrow.

"They're not for me."

She shrugged as if to say "Sure they aren't" and took my money. Since my jaw was aching, I was glad to head for home.

By the time I unhitched the trailer and checked on all the cows and horses, poor Beatrice had passed indignant and gone straight to pathetic, holding her head low. She perked up with a little extra sweet feed and an apple. As I walked past the tree where the dogs had been chained, the eerie silence caused something to crawl up and down my neck. Even worse? There was Curtis leaning against the rotting back porch of the trailer, the orange tip of his cigarette glowing eerie against the long shadow of dusk.

"Well, well, Mr. High and Mighty. Seems that my dogs had to go because they had the audacity to bite your *girlfriend*."

I kept walking. The little beagle hound nosed up beside me. I refused to pet her. If Curtis saw I loved her, he'd be sure to take her away.

And if I show any emotion whatsoever now, there's no telling what he'll do to Romy.

"Goat Cheese said you gave *my* dogs to Pete Gates."

And if Curtis knew Romy was my wife? My heart hammered ninety to nothing. "What else did he tell you?"

"That he was sorry to hear about my eyesight," Curtis sneered.

Relief washed over me. He didn't know. For some reason, Goat Cheese had actually held back a piece of information.

"That why you jumped at the chance to take the farm out from under me?" Curtis continued. "Thought maybe she'd take your sorry ass back in if you had some land like those do-gooder Satterfields?"

"As I recall, it was your idea. I already do all of the work around here. Might as well get paid for it and get rid of you, too."

Just before I slammed the door behind me, I heard chairs being thrown and, possibly, the screen door being swung off its hinges. It wasn't wise provoking Curtis like that, but the way he said "girlfriend" made me want to throttle him. Instead, I hoisted up my punching bag with a new chain and strapped on my gloves.

I threw my punches, slowly at first but quickly picking up speed.

It's only a matter of time before he finds out the two of you are married. Hell, everybody'll know. Then she'll be done with you for sure.

But I was supposed to be done with her. Wanting to kiss her outside The Fountain? That was just something you felt for an old flame.

To you, she's never been an old flame. She's been the only flame.

I pounded away at the bag, dust motes flying through the air and catching the last rays of evening sun. Sweat trickled down the side of my face and still I punched. The worst part was that I'd probably just thrown away any hope I had of becoming Curtis's power of attorney.

He's going to hang on to the place to spite you. Bastard'll probably live to be a hundred.

No. He couldn't. He wouldn't. He couldn't see for shit and no amount of meanness could change that.

But he could put Uncle Charlie in charge.

I punched and punched until I could hardly catch my breath. If Curtis was bad, Uncle Charlie was worse.

They can all go to hell, I thought as I leaned against the punching bag.

It was stupid for me to feel so bad about something that was so clearly Curtis's fault, but I did. I took off my gloves and unwound the tape. I couldn't fix things, but I could make them better. Grabbing the boots, I started walking up the road, my little beagle bounding after me. She sniffed her way up the road ahead of me, her tail straight up at attention.

"We are on a stealth mission here," I scolded her when she bayed at some invisible creature down in the dip between our two farms. She whined at me like she understood and didn't say another word as we walked up the driveway.

I tiptoed onto the Satterfields' porch. Looking through the window, I saw Romy take dishes off the table then disappear out of my line of sight. I laid down my gift and rang the doorbell before hightailing it off the porch.

Romy

When I stepped out of the bathroom, the smell of fried country ham bowled me over. My stomach growled a reminder I'd somehow managed to skip lunch. For an irrational second I thought I'd walk into the kitchen and find my own mother, wearing the same pink checked apron she'd helped me sew for 4-H. She'd draw me into a hug and promise me she wouldn't cook so many fried foods . . . next time.

Instead I saw Richard leaning awkwardly against the upright freezer that sat beside the door that led to the kitchen. He held a white freezer-paper-covered bag of purple hull peas to his left eye. I doubted the tightly packed, home-frozen peas were as good at bruise prevention as the floppy store-bought bags.

"It says peas on here," he said with a shrug.

I put my stuff on the cane-bottom chair by the door. "Oh, Richard."

He looked so out of place, so out of his element holding that package of peas up to his face while standing on the porch my granddaddy had added.

"I'm sorry about this afternoon," he said. "This has all been such a mess. Things were so much simpler back home."

Home for him was Nashville. Home was a Starbucks and a

Target on every corner, one traffic light after another, and a round of golf at the Brentwood Country Club. Things *had* been simpler there. My alarm told me when to get up and get ready for school. I constructed my lesson plans to tell me what to do each minute of each class period. We shared an online calendar, and he sent me reminders about date nights, fund-raisers, and galas.

Oh, the places we went without a care in the world! Wine tastings, concerts, horseback riding, antique shopping—you name it. We had brunch each Sunday after early Mass, then he would let me work the crossword puzzle in the Sunday paper. But then he would leave, and I would stay up all night grading papers and constructing new lesson plans that would fill up each second of class and plan for any contingency like the knife fights that sometimes forced us into lockdown.

And suddenly I was tired, so tired of that ceaseless, scripted activity.

"This isn't working, is it?" He switched the bag of peas from one side to the other.

I sighed. "I don't think so. I don't know."

"For what it's worth, I'm sorry about the cow thing."

"I'm sorry I yelled at you," I said. "You didn't know."

He reached out to caress my cheek. "But I should've trusted you. This is your world, not mine."

My world. This wasn't my world. Not anymore. I'd snagged myself on the electric fence. Conversations with people I'd known all my life were stilted. I'd had the audacity to leave, and they eyed me warily.

But Nashville wasn't my world, either. Richard's private-school friends tittered behind my back. The other teachers at my school—even the students—eyed me suspiciously, as if wondering what the white girl was doing working at a fenced-in school with metal detectors. Sure, I had loans that would be reduced if I taught in an at-risk school, but I wanted more than anything to make a difference, to help kids love literature as much as I did.

I had no world.

No, I was stuck between two worlds. My commitment to education was often frowned upon in Ellery, but my humble roots meant most people in Richard's social circles couldn't quite accept me. I was the ultimate oxymoron: an educated hick.

"Hello? Earth to Romy? I was going to stay until your birthday, but I'm leaving. I've made things worse."

"No, you didn't. I should've told you everything from the start."

"Well, on that much we can agree." He put the bag back in the freezer, then advanced to kiss me. Part of me wanted to run. Another part of me wanted to see if it felt any different from how it had before.

He didn't brush my lips first like he sometimes did. Instead he pulled me tight and crushed his lips against mine, his tongue forcing its way in like a battering ram. I whimpered when he crushed my injured arm against me. He broke off the kiss. "I love you. You know that, right?"

"I love you, too," I echoed automatically, but I was marveling at how little I felt. Mainly annoyed that he'd kissed me so possessively without asking. Of course, wasn't that how it was supposed to be with husbands and wives? Were husbands supposed to ask before passionately kissing their wives?

"Put your ring back on," he said as he stepped outside. "We'll work this all out once the craziness subsides."

"Drive safely," I said.

He nodded and let the door close softly behind him.

When I turned back to the kitchen, I saw Daddy through the wavy panes of that ancient door. He awkwardly turned in his wheelchair to reach into the oven for a pan of biscuits. He leaned up and to his right but bobbled the pan at a dangerous angle, causing me to gasp. I shoved the door open to give him a hand.

"Daddy, I didn't know you could cook," I said as I rummaged for a pot holder to take the biscuits from him.

"Didn't think I was starving, did you?"

"But you never cooked before."

His eyes shifted to the corner of the kitchen as though learning to cook was akin to keeping books for a mafioso. "Took some lessons. Where'd Richard go?"

"He went back to Nashville."

Daddy nodded and I put everything on the table: country ham, biscuits, fried potatoes, green beans, fried okra, sliced tomatoes, and . . . red-eye gravy? "Where'd you learn to make that? Even Mom couldn't make that."

"Rosemary, you could write a book with all the things you don't know about me."

That was my cue to sit down and start eating.

"Proud of you," he said after a while. "You did your best to get Maggie to take her calf."

I blushed. Compliments from Hank Satterfield were few and far between—and never exaggerated. "Thanks, Daddy."

"And to think I thought you were all citified."

I opened my mouth to make a smart-aleck comment, but I shut it. True, I was sore and tired, but there was a genuine satisfaction from working the garden and especially from taking care of the calf. I might be going back to Nashville in less than six weeks, but my life there seemed far away. This house, my home, suddenly seemed far cozier than my apartment. I thought of Richard's condo with its sleek lines and modern furniture of metal and glass—in my mind I seemed as out of place there as he'd seemed leaning against my granny's antique freezer.

Daddy leaned forward, and I wanted to tell him what he so desperately wanted to hear, but I couldn't. After all, I was engaged to Richard but married to Julian. And Julian was a fine reason for me to *never* make my home here again.

Finally, Hank lowered his eyes and sopped his biscuit in gravy. "Genie must've called four times today."

I closed my eyes. No doubt she wanted to finish our discussion from earlier in the week. "I'll call her after supper."

Daddy nodded, his jowl jiggling.

We finished supper in silence, then turned to the one routine that had held us together after Mom died. I washed the dishes. He dried. Even right after she died when people brought us enough desserts and casseroles to feed the entire Hun army, I washed and he dried, sometimes emptying containers prematurely so we could keep washing and drying.

We hadn't been able to find the words back then because she'd been the glue that held us together, the person who bridged the gap between the person he was and the person she wanted me to become. Without her, we were only this routine minus the person who had cooked our meal then sat at the table playfully heckling our efforts to clean up her mess.

That last mess she left us was one we hadn't been able to clean up yet.

I started to put the stack of plates in the cabinet, then remembered Daddy couldn't reach them there and set them on the counter instead. He placed his old, rough hand on top of mine. "I still miss her, too, you know."

I nodded, but turned before he could see the tears threatening to spill from my eyes. I squeezed out the dishrag to wipe down the table. After supper would be a great time to tell Genie I couldn't help her out after all. I could shift my duties to just taking care of Daddy, maybe picking and canning the garden yield so nothing went to waste. There had to be farm boys—other than Julian—who could be paid to put up hay for the cows.

The doorbell rang as I leaned over to wipe the table. I tossed the rag down.

When I got to the door, no one was there, but on the mat was a brand-new pair of steel-toed rubber boots in just my size.

Julian

Imagine my surprise the next morning when I ran into Curtis on my way back from the garden.

"Looks like some mighty fine corn you got there," he said.

I didn't even slow down. If he was tossing out compliments, he wanted something. "Silver Queen did really good this year."

"Your mama might want some," he said.

"She got some," I answered as I paused at the back door to take off my boots. "She's still out there picking beans and getting some tomatoes."

"Some things I wanted to talk to you about."

He'd followed me. At least he wasn't trying to go into the house. He knew how I felt about that. I put my buckets of corn just inside the back porch and turned to face him. "What do you want?"

"Well, now. I went over to The Fountain and heard from Bill that you and that Satterfield . . . girl actually got hitched."

I forced myself to stare him down. "We did, but we're not going to stay that way."

"That's a shame," he said as he pulled on his chin. "Seems to me like combining the two old farms might be a good idea."

I snorted. "Since when?"

He clapped a hand on my shoulder. "I know I've been tough

on you, boy, but I'm not going to live forever. Maybe I've been thinking about what's going to happen to you and your mama when I'm gone."

"Last night you wanted to kill me."

"Oh, I'd had a few nips too many. I got a good night's sleep and decided I needed to have your uncle Charlie draw up those papers that would sign this place over to you. Since you were right about my not being able to see and all."

Looked like the same jackass, but Curtis was acting like he'd been abducted by aliens. If this kinder, gentler version was what they left behind, I wasn't complaining.

I also wasn't stupid enough to trust him.

"Why don't you bring those papers over to Ben's office next week, and I'll sign them."

"Ben's office?" Something flashed behind his eyes, but he quickly tamped it down. "He mainly does that stuff with the juvie kids, doesn't he?"

"Yep."

"All right then. I'll be there Thursday at nine."

"That ain't next week. He might be busy," I said.

"Then he can get unbusy. This can't wait another minute."

Curtis flashed me a smile. If I hadn't already known he was up to something, I would've known then. Still, it was worth a shot, wasn't it?

Romy

"Did you do all that?" Genie asked as she looked at an array of quart jars full of green beans and tomatoes. Calling her hadn't been enough. She'd decided to stop by a couple of days after our call.

"That I did. Only lost a jar or two." I'd spent the day before canning and even froze a few packs of butter beans.

At first I'd been scared to death I would blow up the house with the pressure canner, but the instructions were easy to follow. Freezing hadn't been too bad, either. It would've been easier if Daddy hadn't been giving a running commentary to Mercutio on everything I was doing wrong. Now the cat sat in a beam of light on the kitchen floor napping as if he'd been doing all the heavy lifting.

"That's pretty awesome. My mom did some canning, but I never picked it up," Genie said.

"I followed the instructions," I said with a shrug.

"Ha! I'd have to have something to can. These crazy shifts keep me too busy to fuss with a garden." Genie fished around in her bag for all of the reunion paperwork while I fixed us each a cup of coffee.

At the whirring of the Keurig, Daddy rolled in from the living room wanting a cup. Once he got one, he rolled right back out since Genie and I were discussing reunion particulars. She wanted me to search the Internet to see if I could find addresses for a few more people she hadn't been able to find on Facebook.

"We're already past the deadline," I said.

She winced. "I know, but I want everyone to have a chance to come if they want to. Besides, this will all be over and done in three weeks," she said with a sigh as she closed her notebook and slid all of her information back into her bag.

"I'm actually beginning to look forward to it," I said.

"Well, I would hope so! Is Richard going to be there?"

I thought of our last conversation. "Maybe?"

"What about Julian?"

"He didn't pay for a ticket so I can only assume he's not coming." Not that I had checked specifically for his name or anything.

"Shocker," Genie said.

"And you're bringing Ben?"

She smiled. "I don't know. I think I will."

She gathered her things and started for the door, but stopped to tell me one more thing. "You know, this country thing is really suiting you. I wondered if you'd be able to make this work, but here you are working in the garden and canning and"—she nodded toward my arm—"taking care of cows. It's pretty impressive."

"Thanks," I said as I walked her to the door. Life had been easier once I'd relearned how to walk in a pasture. Coffee had helped, too. Apparently, one had to be alert to avoid the cow patties of life.

I followed her out on the porch and onto the lawn barefoot. The grass tickled my overly sensitive feet. But those feet were getting tougher, remembering the freedom of wiggling bare toes in the grass.

I waved to Genie as she left.

My hand felt lighter. I hadn't put my ring back on despite

what Richard had said. At first, I told myself I didn't want to lose such an expensive piece of jewelry in the garden or get it caught on anything. Now I was beginning to see I didn't want to wear his ring because it might get in the way of other things.

Julian

Pushing away any thoughts of Romy, I kept my head down and worked hard through the rest of the week including two days changing oil and such for Leroy. Finally, Thursday came, the day to sign the power-of-attorney papers.

I got to Ben's house early. He was all business, but not anywhere near as optimistic as I was. "You sure he's actually gonna show this time?"

We both knew how Curtis liked to string people along.

Ben pointed a long finger at me. "You owe me."

"I know, I know. We're up to an evening with the Swedish Bikini Team, I believe," I said.

"Yeah. And a six-pack. And free oil changes for life. You can start with the six-pack."

I nodded. This was the game we played.

He went back to his desk and started arranging all of the papers in piles. I wanted to be jealous of him because he'd made something of himself. There Ben Little stood in a crisply pressed dress shirt, his dark skin contrasting against the white of the shirt. It might be a new millennium, but folks still asked how we could be friends. Easy: We both knew poor. We both knew bullies and bad fathers—though he'd been lucky enough to escape his. City or country, white or black, those weren't the things that defined us. Knowing what it was like to be overlooked or under-estimated—that's what united us.

Besides, I was there when he needed me, and he was there when I needed him. Only he and Hank—of all people—knew my darkest secrets.

"He isn't coming."

"Ben, he'll be here. He's desperate this time." I leaned back into the leather chair. *He has to come.*

"And I guess he's bringing that asshole who gives a bad name to lawyers everywhere?" Ben raised one eyebrow. I couldn't blame him for disliking Uncle Charlie. He was my uncle and I couldn't stand the sonuvabitch.

"Of course he's bringing Uncle Charlie."

Ben muttered under his breath and pointed at me again. "Big-time."

"Next time I change your oil, I'll rotate your tires, too."

"And find a new hubcap for the town car?" Ben said.

"Yeah, fine." I wanted to go through car junkyards about like I wanted another hole in my head, but one way I'd been able to pay Ben back was helping him fix up the 1986 Lincoln Town Car that had once been his grandmother's pride and joy. Damn car guzzled gas, but it was stout. Even if it was a Ford.

I figured Ben had a soft spot for the old car because it's the one that his grandmother drove to get him out of Chicago, where his parents had been hip-deep in drugs and gangs and who knew what else. I kept the thing running, and Ben made sure my uncle Charlie didn't pull a fast one.

"There the jackass is," Ben muttered under his breath.

He opened his mouth to speak, but I spoke for him: "I know. I owe you. Big-time."

Ben went to get the door, opening it before Uncle Charlie could ring the doorbell. Uncle Charlie and Curtis could've been twins: same shock of thinning gray hair, same craggy nose, same paunch, and same mean expression. Curtis had put on his Sunday best overalls, though, while Uncle Charlie wore a cheap, crumpled suit.

"*Mistah* Little," Uncle Charlie sneered in an affected Southern drawl.

"*Mister* McElroy," Ben returned as he gestured to the house's dining room, the room he used as a conference room. "Have a seat, gentlemen. Can I get you any coffee?"

I snorted at how polite Ben was being. He shot me a dirty look.

"No thank you," Curtis said.

"Let's get down to business then." Ben leaned out in the hallway to the parlor, where his sometime secretary sat. "Hey, Lydia, I'm going to need a notary on this one."

Lydia, a sturdy brunette, took a spot along the wall to watch the proceedings.

Uncle Charlie took papers from his attaché case with fat fingers, the exertion causing him to huff. Ben put on his glasses and began reading each paper. Carefully.

Uncle Charlie ran a hand through his hair, and I thought I saw a tremor.

Ben looked up over the rim of his glasses, his eyes burning through Uncle Charlie. "What do you take me for?"

Uncle Charlie opened his mouth to say one of the most hateful words in the English language but stopped short at the look in Ben's eyes.

Ben pointed to the papers. "My client won't be signing these."

"What?" The word came out before I could stop it.

Ben nodded his chin ever so slightly in the no direction, and my heart sank down to my stomach. I'd known it was too good to be true. Just because Curtis was getting blinder by the day did not mean he was getting any nicer.

Curtis walked right into a table and knocked off a couple of file folders.

"Looks like Mr. McElroy has some trouble seeing," Ben said quietly. "Maybe you should draw up the papers you said you would."

"Look, asshole," Uncle Charlie said. "I ain't gotta do nothing but be white and die."

Lydia gasped.

Ben took off his glasses and laid them gently on the table. He stood, an impressive six-three. "I think it's time for you to leave."

"Ain't no ni—"

"Don't." Ben edged around the table and stood over Uncle Charlie.

Uncle Charlie turned to the side and spit. Tobacco juice just missed Lydia's shoe and the Oriental rug in the foyer.

"Go. Now." Ben's hands clenched into fists at his sides. He knew Uncle Charlie was baiting him, knew the old man wanted him to throw a punch. Uncle Charlie would happily take a fat lip or a shiner if it meant he could take someone to court.

Uncle Charlie turned to spit again, but I stepped up beside him.

"What you gonna do, boy?"

"Get out," I said. "Both of you bastards get out. Or I'll *help* you out."

"Bastards, huh?" Curtis laughed as he sidled up to his brother. "You know a lot more about bastards than you think. Guess you'd better figure out a way to convince the Satterfield girl to take you back. Before this is over, you're going to be selling your clover patch to me."

I involuntarily leaned forward, but Ben clamped a hand on my shoulder. "I'm not bailing you out, Jay," he said through clenched teeth.

I lunged forward anyway.

Uncle Charlie flinched. "C'mon, Curtis. I think we're done here."

Curtis and Uncle Charlie eased out of Ben's house, leaving the door wide-open behind them.

Lydia slammed it shut and disappeared into the parlor. Ben tossed me a wad of fast-food napkins. "Your family. Clean up their mess."

"Is it too late to find a new family?"

"I don't want to say I told you so, but I told you so. Add entry to the Playboy Mansion to my bill. And Hef's girls are going to rub the tension right out of these shoulders."

I dropped the stack of napkins over the wet spot and stepped on them. "What the hell's going on, Ben?"

"That son of a bitch drew up papers that would make Curtis *your* power of attorney," Ben said as he leaned against the doorway and watched me clean. "I can't believe he thought I wouldn't catch that."

"No, he hoped *I* would be stupid enough not to catch it." They knew I couldn't read well, especially not the tiny print Uncle Charlie had chosen. "But why?"

Ben shrugged. "He must want something you've got. Something he could sign over to someone else—and he's got to be desperate if he's willing to try something that stupid."

The only thing I had was my third of the farm, the part Mamaw had willed me. But why in the hell would he want that? I mean, he needed the money, but who would pay for our place? The McElroy farm was only a fraction of the Satterfield spread.

"You need to get away from those people," Ben said. "Too bad I can't send you down south to live with your grandma."

"Ain't got a mamaw anymore and if I go any further south I'd have to retake Spanish."

Ben sighed. "You are one literal son of a bitch, you know that? I'm saying you should've left. You still can if you'll—"

"Leave my mama on her own with *him?*"

Ben came around and sat on the corner of his desk, and I was jealous of him in that moment. Jealous as hell because he'd made something of himself while I was still beholden to Curtis.

"You don't owe her one damn thing."

I met Ben's gaze, his dark eyes hard and unyielding. He was right except I did owe her for bringing me into this world. And the only way I was getting out of this conversation was to change the subject. "So, what do you know about getting an annulment?"

Romy

I knew I had to go into town to see Dr. Malcolm on Thursday, so I finally made that appointment to see Delilah about a haircut and getting what was left of my nails removed. I spent the rest of the week lounging around the house with Daddy for the most part, but I did manage to do some reunion work for Genie and to keep feeding my little calf. I'd decided to name her Star for the black shape on her white head. In a sort of homage to my mother, I'd go down to the little pen each morning singing to her about being a shining star.

She didn't particularly appreciate my singing, but she had taken to the bottle and trotted around the pen all fat and sassy. Tuesday morning I was especially glad for the boots Julian had given me because little Star loved to step on their steel-toed tips. Daddy had no sympathy for me, snorting that any idiot ought to know to feed the calf from the other side of the gate.

Wednesday morning I tried to call Richard, but he didn't answer. I debated for a long time and finally put on the engagement ring he'd given me. That was the day Daddy sent me for an actual litter box, litter, and copious amounts of cat food. Mercutio aka Freddy Mercury was officially a part of the indoor family. I was more than happy to be done cleaning up the makeshift sandbox. At least Mercutio knew to go to the bathroom there instead of other places. Not that it was going to be this particular idiot's problem for any longer than the next few weeks.

"What are you so chipper about?" Daddy asked when Thursday finally rolled around.

"It's a big day. I've got to go to the doctor, I've got lunch with Genie, and I finally got an appointment with Delilah."

"Delilah, huh?"

"Yes, Delilah."

"Gonna get her to take off those claws?"

Instinctively, I looked at my hands. I'd broken off a couple and a few more were loose. One nail in particular was still red and ragged. They looked like Frankenstein hands. "Yeah. These have to go."

"Well, Julian's coming over to change the oil in the new truck, so you'll have to take the old one."

Good. I'd probably miss Julian.

"Wait. What?" The old truck was old. Very old. It was so old it had power nothing, not even a tape deck, only an AM radio, and no air-conditioning. Last time I'd checked it also had a wasps' nest hanging from the rearview mirror.

"You heard me. I didn't know all your big traveling was going to be today." Hank picked up the paper and went back to his favorite pastime. Mercutio pounced into his lap with a guttural mew.

"Fine. I've driven it before," I muttered as I took the keys from the hook. I should just be thankful that Daddy'd agreed to let someone else change the oil in the truck rather than attempting to do it himself. I tromped through the tall Johnson grass to the shed beside the barn to get the old truck. The grass smacked at my legs, making them itch, so I muttered under my breath the whole way. If I'd known I was taking the ancient truck, I wouldn't have bothered dressing up for town.

The old Ford hiccupped from having sat for so long, then rolled over with a steady, satisfying rumble. I put it in park and yanked the seat about a foot forward. Once in that position I could see all around me. Well, there was the matter of the missing passenger-side mirror, but I thought I could manage a trip to town without that.

This was the truck I'd learned to drive in, the one I'd driven to help Daddy haul hay from the time I was thirteen. After the little Civic I'd bought with my first teacher's paycheck and Richard's roadster, I felt like the queen of the world in the old pickup. Sitting up high had its advantages, I decided.

And Julian tried to tell you Chevy was better. Ha! I hadn't seen his old Chevy anywhere around. In my mind I saw young Julian, arrogantly sure of himself and his truck. One night as we lay on a quilt in the back of his pickup he said, "Heck, the only thing you have to watch out for is the alternator giving out at about seventy-five thousand miles. Other than that she'll run forever with your regular maintenance."

"Shut up and look at the stars," I'd said.

But when I looked his way he was staring at me instead.

No more of that nonsense. That part of your life is over.

Pausing at the edge of the driveway, I reached over to roll down the passenger-side window. No air-conditioning, all right. Delilah was going to have a cow of her own once she saw my hair. It was bad enough it had started to frizz, but riding with the windows down would tangle it sure enough. Somehow, though, it was worth the fuss for the feel of that cooler air on my face as the wind whipped tendrils free from my ponytail.

I turned the old AM radio on and paused at a Tejano station before finding some Hank Williams. The old-school country went along perfectly with my mood, and I inhaled deeply, enjoying the smell of the freshly cut hay on the side of the road. There was something to be said for fresh air and no traffic even if that did mean the only radio station you could find was country.

The fields gave way to a few houses and then to town proper. The truck sputtered a little bit at the light I'd run not so long ago, but she decided to continue into town. I crossed Main Street and turned behind the row of stores that faced it. The backs of those buildings looked nowhere near as friendly as the fronts. Rickety porches crumbled from the walls, and cardboard and corrugated tin covered broken windows. There was a metaphor in there somewhere, but I couldn't find it. Picking apart real life wasn't as easy as finding the symbolism in literature.

A glance at my watch told me I was already three minutes late for my appointment as I headed for the nicer of the entrances. Delilah had added a sign since my last visit, a hand-painted one that read BACK DOOR FRIENDS ARE BEST. I walked down the long hall thinking of all the times I'd come to this salon with my mother. She'd always been one to color and perm her hair, almost religious about its upkeep. At least when she had hair to keep up, she was.

When I rounded the corner to the salon proper, the room that looked out on Main Street, I half expected to see her sitting in a chair thumbing through a magazine with her hair covered in foil folds. Instead, Delilah looked up from where she was sweeping as if I'd only been away for a few weeks, not a few years. "Afternoon, Little Hank."

"Afternoon," I mumbled back. Delilah had gone to school with my father and swore I was his spitting image. She looked the same as I remembered: still heavyset with bleached blond hair that was cut ever shorter, as though she was always too impatient to try something new and couldn't wait for her hair to fully grow out.

"How's your arm?" she asked as she guided me to the front portion of the salon and had me sit and soak my fingers in a bowl of acetone. I was careful to hold my injured finger out. I didn't have much of any kind of nail left on that one.

I looked over at the layered gauze that held the bandage in place. "Better."

The only folks in the salon were a lady I didn't recognize and an elderly lady I only half recognized. Delilah motioned for the older lady to take a seat in her chair and headed back in that direction.

"Quite a rock you got on your finger there," she said as she took out a fresh cape and draped it over her next customer. Only Delilah could manage a conversation starter as a simultaneous scolding that I hadn't led with the best piece of gossip.

"Yes, I got engaged to Richard Paris. I met him at Vandy." My words didn't come out as brightly as I had hoped. *At least I hope I'm still engaged to Richard.*

Delilah nodded as she pulled up long strands of the stranger's hair and snipped them in an even line. Pull and snip. Pull and snip. "How's ol' Hank feel about that?"

"He's getting used to the idea."

"Gonna live in Nashville after you get married?"

I hesitated. Delilah, meanwhile, had stopped her snipping. Her beady eyes bored through me. Why the heck would she care where I lived? "I don't know yet. Probably."

She nodded and released a breath as if relieved there was some doubt in where I'd be living. Weird. I opened my mouth to ask her a nicer version of "What's it to you?" but I couldn't find the courage, watching her rhythmically snip the hair of the lady while my nails soaked. After what felt like an eternity but couldn't have been more than thirty minutes, the front door opened with a tinkle of bells. My eyes automatically traveled in that direction.

Not Shelley Jean. The nail tech could not possibly be my cousin Shelley Jean.

"Sorry I'm late," she said brightly as she placed her jacket on the chair behind the little white table she'd be using to work on nails.

Delilah grunted. "You and your two-hour lunches! I told Rosemary here we'd squeeze her in."

Shelley Jean looked through me a good thirty seconds before she recognized me. "Romy! So good to see you. How's Uncle Hank?"

"Same as always. How's Aunt Bonita?"

"Still on my case wanting me to be more like you." Her smile said she was joking. Her eyes did not.

She patted a seat on the other side of her table. "Come on over and let's see what we can do for you."

I'd rather take up snake handling, but I had to do something about my broken nails, so I left the acetone behind and went to sit across from Shelley Jean in front of the picture window that looked out on Main Street. She picked up my nails and clucked, "Good heavens, what did those acrylics ever do to you? What have you been doing with these nails?"

Driving trucks, picking beans, fighting off dogs, carrying calves—you name it. "A little farmwork."

Shelley Jean wrinkled her nose as though she'd been the one to fall in a pile of cow manure earlier yesterday. "And you want to replace these?"

"No, I think I'd better get rid of them."

"Next time you ought to try this new gel polish they've been coming out with."

"Maybe I will." *But I probably won't because getting dirt out from under long nails is a pain.*

She tested a nail to determine they were ready and got to work. "So. I hear you went to The Fountain and sang your little song with Julian."

I gritted my teeth. Shelley Jean had been in my business since kindergarten when she tattled to the teacher I was wearing the wrong day of the week on the back of my underwear. "Just a little karaoke."

She chuckled. "I know that's right. I had a little run-in with Julian a few years back myself."

I stiffened in spite of myself. The thought of Shelley Jean so much as holding hands with Julian made me want to rip out her throat. Thanks to her never-ending whispers during high school World Geography, I knew exactly where she'd been—and that was just in high school. Julian might not be my favorite person in the world, but I didn't want him to catch any communicable diseases.

Of course, it shouldn't have come as any surprise to me because Shelley Jean had dated every starter on the football team but two: the kicker and Julian. Apparently, as a cheerleader, her philosophy had been that each player needed some one-on-one encouragement.

"I guess you're totally over Julian now that you're marrying a

Paris, huh? And once upon a time I thought you and Julian were going to last forever."

I gritted my teeth. "Nothing lasts forever," I said before I could stop the words.

Shelley Jean, almost a bleached blonde mini-me of Delilah, looked up at me with pursed lips and an arched eyebrow that was about twenty shades darker than the rest of her hair. "Well, let me tell you one thing: You dodged a bullet with Julian."

I don't want to know. Don't tell me.

She had finished with one hand and was starting on the other. If I could just keep my mouth closed, maybe she would finish getting the rest of my nails off and I could leave before I gave in to the urge to punch her pug nose.

Please tell me he didn't. Not with her.

My left hand curled into a fist in my lap, feeling oddly naked without the nails I'd been sporting for so long. Shelley Jean made it all the way to my middle finger on my right hand, but she couldn't hold it in anymore. She leaned across the nail table conspiratorially and whispered, "He's just awful in bed. We didn't even make it to the bed. He's impotent or something."

"He's *what?!*" My face flamed as soon as I said it. If there was one thing in this world I knew beyond a shadow of a doubt, it was that Julian McElroy was the farthest thing from impotent. Unless . . .

"Shelley Jean, you quit your gossiping and worry about what you're doing," Delilah snapped. As her charge left the seat, she snapped out the cape as a double warning, and the sound made us both jump.

Shelley Jean cast a sideways glance at Delilah, then leaned forward again. "See, I knew you were one of those 'good girls' who waited until marriage."

A good girl. About that . . .

"Good thing I did a little legwork for you a few years back. Met Julian over at The Fountain and thought he could use some cheering up. . . ."

Ever the cheerleader.

"Only when we got back to my place, he got all freaky and made me turn out the lights. I heard him taking off his shirt, but then he just turned and walked away."

This is a nightmare. Make it stop, make it stop. I wanted to pull my hand away, but she had a vise grip on it.

Shelley Jean clucked as she took off my pinky nail. "Such a shame, too. That man is *built*, I'm telling you. I could feel the muscles underneath his shirt—"

"Shelley Jean!" Delilah warned.

I fished through my purse until I found a five and a ten. It was more than Delilah had quoted me for acrylic removal, but I couldn't breathe. "Thanks. Good talking to you."

Shelley Jean muttered something about some people having more money than sense but it was no skin off her nose.

I bolted, but Delilah reached out to grab my arm as I passed her. "Where do you think you're going?"

"I don't know if I have time to do my hair after all."

I pleaded with my eyes even though I knew Delilah was not known for mercy. She went through beauticians and nail techs faster than Henry the Eighth went through wives, and their departures were usually just as brutal. Customers only put up with her because she was an absolute wizard with hair.

"I am *not* going to let you walk out of *my* salon looking like that."

I exhaled deeply and took a seat in her chair. Delilah leaned the chair back and started to wash my hair, massaging my scalp with her unforgiving nails. I could almost forget about Richard and about Shelley Jean gossiping. . . . When Delilah sat the chair up and began to towel off my hair, I noticed Shelley Jean was absorbed with a different customer, a middle-aged woman whose lips were pursed as though she'd taken a sip of vinegar.

"All right, what do you want to do today, Little Hank?"

"I was thinking you could take about three or four inches off."

Delilah twirled the chair one way and then the other. "Five would be better."

No arguing with her. If I had really wanted control over my haircut I would've been better served going somewhere else.

"Uncross your legs!"

If I had a dollar for every time I'd heard Delilah say that. Mom used to silently motion to me from across the room, but I'd always forget and cross them back again.

"How's Hank doing?" Delilah asked as her scissors whooshed and snipped close to my ears.

"Well, I think. He's not got too much longer before they can take the cast off, so he's getting especially ornery."

Delilah chuckled at that. "Well, I bet he's glad to have you home."

Was he? Had Hank Satterfield said yet that he was happy to have me home?

The older lady whose name I still couldn't remember started a conversation with Delilah about the evils of being a Democrat, and suddenly I didn't have anything else to think about but what Shelley Jean and Julian did.

Impotent? I didn't believe it. Not for a minute.

And why should you care? I shouldn't. And just because Julian didn't have sex with Shelley Jean didn't mean he hadn't had sex with someone else. Avoiding Shelley Jean just made sense.

You care because you did *have sex with Richard.*

What did that matter? I wasn't going to beat myself up over it. Sure, I should've got a divorce first, but Julian and I had broken up for a while by the time Richard and I got horizontal.

I looked instinctively at my lap to see my engagement ring, but my hands were clasped underneath the cape. Richard was Julian's opposite in every way, and I did mean every way. But Julian had stayed true to our vows, and I hadn't. . . .

O, that way madness lies.

"What do you think about that?" Delilah's voice brought me back to the hair salon where my body had sat quietly while my mind went through a gymnastics floor routine.

"Huh? What?"

"Take a look in the mirror and see what you think."

Cutting off a few inches seemed to take the weight off my hair, allowing it to bounce up in waves instead of living somewhere between straight and frizzy. Much better.

And with a fresh face sans makeup, a lot more like me.

I smiled. "Thanks, Delilah. I always feel lighter when you get done working your magic."

Her lips hardly tugged up at the corners, but her eyes twinkled. "Quit messing with that flat iron. You're frying your hair. And get you some of that shampoo in the blue bottle before you go."

"Yes, ma'am." I dared to swish my hair a little to each side. Much lighter, but still long enough to pull into two ponytails if I needed to get the hair out of my face. I frowned at the mental image of me with two ponytails. Seemed I was turning into Elly May after all.

"You tell Hank I said hello." Delilah's gray eyes were back to steel. She shook out the cape. "And don't mind anything Shelley Jean says."

Too late for that.

Paying Delilah even more generously than Shelley Jean, I headed back out to the truck. I had the most ridiculous urge to drive straight up to Julian McElroy and ask him if what Shelley Jean had said was true. But what in the blue hell did it matter to me? Why did I care?

Guilt gnawed at me. *You need to know he didn't take your marriage seriously. Otherwise, maybe you're the one who did him wrong.*

Julian

According to Ben's preliminary research, poor Richard shot himself in the foot by tearing up those divorce papers because the great state of Tennessee wasn't too keen on annulments. Marrying your cousin? Sure. Wanna get married by the mayor? Why not. But try to prove you have a sham marriage that you haven't consummated? Yeah, Tennessee isn't getting into all that. Basically, it was going to take a better lawyer than mine to get an annulment.

Of course, Richard Paris undoubtedly had a better lawyer than I did.

And Ben Little was one damn fine lawyer.

When I got home, I walked to the back porch instinctively, but one look at the punching bag told me I didn't need it. I didn't want to hit anything or anyone. Instead, I saddled up my old chestnut gelding, Benedick, and went for a ride. Blowing off work and riding seemed like playing hooky, but then I realized I was guiding ol' Benedick along the edges of the farm that was supposed to have been mine. Kinda felt like I was making sure everything was where it was supposed to be. Or a farewell tour.

What in the hell had I been thinking? Or was it hoping? Maybe I'd hoped the sonuvabitch had finally found a lick of sense and decided to let me legally do what I'd already been doing. Or maybe I'd hoped he'd already be dead by now. He certainly drank enough, smoked enough, pissed off enough of the right people. But there he was, always needling me. Fact was, I, like Tom Cruise's character in *A Few Good Men*, couldn't handle the truth: That bastard was going to live forever, and I was a fool for staying here and hoping for anything else.

Just as I came to that conclusion, I heard the pitiful bleat of a calf and urged Benedick ahead. That had to be Romy's calf bawling on the other side of the fence. Hank had mentioned something about how his newest calf was half-Hereford when I went over to change the oil in his truck. Our bull had gotten loose a while back. Little black cow with a white face? Yep. Half-Hereford and half-Angus.

I weighed my options. Getting the calf back to where she belonged would take half the day if I tried to chase her. I tossed Benedick's reins over the branch of a nearby maple tree and stepped over the electric fence. The calf skittered back.

Well, shit. "You would wander as far away from your barn as you possibly could."

She popped one ear back in answer and lifted her nose to smell the air around me, but she didn't know me, so I wasn't getting anywhere close. I fished my cell from my back pocket, hoping I could get enough bars to make a call. Hank answered on the third ring and said he'd send Romy right over just as soon as she got back, which shouldn't be too long.

Hank's idea of "not too long" and mine were very different things, but I sat on a stump and dug rocks out of my work boot with a pocketknife until she finally showed up in their ancient Ford pickup.

"Get lost?" I asked.

"Nope. I had some things to do in town," she said as she slid out of the truck, bringing a bottle of formula with her. The little calf ran to Romy with tail wagging like an overgrown dog.

"Hair looks nice," I said. It was shorter but not as perfectly straight as it had been. I used to give her a hard time when she cut her hair, but this looked more like her.

The calf soon backed her into the grille of the truck, and she giggled, holding on to the bottle for dear life. Something inside me cracked and broke. That beautiful woman was my wife. Now that she'd cut the city off her hair and taken off the ridiculous nails, she looked at home in an Alan Jackson T-shirt and cutoff shorts, her killer legs ending abruptly in the boots I'd bought her.

And she, like the McElroy farm, was yet another thing I couldn't have. "Need some help getting the calf back up?"

She brushed back her hair. "You gonna hold her in the back?"

"Hell, no. One, she doesn't like me. Two, she'll jump out. We'll put her in the cab. I'll drive, and you can keep her calm."

She arched an eyebrow at me but couldn't come up with a better plan. "I thought you'd die before you drove a Ford. Only thing that'd ever go wrong with a Chevy would be the alternator at seventy-five thousand miles, give or take, and—"

"Hand me the keys."

I hoisted the calf into the truck and helped Romy inside before rounding the truck and climbing inside.

"I can't help but notice you aimed the dangerous end in my direction." She leaned back against the seat as far from the twitching tail as she could. She put her right hand on the calf and rested her left arm on the top of the seat. Her bandage was a little smaller.

"It's a short trip. Maybe you'll be lucky," I said as I started the ignition. Suddenly, the calf had her wet nose all in my business. "You're not driving, I don't care how curious you are."

Romy giggled again. "Her name is Star."

A quick glimpse and I saw the little black star on the forehead of an otherwise white face. "Nice to meet you, Star, but I'd prefer you stay at home next time."

The calf slobbered on me then almost sat on Romy as we went through a dip in the pasture.

"Thank you for the boots, Julian," Romy said softly.

"You're welcome."

"And for looking out for little Star, here."

"That's what neighbors are supposed to do, right?"

She didn't answer. Mamaw once told me the whole McElroy-Satterfield feud had begun before the Civil War over a lost calf that had wandered from the Satterfields to the McElroys. Some young McElroy who was, no doubt, directly related to Curtis, had quickly cut a notch in the calf's ear to "prove" it belonged to the McElroys. They'd been squabbling over property lines ever since.

And here I was giving a calf back.

I pulled up in front of the pen, and Romy cajoled the calf back inside while I walked the perimeter looking for the spot where the calf got out. Romy was the one to spot it first. The fence around the pen was ramshackle, parts of it twice as old as either Romy or me. Some of the boards between the barn and the gate that led back to the larger pasture had fallen down. Or, more accurately, had been butted down by the calf, who had squeezed underneath.

"If you'll get me a hammer and some nails, I'll fix this for you."

"I'd appreciate that," she said softly. She climbed over the short gate on the other side of the pen, no doubt on her way to the neighboring milk barn to find some tools.

Just a week or so back into the country, and she was walking with purpose, not sashaying as she had on that first day back in town. I liked the country-girl walk better. And I'd always loved to watch her go, especially when I knew she was coming back.

Romy

I rifled through Daddy's toolbox looking for a hammer and then through the scattered cardboard boxes looking for nails.

I will not ask him. I will not ask him. I will not ask him.

No, I'd heard about the cat and curiosity, and I would not ask Julian if what Shelley Jean had said was true. After all, we were in the middle of an uneasy truce now that he'd taken care of the dogs and been kind enough to buy me the boots. No. What Julian did in his private life was no business of mine.

Well, that and you don't want him turning the tables on you.

Stomping across the side yard and back to the pen, I repeated my mantra. I clambered over the gate, rubbed Star's head, and surprised myself by saying, "So, guess who I ran into today?"

"The Queen of England," he said as he took the hammer and nails.

"Shelley Jean."

Was it my imagination or did he flinch at the mention of her name? If so, he shrugged it off quickly and began to pry off boards and then hammer them all back in place. By the time he finished I practically itched with curiosity. "Don't suppose you're interested in what she had to say."

"Dammit, Romy, I wouldn't believe a word of it." He tried to brush past me, but I grabbed his arm. Somehow I expected

Richard's arm, but instead of a trim yet soft arm, I got a hard bicep.

"Care to let go? I need to go get Benedick from the maple tree. I'd appreciate a ride back over there."

My cheeks warmed, but I removed my hand. "She said she'd done me a favor because you couldn't get it up."

He laughed. "Of course she did. She didn't want to tell you I got sober enough to come to my senses. Now what the hell do you care?"

I swallowed hard. Reading between the lines, I heard, "You didn't come back for me? What's it to you?" And, really, why did I care? I was going to marry Richard just as soon as I got an annulment from Julian, so it was none of my business. We were only married on paper, having never lived together. Still, the truth bubbled up to the surface: "I guess I didn't like the idea of you with her." *Or anyone else for that matter. Not that I can admit that.*

"Hell, you're about to marry another guy. What the—?" The truth smacked him halfway through his question. "I've done a lot of shitty things in my life, but cheating on you is not one of them."

His words hit me like a punch in the gut.

Oh, God. He considers it cheating. "No one?"

He grunted something that sounded a lot like "no one," then added, "And, for the record, I don't really like the idea of you with him."

We stared each other down for so long, I thought tumbleweeds might roll through along with a Wild West whistle. He was the first to look away, but I didn't feel all that victorious.

He stood you up and didn't answer any of your calls or letters. He did not follow you to explain himself. You do not *owe him any explanations.*

He unlatched the gate rather than climbing over it, and walked the tools back to the milk barn. I trudged behind him, stopping to latch the gate once I was on the other side. Only then did it strike me as odd that he'd walked right into the cinderblock milk barn as though he owned the place. I drove him back through the pasture to the low spot in the fence and the creek where we'd always played together. We didn't say anything, and I couldn't tell if I'd ruined something by my questions or somehow made it better.

"Thanks for the ride," he said, pulling up his ball cap and putting it back on his head. I realized the straw cowboy hat he'd smashed must've been his only one.

"Thanks for fixing the fence," I said.

"Well, you'd better keep an eye on it and keep that calf on your side," he said with a grin that made the thin white scar on his chin go tight. "Feuds have started over less."

I was still confounded by Julian, by us, by the ridiculous predicament we were in when I made it back to the house. "Hey, Daddy, you want me to fix some supper or—?"

I didn't finish that sentence because the muted conversation from the living room registered. We had company.

"Rosemary, quit your yelling and come in here and meet Mr. Marsh."

Slowly, I crossed the worn linoleum of the kitchen and entered the living room. Sure enough, a pudgy, balding man sat on the edge of the world's most uncomfortable couch, a beret in his hands. He stood to shake my hand. "Miss Satterfield, it's a pleasure."

"Nice to meet you, and please call me Romy," my manners insisted I say. The hackles on the back of my neck suggested it wasn't nice to meet him at all.

"Go on. Have a seat over there." Hank lifted his hand from the cat long enough to point to Granny's rocker in the corner. I eased into the low chair, waiting for the enigmatic Mr. Marsh to speak. He could be a Jehovah's Witness come to preach the Kingdom of Heaven, but I didn't think so. For one thing, Daddy would've already run him off. For another, his shifty eyes made me think he wanted something.

"Well, Romy," he said. "I've been talking with your father for some time about the possibilities of this farm."

"Possibilities?"

"Yes, up until now, Hank has been determined to hang on to the place even though I'm sure he's having a hard time paying the property taxes with only the income from renting out the land and the few head of cattle he has. Probably spending more than you're making, aren't you, Hank?"

He nodded with his eyes mostly closed. "Pretty much."

"So, I think I've just about talked him into selling the farm to one of my holdings, a company that develops golf course communities. Together with the farm next door, the rolling hills would make a really nice course, and we could keep this house as a sort of clubhouse. After all, it would be a shame to tear down such a lovely old place. You see . . ."

He kept talking, but I tuned him out, even pinched myself to make sure I wasn't in the middle of one of the worst nightmares ever. *Well, what did you think, Romy? Did you think Daddy was going to live forever?*

Damned if I didn't think he would.

Most of my life Hank Satterfield had stood tall. He worked so hard at everything he did that I couldn't imagine him ever stopping. He was my daddy, and if ever he did anything wrong, then somehow it still had to be right. But if there was one thing this summer had taught me, it was that my father wasn't invincible. One of these days I was going to lose him, and I didn't have any brothers or sisters to share that grief or to share the load of what to do with all of the things he left behind.

Holy hell, I'm the last one. I'm the last Satterfield of Yessum County.

"I'm sure you're going to need some time to think it all over," Mr. Marsh was saying. "I've put all of the literature in a folder for you with some quotes, but my company is open to ensuring that this structure remains on the property and intact—"

Damn right my house is going to remain right here and intact! If it survived the Great Depression and the infamous tornado of '52, then you're sure as hell not going to tear it down.

"—and maybe I'll come by early next week to see where we are on the deal."

It seemed as though Mr. Marsh could sense my hostilities because he was backing to the door, his ridiculous beret still in his hands.

"All right, Mr. Marsh, you have a good day now, you hear?" It took every ounce of my willpower to hold on to the screen door and not let it slam behind me. "Daddy, what's this all about?"

"Romy, baby. Have a seat."

It was my turn to take a seat on the ridiculously scratchy couch.

"I've always told that Marsh fellow where he could stuff it, but he still comes around once a month or so—probably hoping I'm dead and gone. Then Richard came in and proposed and it got me to thinking. I know I promised you a spot to build a house, anywhere you liked on this whole farm, but you're going to want to go live with him. You're not going to want this old place."

"But, Daddy—"

"Now, hush, and hear me out. I ain't dead yet, but this old bone is taking one helluva long time to heal. I'm not as young as I used to be, and I can't keep messing with these cows forever. Maybe it'd be best if I went on and moved into town close to everything for when I can't drive anymore."

The tears came unbidden. My daddy? In town? "But, Daddy, isn't town where all of the 'idiots who don't like space or clean air' live?"

"Baby, I gotta be practical. I guess some part of me hoped you would someday come on home, but you've gone and got yourself engaged to a Nashville boy. He seems like a . . . decent fella. I don't want to be a burden to you."

"A burden? Are you serious?" I could hardly choke out the words from beyond the lump in my throat. "No. There has to be another way. We'll find another way."

"Rosemary, sweetheart. The ol' Vandiver boy ain't making nothing on the cotton. I don't have any hay put up for the cows, so I'm going to have to sell them at the end of the summer anyway. It's the right thing to do."

One look into his hooded eyes, and I knew it wasn't the right thing to do. The Satterfields had made it through the Civil War, the Great Depression, World War II, and living next to the biggest bunch of assholes the world had ever seen. We couldn't stop now just because Richard Paris had asked me to marry him. Hell, the Paris family had law schools named after them. And streets. And public buildings. This little patch of land in West Tennessee was the whole reason my Daddy existed and thus the only reason I existed.

"I'll bale hay. I'll move home and teach here in the county."

"But what about Richard?"

What about Richard?

"We'll just have to postpone the wedding. We can make long distance work for a little while." I stared through my father, daring him to tell me to go one more time.

Instead, he sighed. "I hate it when you give me that look. It reminds me of your mother." Mercutio leaped out of his lap and landed with a thud. Daddy didn't know what to do with his hands then. "Tell you what. We'll just talk about this at the end of the summer. See if you still feel the same way then."

The end of the summer. I could do that.

Then Mr. Marsh's words came back to me: "*Together with the farm next door . . .*"

I would've sworn Julian wouldn't give up his place in a million years. But his father, on the other hand . . .

"Daddy, I gotta go."

Julian

After checking on the rest of the cows and horses as well as the garden, I headed back to the house. The beagle came out to meet me halfway and trotted beside me with her tail wagging. "I guess I'm going to have to give you a name if you're going to insist on following me around, huh?"

She whined in response and jumped up for me to scratch behind her ears.

"I will tell you one thing," I said to the dog. "I sure as heck ain't naming you Shelley Jean."

Even she didn't like that idea. She jumped down and started trailing something with her nose to the ground and her tail in the air. Kinda reminded me of Little Ann in that *Where the Red Fern Grows* movie.

You can be Little Ann.

But naming the dog something else didn't keep my mind from wandering back to Shelley Jean and, more importantly, back to Romy. It had been ridiculous to think she would be a nun while she was gone, but that didn't make it hurt any less.

I mean, I'd made it through the first few years thanks to too much booze and whatever pain pills I could find. Mama always had a ready supply. When I'd broke myself of the worst of those habits, I'd watched some movies I didn't want to quote to Ben.

Then I realized I had to break myself of that habit, too. Finally, I'd settled into feeling low, not feeling much of anything at all.

Little Ann bayed at something invisible, then disappeared around the trailer. I started to call after her, but I heard voices in the front yard. Then Curtis told her to "Git!" and she yelped, which told me he'd given her a good kick.

I walked around the front of the trailer ready to kick him until he yelped. He'd only kicked her because she was mine, but she'd picked me—not the other way around. She dashed past me, head low, and hid underneath my porch. Anger welled up inside me. I was sick and tired of how he hurt things just because they belonged to me.

"Curtis McElroy, we need to have words."

I stopped short at the sight of the tiny red convertible in the driveway. And the paunchy guy in a beret beside Curtis.

"Son, here's someone I'd like for you to meet. Mr. Marsh, this here's my boy, Julian."

Mr. Marsh extended his hand, and I shook it. It was pale and limp. "Julian, what a pleasure to meet you. I called your father last night to tell him, unofficially, that our deal is on. Your family is about to become a very wealthy one."

I shoved my hands in my pockets so I wouldn't punch someone. "How's that, Mr. Marsh?"

"Well, I've been after both your father and Hank Satterfield for a couple of years now wanting to buy these two farms and put them together to make a world-class golf course community. Hank Satterfield is finally on the verge of agreeing."

He beamed. It was all business to him. I stared through Curtis instead. "Let me guess: You're offering a lot of money for his part of the farm."

"One fifty, actually. Curtis says that you own the other ten acres. I'd be quite willing to offer you a generous twenty just for your little portion."

That's all I needed to know. "My land's not for sale."

"Fine, fine. How about thirty? Surely, everything has a price, Mr. McElroy."

Oh. So now I was Mr. McElroy, was I? "I'm not selling. I was born here. I'm going to die here. If all I have are my ten acres, then that's all I have. Some things are more important than money."

As I walked off I could hear Curtis putting on the charm he brought out for special occasions: "Don't you worry, Mr. Marsh. I'll get him straightened out yet. Just young and stupid, you know?"

I slammed the door behind me so hard the pictures on the opposite wall fell. By habit or instinct, I couldn't tell which, I walked straight back to my punching bag. I threw a punch without taping up, but it didn't help. Instead I sank down into the glider rocker that'd been Mamaw's.

How in the blue hell had such a sweet woman produced such an asshole of a man? I meant every word of what I'd said, too. I would squat in this old clapboard house until the day I died. Or the day I finally snapped and shot Curtis McElroy then had to go to jail. That was assuming a jury of my peers would ever convict me.

And then the bastard started banging on the front door. I stomped through the house and flung open the door. "What the hell do you want now?"

Romy shrank back. She'd already been crying.

"I'm sorry, darlin', I thought you were Curtis." I clamped my mouth shut. The "darlin'" had slipped out because nothing hurt me more than seeing Romy Satterfield cry.

"Julian . . ." She tried to say something, but the words were lost in a hiccup as she started crying again. I leaned toward her, already about to take her in my arms when I remembered I couldn't. Or I shouldn't.

"Did that sonuvabitch do something to you? I told him I'd kill him." More words I shouldn't have said, out before I could stop them. She shook her head no. I gestured for her to come in. Instead she flew into my arms.

Ah, God, the feel of her arms around me and my arms around her. Then the smell of her shampoo and I was dizzy, so dizzy, like that time I rode the Tilt-A-Whirl after sneaking a flask into the fair. I drew her closer into me, smoothing her hair away from her face while she sobbed into my chest. God had made me to hold her but I'd screwed that up, so I gently pushed her away and guided her to the couch.

If it had felt right to hold her close before, now it felt so wrong not to. The world felt cold without her. "So it's not Richard?"

She shook her head no. And with a sickening thud in the pit of my stomach, I knew. "It's about Hank wanting to sell the farm, isn't it?"

She bit her lip, tears still coursing down her cheeks.

I ran a hand through my hair. "How bad is it?"

"He's letting me have until the end of the summer to make a decision." Her shoulders heaved up and down, and my palms itched from wanting to take her into my arms again.

"Okay, well, what do you want to do? Have you told Richard about all of this?"

"Richard." She said the name as though she'd forgotten who he was. I was seized by an overwhelming desire to help her forget him.

She is still your *wife.*

"Yeah, he could probably buy the whole thing outright."

Her eyes narrowed. "I'm not asking him to buy our farm."

The way she said "our farm" caused my heart to skip a beat.

She is *still your wife.* . . .

Romy stood and paced, which was a good thing considering she had no idea where my mind was going. She hesitated a moment before walking down the hall, but I heard her blow her nose before I could remind her where the bathroom was. Slowly, she trudged back into the living room and flopped beside me. "It's because Richard proposed, isn't it?"

I started to answer, but she cut me off. "All that talk about a fancy storybook wedding in a cathedral in Nashville's got Daddy afraid I'll move there and never come back and—"

"How long has it been since you came home, Romy?"

"Almost a year. And two before that," she whispered.

I swallowed hard. I didn't want to say what I had to say next. "So is it fair to ask Hank to hang on to the place when you only come home once a year? If that? He is getting older—"

She leaped to her feet and resumed her pacing. "No. I'm through with that. I thought I was staying away because home made me think of Mom. Now I know I was staying away because I was afraid I'd run into you, but here I am. We're both still standing. I won't make that mistake again."

"Still, I don't want to see the man get run over by another bull, and it takes a lot of money to keep paying the property taxes when—"

"God, Julian! Whose side are you on anyway?"

Yours, always.

She stared holes through me, her mood moving quickly from sadness to righteous indignation and stopping shy of mad as hell, which, as I recalled, always resulted in some truly incredible sex. I cleared my throat as a reminder to myself that I was strong enough to handle both the appeal of mad as hell and pear shampoo.

She resumed her pacing. "I need help putting up hay for the cows."

"I can do that."

"Great. Then I . . . no, not great." She stopped there beside me then slugged me in the arm. "I'm in this predicament because Mr. Man up the road never taught me how to drive a tractor. I need someone to teach me *how* to do it, not do it for me."

I took a deep breath and sighed. The time I'd tried to teach Romy how to drive a stick shift had been . . . interesting. "Fine. I'll teach you. What else?"

"I don't know."

She started chewing on a hangnail on the side of her thumb. It wasn't my favorite habit of hers, but it was endearing because she only did it when she was really nervous about something. It was a part of her that hadn't changed. Or a part of her, like her accent, that she'd forgotten to hide.

"I'll do whatever you need me to do, but I'm not going to help you break that old man's heart." I almost added "again," but I'd already given too much of myself away because she studied me with her head turned sideways.

"And since when have you and Hank Satterfield become such bosom buddies?"

I stood and crammed my hands in my pockets. "We're not buddies. He's just a decent fellow."

Her eyes narrowed. "That's not what you said when we were in high school."

I shrugged. "A lot's changed since then, I guess."

"And I don't guess you're going to tell me what changed?" Her hands moved to her hips.

"Nope."

"Fine. We can start those tractor lessons tomorrow at seven."

I gave the little night owl a double take. "Seven? You're going to be up and ready to go at seven?"

"What else can I do, Julian? I've got to feed Star, go through the garden, learn how to drive this tractor, and figure out how I'm going to get this all together. I've got another meeting with Genie, and I'm going to have to call Richard to tell him we're postponing the wedding. If he'll still have me."

"If he'll still have you?" My fists were already out of my pockets and clenched.

"Yeah, this hasn't been a good week for him, what with finding out we were still married, getting into a brawl over at The Fountain, and"—she crinkled her nose—"then he and I sorta got into it over the calf."

"What?"

"I was trying to get Star to take the bottle, and he came in guns a-blazing and scaring the poor thing. Then he told Hank that we were still married, and—"

I closed my eyes. If Hank Satterfield knew I'd kept a secret from him, he would have absolutely no incentive not to tell Romy the one thing I didn't want her to know. Blessedly, Romy was still carrying on about what had happened with Richard and the calf.

"All right, Romy," I said to get her attention. "You've got a lot to do tomorrow. I understand. Why don't you go get started to-day? As long as you're all right."

She treated me to a grin, a dazzling smile that took my breath away. "I'm going to be fine now. Thank you, Julian."

"You're welcome. Seven tomorrow."

"Are you trying to get rid of me?"

Dear God, yes. Because if you keep looking at me like that with your hip cocked to one side, I'm going to kiss you.

"I've got stuff to do. And so do you." My voice came out gruffer than I intended, but that teeny bit of hurt behind her eyes might do her some good, might remind her to stay away from me.

"Fine. Tomorrow at seven," she snapped before flouncing out of the house.

For the second time in one day I caught myself watching her go. This time I had to remember she wasn't coming back. At least not permanently.

I wandered through the house, finding myself standing in front of my friend, the punching bag. This time I was ready to give it a go for a whole different reason.

Romy

"Where've you been?"

Daddy was trying to stare me down, but I wasn't going to let him. "I went to see Julian, if you must know."

He frowned. "Don't reckon that's a good idea."

I dug in for a fight. "And just why's that?"

"Well, Richard's called about four times, for one."

And I'd left my cell phone upstairs to charge all day. Muttering some distinctly unladylike words, I didn't stay to find out any more reasons why Daddy thought I shouldn't go see Julian. Instead I ran upstairs for my cell—the Satterfields didn't believe in unlimited long distance on the landline, either.

"Supper'll be ready in thirty minutes," Daddy hollered after me. He was puffing from the effort of trying to cook from the wheelchair, but I knew better than to try to stop him. He'd tell me he had to feel good for something.

I didn't answer. Now it was time to tell Richard we might have to postpone the wedding. He, however, didn't need to know I'd gone to Julian for help. His response would be, "Why don't you just buy some hay?" He wasn't following the news about the drought. He didn't understand that people like my father and Julian were the ones who *made* the hay. He sure as hell wouldn't understand my sudden desire to learn to do some of these things for myself. I didn't understand it, either, but there were some things I had to prove to myself.

Like how you proved to yourself you could ask Julian for help without falling all over him? How did that go?

I hugged myself at the memory. I wasn't too proud of my actions, but letting Julian hold me had felt so good. Once upon a time I'd believed there was nothing I couldn't stand as long as I had him to hold me and tell me it was all going to be okay. It was a momentary lapse because I was still upset about the farm, and it wouldn't happen again.

I checked the bars on my phone, but it wasn't happening. Instead I had to tromp downstairs and go sit on the edge of the front porch to make the call.

"There you are!" Relief whooshed from Richard when he answered the phone. "I've been missing you so much. I don't like the way we left things."

I felt a twinge of something behind my breastbone. I had missed Richard, at least our easy companionship. I missed the steadiness of life with him, of what should have been a lazy summer of sleeping in and catching up on the housework I'd neglected during the school year. "I've missed you, too."

"So, we're still engaged?" He sounded so small, so vulnerable on the other end of the line.

"Of course, we're still engaged! But . . ."

He sighed deeply. "I don't like the buts. Please tell me you don't have a child somewhere."

"Richard! Of course not! No, Daddy's thinking about selling the family farm, and—"

"That's great! He can come to Nashville and live closer to us!"

My mouth went dry. No, not great. Hank Satterfield wouldn't last a day in Nashville. In his not-so-humble opinion, Memphis and Nashville were the Mecca and Medina of idiots. "No, Richard. Not great."

"What do you mean?"

I flicked chips of paint from the porch post.

"He's a farm boy, Richard. This farm has been in the family for . . ."

"What'd you say? You're breaking up."

But I wasn't. I had run out of words to explain how Daddy felt about the farm. Hell, how I felt about the old place. Finally, I said, "This farm has been in the family for six generations, and he's only selling it because I'm going to Nashville."

I could almost hear Richard frown as he tried to puzzle through what could possibly be wrong with what I was saying. "But that's a good thing, right? I mean, he's getting older and he can't really take care of things by himself, so—"

"Richard, I don't want to lose the farm, and I sure as hell don't want him to sell it just because I choose to live in Nashville."

"Oh."

"I was thinking maybe we could postpone the wedding? I might need to stay here for a year and help him see that he can manage the place or at least find some help for him."

"Oh."

Oh, indeed. Now that I'd said the words, they sounded ridiculous even to me. What could really change in a year? My father was still getting older. I'd still have to choose between home and Nashville. We'd be right back to this place sooner or later.

"This is about having the wedding so soon, isn't it?" Richard asked.

I chewed on my lip. "No. Maybe. I don't think so." I didn't want to be a Christmas bride. I wanted to get married in May on the day that my parents had married.

You mean the day that you and Julian got married? You'd scoffed at the saying "Marry in May and rue the day." Look what that got you.

"Well, we can wait a little longer," he said.

That gave me pause. Richard wasn't one to back down.

"Say, Richard, did you find out anything about getting an annulment?"

His pause told me more than words would've. "It's looking like you won't be able to get an annulment through the state. It'll have to be a divorce and then we'll have to petition for an annulment through the church."

So that's why you're willing to postpone the wedding. And you tore up the papers for nothing.

"I'm sorry I let my temper get the better of me that day," he said as though reading my mind. "I'll text you my lawyer's number in a few minutes. You can get him to draw everything up."

"Well, how about having the wedding here? Say, next May maybe? We don't have to get married in the Catholic Church, do we?"

Silence yawned between us, and I wondered if I'd stretched him as thin as he could go. "You know what? Let's just postpone the whole thing indefinitely."

His words slammed the breath out of me. "O-o-kay. If that's what you want. . . ." Tears stung my eyes for the second time that day.

"Rosemary, getting married shouldn't be this difficult. I'm beginning to wonder if you even want to marry me at all. Ever since you've gone . . . *home*, you've been a different person. Maybe you need to sort some things out."

I swallowed hard. His words hurt more than yelling would have. So calm, so reasoned, so Richard. "I'm sorry."

"Oh, and now I've made you cry. Honey, I don't mean to make you cry, but it's so frustrating. Why didn't you just tell me you were married?"

I was too ashamed, too hurt, too betrayed.

"We could've taken care of the whole thing years ago." He paused, waiting for me to say something, but I couldn't push the words over the lump in my throat. He continued, "Look, just take some time for yourself. Think everything over. I'll be here when you're ready."

We murmured our good-byes, and I realized *that* was one of the reasons I was with Richard. He would always be there when I was ready. In that way and every other he was the complete opposite of Julian McElroy.

To be fair, Julian was always there for you right up until your wedding night.

I frowned down at my engagement ring. It winked at me with the last rays of the setting sun, not aware of the drama that surrounded its beauty. I wrenched it from my finger and took it inside and upstairs to put back in the velvet box that still sat on the end table.

My hand felt lighter. My heart felt lighter. Maybe Richard was right. I needed time to think, time to figure out how to keep the farm and Richard, too. That light feeling continued as I walked down the stairs and into the kitchen for supper. A peculiar happiness welled up inside me, and I giggled. Lightness of being wasn't so unbearable after all—take that, Milan Kundera!

"What are you so happy about?" Daddy grunted as he took meat loaf out of the oven. "Did you and Richard coo at each other?"

That thought sobered me up. Having space and time away from Richard should not make me this happy. After all, my first semester at Vanderbilt without Julian had been miserable. "Not exactly. We've decided to hold off on the wedding until we figure some things out."

"Might be wise," Daddy said.

"You don't like Richard much, do you?"

He looked up from his plate of meat loaf and corn bread. "Don't much matter what I think. I don't have to live with the guy."

We ate in companionable silence for a while. "Are you still mad at me for not telling you about marrying Julian?"

"Why didn't you?" His question surprised me because I thought for sure he knew the answer.

"I was afraid you'd say no."

"Damn right I would've! You were eighteen and headed off to college. Marriage could've waited until you got your education."

I had to stop eating at that answer. "But you wouldn't have said no to Julian?"

He thought about it for a moment. "Yeah. I probably would have. Back then."

Back then? But, in retrospect, he wouldn't now?

"What happened between you and Julian after I went to college that the two of you are so chummy now?" The question came out before I could stop it.

Daddy chuckled. "I wouldn't say we're chummy. We just understand each other better now."

"But, Daddy—"

"Nope. You'll have to ask him if you want to know more. Now come give me a hand with these dishes."

And that was all I'd get out of Daddy.

For now.

From Rosemary Satterfield's
History of the Satterfield-McElroy Feud

When your granddaddy first married your granny they lived in a little frame house by the sweet gum tree. When Pearl Harbor happened, nothing doing but your granddaddy had to volunteer. He could've gotten out of it since he was almost thirty, but men of his generation had a strong sense of duty. He was as healthy as a horse, and he ended up fighting in the Pacific.

Anyway, Exie McElroy DeWitt came by one day to help your granny out. They had been friends at the old one-room schoolhouse so your granny didn't think much of it. She'd had her hands full with your aunt Joy and aunt Glenda, then your aunt Nancy was born, a sort of parting gift from your granddaddy. Exie McElroy soothed each and every one of the older girls and put them upstairs to take a nap while your granny nursed the baby. Then she hummed as she put a stew on the old woodstove to cook.

And just as soon as your granny nodded off, Exie set the house on fire.

Julian

I sucked in a breath at the sight of Romy perched atop her father's John Deere. She frowned at the manual in her left hand as her right waved over the stick shift in the proper order it would need to go to progress from gear to gear.

You're an idiot, Julian. What in the hell were you thinking agreeing to this?

I hadn't been thinking. Now I saw only too clearly how small and fragile she looked while sitting in the driver's seat of the tractor—especially with the white bandage on her left forearm. It was too dangerous. Did she even have any idea how many people hurt themselves each year by turning over a tractor or getting thrown and running over themselves with their own machinery?

"Romy, I don't know about this."

She jumped out of her skin, dropping the manual. "Julian! You scared me half to death—don't you know better than to sneak up on people?"

I bent to pick up the manual and made the mistake of looking up at her. She'd pulled her hair back into two ponytails, but she was wearing a tank top and practically nonexistent shorts. I looked at the wheel well. "I'm serious. I'm thinking this might be too dangerous for you."

"Gonna protect the little woman from learning something useful? Fine. I'll teach myself. Hand me that manual."

I held it just past her reach. "This ain't something you can learn from reading a book."

"Wanna bet?"

She rammed the key into the ignition and I grabbed her wrist. I didn't need her barreling through the barn and getting herself killed. "Fine, fine. At least let me back 'er out of the barn so we can make sure you don't hit either of the posts and knock the whole thing down."

"No way." She crossed her arms over her chest, and I tried to ignore what that did to her cleavage. "How am I supposed to learn if I'm down there and you're up here?"

A vicious idea came to me. "Guess you'll be sitting in my lap then."

"Oh, no. I don't think so. You can tell me what to do while you walk beside the tractor."

I leaned against the wheel well knowing I had her. "Yeah, that's a great idea. I've always wanted to get run over by a tractor. If that doesn't pan out, maybe later I can walk barefoot down by the pond. Maybe see if I can step on a cottonmouth."

She stared through me, but I stared right back. I had something she wanted, and she knew it.

"Fine. Whatever." She balanced on the step on the far side of the seat and let me jump up beside her. I put my hands on her hips to balance her as she sat—and did my best to forget every other time I'd had my hands there.

She sat back gingerly, landing on the middle of my thigh instead of all the way back. Her knees bumped into the steering wheel so I pulled her back against me despite her squeak. "Look, you can't drive with your knees in the way. It's not like we haven't done this before."

"That was different. And you can move your hands from my waist now."

Well, where the hell else can I put them?

My brain surprised me with entirely too many suggestions, but I shook them off. Instead I explained all of the steps she would need to take, talking her through when to press down on the clutch and when to let up. As she turned the key, the breeze blew her hair into my face. Those damned pears again.

The engine stalled out twice, but finally the tractor lurched backward, almost backing into the makeshift fence around the garden. She giggled then shifted into first with a lurch.

"Easy on the clutch, darlin,' or you'll give us both whiplash." I put a hand on each of her thighs, feeling the muscles tense. By lightly pressing on one leg then the other, I guided her on when to press one pedal and release the other. We rounded the sweet gum tree, and she shifted seamlessly from second to third then gave a victorious whoop.

I finally drew my hands from her thighs but accidentally knocked against her sore arm. She sucked in a breath and lost control of the steering wheel for just a minute when she jerked her left hand away. The right wheel of the tractor came off the ground and the tractor lurched dangerously to the left. I clamped my arms around her even as I wedged my elbows against each wheel well. She pulled her feet back and killed the motor. The tractor landed on all four wheels with a sputter and a thud.

"Maybe you should drive back, and I can walk."

She was shaking.

I could stand a lot of things, but not the sound of defeat in her voice. "Oh, no. No Satterfield I know would give up after one little mistake."

Her hand hesitated over the ignition.

"C'mon, Romy. It's like falling off a horse. You gotta get back on."

"Wasn't allowed to have horses. You know that. They're too expensive."

"All right. It's like falling off a bicycle, then. We both did that plenty of times, now, didn't we?"

I felt her grin rather than saw it. No doubt she remembered the time we played *The Dukes of Hazzard* and attempted to jump the low spot in Bittersweet Creek with our bicycles. She'd skinned both knees and an elbow. I'd skinned a knee and sliced my chin open on that stupid license plate Mama had attached to the handlebars. We'd gone to her granny to patch us up. We knew she'd use alcohol instead of hydrogen peroxide, but she'd also give us tea cakes.

"Yee. Haw," she deadpanned before setting her shoulders and turning over the ignition. The tractor lurched forward with a sputter, then jerked into first gear with none of the speed or joy of before.

Just then we hit a particularly deep dip and the seat beneath us inched forward, sending us even closer together. Too close together. My arms closed around her and my forearms brushed up against her breasts. She now sat squarely on my lap with her stiff back against my chest. I could've asked her what she wanted for Christmas. She didn't have to ask what was on my list.

She guided that tractor just as pretty as you please up to the side of the barn and killed the motor. Without the rumble of the engine, I heard birds, cows lowing in the distance.

She's not going to say anything.

Then she turned with that hell-to-pay glint in her eyes. "Well, maybe you've missed me after all."

Romy

What possessed me to say that?

Why couldn't I leave well enough alone? In my defense, the shifting seat had taken me off guard, too. At first, I'd been smug because Julian wasn't so impervious to my charms after all.

Then I realized I wasn't so impervious to his, either.

I clambered over Julian, not daring to meet his eyes. I almost tripped over his boot, and he reached out to steady me. I shot him a dirty look, irrationally angry. His eyes held what they'd always held, an expression I couldn't quite read.

And you need to remember that. Mr. Enigma stood you up. On your wedding night.

I looked down at my ring finger as a reminder, but I'd taken off the ring. Instead I was reminded of how Richard had told me I needed to sort some things out.

Julian jumped down from the tractor with languid ease. He put a hand on my shoulder, and I made the mistake of looking up into his eyes again. They crinkled around the edges now. "Romy, I . . ."

His smile reached all the way to his eyes, an embarrassed, crooked smile that revealed the thin white line of the scar on his chin. For a minute I thought he was going to kiss me. For a minute I was going to let him.

Nope. Not doing that again.

I stepped backward.

His beautiful smile transformed into a scowl. "Aw, Romy, c'mon."

I pushed back on one strong shoulder. "C'mon yourself, Julian."

He didn't say anything, so I shoved the other equally strong shoulder. "You know what I think? I think you didn't just 'change your mind.' I think there's something you're not telling me."

His Adam's apple bobbed, but that's all I got. Damned if I didn't hate Julian's silent treatment more than anything. I would've happily taken bamboo splints under my fingernails if he would only tell me *why*.

I pushed both shoulders this time, hard, finally forcing him to take a step back. "Don't you think you at least owe me a reason?"

"Maybe I ought to take a look up in the loft. See how much hay you've already got up there."

Go up to the barn loft? What kind of ridiculous non-answer was that?

He turned for the barn, each of his long strides easily equaling two of mine. "Oh, no you don't. Don't go changing the subject on me!"

But he was already at the top of the ladder that led to the loft. I scrambled after him, but he'd already taken his count, kicking a bale in the corner to see how many mice ran out from under it.

"Julian, I am having a conversation with you!"

He stopped, serious deliberation going on behind his eyes. Then he clamped his mouth closed, his decision made.

"Well, I'm not having one with you," he grunted. He took a step toward the ladder but I blocked his way. I planted my hands on his chest, and my fingers curled of their own accord.

"Just tell me why," I whispered.

His heart beat frantically under my fingers, and he leaned toward me. I leaned toward him, suddenly wanting nothing more than one last kiss. Just one. Just to see.

His lips brushed mine, so gentle despite the fierce grip of his hands on my hips. The world went black for a second, and leaning into his familiar kiss was coming home. Here, we'd made love and pledged to join our lives together. Here, we'd found each other once again.

Julian broke the kiss, his forehead touching mine. "I can't do this to you."

And he left me.

I trotted to the open loft door to see his long legs taking him back to his stupid Chevy. I felt ridiculously akin to Juliet pining from her balcony, my body thrumming for him with all of the need of a hormonal teenager.

"Julian McElroy, wherefore art thou such an asshole?" I yelled down.

"Heredity," he yelled back before sliding into his truck with languid ease.

A chicken snake slid out from under the bale he'd disturbed, and I kicked the snake out the window. Belatedly, the feel of my toes connecting with its freaky coiled muscle of a body made me shiver.

Stunned, I sat down on a bale of hay then jumped up to make sure the snake didn't have angry relatives before sitting down again.

And now all I could think about was Julian and his proposal.

That spring break when almost every other senior had skipped town for Mobile or Biloxi or even Panama City, we stayed home. We spent a lot of quality time out at the barn. Just the thought of those lazy days gave me goose bumps.

Damn my hormones. Damn Julian. Damn them all.

Still, I couldn't help but remember that Wednesday. He'd followed me up to this very loft, and I'd already grabbed the hem of my shirt ready to pull it over my head. I'd worn my prettiest bra with matching panties and was anxious to show them off. When I turned around, Julian was on one knee. I let my shirt fall back into place.

"Romy, I don't have much to give you," he said. "But if you would do me the honor of being my wife, you know I'll love you forever."

Then, with trembling hands, he held out a black velvet box.

My heart pounded. Silly as I was, I was only worried about him spending money he didn't have, not whether or not it was a good idea to say yes. When I opened the box, I saw the thin band with the engraved orange blossoms that had almost worn away. "Oh."

He looked away, disgusted with himself. "Like I said, it ain't much."

Tears pricked my eyes. "But it's your mamaw's."

He gave one curt nod.

"Yes." The word was a whisper as I took the ring from the box, my own fingers trembling. The worn band was too large for my ring finger but fit my index finger perfectly. That didn't matter, though. The ring had belonged to Julian's Mamaw Louise, the only person in his whole family who loved him and loved me.

That afternoon, as a spring shower pattered against the barn roof, he made love to me so slowly and so tenderly I thought I might die.

Julian

I thought if I took her up to the loft of the barn I could tell her, but when I got up there my courage left me. The good memories up there outweighed the bad, but there were some things Romy never needed to know. Instead, I went home and got to work on the old punching bag on the back porch. At some point I finally looked down at my bruised and aching knuckles. I'd forgotten my gloves. I'd also been punching out of frustration instead of anger. And, for once, I didn't feel any better for all the hitting.

I took a shower, got some frozen vegetables out of the freezer for each fist and a bottle of beer for some wound deep within. I needed to work in my own hay, to mow the lawn, to go through the garden, and to check on the cows and horses because I owed tomorrow to Leroy and the dealership.

I didn't feel like getting to work. What was the point of taking care of the farm when Curtis would sell his part along with Hank's to that Marsh guy? He'd figure out a way to take my part and sell it, too. I'd end up mowing lawns for the eventual golf course. Or, worse, as a caddy for a guy just like Richard.

And all because I couldn't seem to get the best of Curtis McElroy no matter how hard I tried.

Fuck that. Truth is, you haven't tried hard enough. At least not in a long time.

Just the thought of Curtis winning was enough to get me out of my chair. Vegetables went back in the freezer. The beer down the sink. No sense in sitting on my ass feeling sorry for myself— I wasn't going down that road again. If I got done what I needed to do, I'd have time to cut some hay over on the Smith place. Half for Romy and half for me, and I could stack it in the barn when she wasn't around.

What she didn't know wouldn't hurt her.

From Rosemary Satterfield's History of the Satterfield-McElroy Feud

No one knows why she did what she did. She'd just lost her husband and her favorite brother, Houston, so some said she lost her mind. Others said she hated your granny for having so many children when Exie had had none.

Either way, Exie had lived a very hard life. She never met her grandparents or three of her siblings, one of whom died in the influenza outbreak of 1918. When her husband died after less than a year of marriage, she had to move back in with her father. I think something snapped when her brother Houston died. Maybe she was thinking back to stories she'd heard about the moonshine fight. Maybe her daddy carried scars just like Myron and Benjamin the Third. He probably did.

She and your granny had been unlikely friends at the one-room schoolhouse they both attended through eighth grade. Your granny said everyone told her it would never end well. She didn't believe it until the day of the fire.

Your granny woke up. She ran your aunt Nancy outside and left her under the sweet gum tree then she ran back upstairs to get your aunt Joy and your aunt Glenda. She had the presence of mind to wrap the five-year-old and the three-year-old up in a quilt and managed to get them all out just before the old frame house crashed in on itself. She told me about hoisting the burning quilt and basically rolling your two aunts out of it. Only when she saw all three of her babies safe on the lawn did she notice her dress was on fire.

That's why she had those ugly scars on her arms and legs, and that's why she shut off the upstairs when she and your granddaddy moved into the big house. If there ever was another fire, she wasn't going to have stairs between her family and getting out.

Romy

When I got to the Calais Café, I saw Genie cozied up to Ben. They held hands loosely on top of the table, gazing at each other with those goo-goo eyes that everyone but young lovers despised. I swallowed hard to fight off a twinge of envy.

Looking down at the spot where my engagement ring had been, I realized Richard and I had long ago reached the comfort zone. He was attentive and generous, but he didn't inspire hand holding for the sake of hand holding. His last kiss had been . . . demanding.

I didn't much care for demanding.

Ben stood to go, then turned to give Genie a good-bye kiss to remember him by while smack-dab in the middle of the Former Farmers of America Convention of the Calais Café. The senior citizen farmers there for their daily dose of grease and sweet tea were, for the most part, not amused. Genie watched every step he took toward the door, never realizing there was anyone in the café besides the two of them.

"So, did you find a new boyfriend?" I said as I slid into the booth that Ben had just vacated.

"Hmm. What?" She blinked furiously as she tried to come back from the Land of Love. "Oh, yes. At least I hope so."

"Certainly looks as though you'd found a boyfriend to me.

The two of you trying to stir up the Jim Crow contingent over there?"

Genie looked over at the counter where several of the farmers sat on stools. One, in particular, glared at her. She sighed. "We did just enter a new millennium, right?"

"We did," I said softly. I wouldn't want her to mistake my jealousy for disapproval. Ben was, and had always been, not only a handsome guy but a good guy. "For what it's worth, I think you make a cute couple."

Genie grinned wide enough to show me all of her teeth, a radiant smile that pinched something deep inside me. "He's something, isn't he?"

A waitress appeared out of nowhere with pad and pencil. "What can I get for you?"

I'll have what she's having. "A grilled chicken salad and a sweet tea, please."

"And are you ready to order now?" she asked Genie.

"You know what, I'll have the same thing. Something healthy to offset all of those calories in the tea."

Off strutted the waitress, shaking her head at our creative nutrition.

"Oh! Where's your engagement ring?"

I drew my hand under the table, but the damage had been done. "Richard and I have decided to take a break. It's been a stressful few days."

Genie's eyes narrowed. "So the rumors are true? You really are married to Julian."

I nodded.

"No wonder Ben—" She pressed her lips together quickly, but not quite quickly enough.

"No wonder Ben what?"

She sighed, hanging her head in shame. "No wonder Ben wanted to strand the two of you together. He said Julian's been pining for you for years."

Julian? Pining for me? "He has a funny way of showing it."

She shrugged. "That's all I know, but I suppose in an indirect way I should say thank you. Ben wouldn't have come over to sit with us then given me a ride home if he hadn't been trying to get you two together. We might never have really had that chance to . . . talk, if not for you."

Judging from the beet-red color of her usually fair face, I was willing to bet that Genie and Ben weren't doing a lot of talking these days. My mind wandered back to what she'd said. *Julian's been pining for you for years.*

Our salads arrived, but Genie could hardly eat hers for all of the class-reunion updates she gave me. In the end I had to get out notepad and pen to write down all of my appointed tasks. A few of them involved the Internet. Trying to get service out in the boondocks was always an adventure. I guessed I could conduct more business from the front porch for the good of the class, though.

"Please don't tell Ben or Julian what I told you," she pleaded later as we were scooting out of the booth to pay our checks. "I'm pretty sure that was something I wasn't supposed to say, and I don't want to mess things up with Ben."

For a moment I got the feeling there was something going on that she wasn't telling me. "Don't worry, your secret is safe with me. Besides, I honestly think you and Ben make a good couple. He's a good man, the best friend Julian's ever had."

She blushed as she smiled with the radiant glow of a woman in love. "Would it be ridiculously smothering of me to stop by his office on my way to my next shift?" she asked.

"Nah." With all the sexual electricity the two of them were radiating, he'd probably meet her at the door. Suddenly, the mental image in my head shifted to me being outside a door, knocking nervously. The door would open wide to . . . Julian, and he would crush me in his arms and—

"Wanna mint?"

And you are out of your mind! One whirl on the tractor with Julian should not be enough to get you riled up. It's not like you to be having moments *in the middle of the Calais Café. Get a grip!* "Yes, please."

Later, as I drove past the McElroy place while still sucking on that mint, I almost stopped and knocked on Julian's door to ask him if he'd really pined for me the way I'd pined for him.

No. Not going there.

But you are still his wife.

And that reminder shouldn't have dredged up all of those plans I'd made up as a senior in high school. The day before he broke his leg, Julian had looked down from where he leaned against my locker. "Romy, what are you going to do with a guy like me?"

I stood on tiptoe and whispered in his ear. "I'm going to marry you, silly."

I pushed him out of the way so I could open my locker and get the books I needed for that night's homework. "You're going to follow me to Vanderbilt, and I'm going to get a law degree."

I was such an idiot. Sure, I'd planned on getting a law degree, but what was Julian supposed to do? He'd finally confessed that he could hardly read, and he wasn't particularly good at math. How would he have ever survived at Vanderbilt? Especially without football.

I'd been so busy thinking about two towheaded children—one boy and one girl—that I hadn't thought about what we would do with the kids while we both worked or what Julian would even do for a living. No, Richard had made me think of those things, practical things. He had talked me into education instead of law. He had reminded me I would want afternoons and summers off in order to be with the kids.

Of course, his brother *had* passed a very unpopular piece of education legislation, so maybe he was thinking it wouldn't hurt to have a Paris who was a teacher.

Bitter and cynical woman. You know you didn't really want to be a lawyer—

Wait. Was that Delilah's shiny gold Buick leaving our house?

The car left the driveway in the opposite direction, and I pulled the old truck up under the Leaning Locust Tree of Pisa, as my mother had always called it. I was in too big of a hurry to roll down the windows, something I would surely regret later, but

I bopped through the back door and into the kitchen. Daddy wasn't there. And his bedroom door, the door that led out of the kitchen, was closed.

"Delilah, honey, did you forget something?"

My not-quite-sixty-year-old father is having a little afternoon delight with my hairdresser. I plopped down at the kitchen table so hard that the chair underneath me groaned. "It's me, Daddy."

Was everyone in the universe *but* me having sex? I was an engaged woman, so why in heaven's name was it bothering me so much?

Because you keep thinking about Julian instead of Richard. That's why.

The high-ceilinged kitchen spun around me dangerously, and I couldn't even look at the multicolored star pattern of the old linoleum floor. Why, oh why had I ever decided to come home?

Hank rolled into the kitchen, not quite centered in his chair with the buttons on his plaid shirt off by one so that his collar stuck up too high on one side. *Oh, God. I will not think about my father having sex. I will not think about my father having sex. . . .*

"I'm sorry. I should've told you," he said softly.

"How long?"

He grimaced. "About a week after I broke my leg, she came by with a pie. We sorta hit it off, I guess."

I nodded. So he hadn't been secretly dating her behind my back for years. "So this is why you want to sell the farm and move into town?"

"Well, up until I realized you were going to marry that Paris boy, I was thinking about asking her to move out here and live with me. If that was okay with you."

My heart twisted. Daddy thought he needed to ask my permission? "Daddy, you don't have to ask me for permission. I just wish you'd told me."

He shifted in his wheelchair, trying in vain to get comfortable. "Well, this was your mama's house."

"It's the Satterfield house," I said. "Mama wasn't the Satterfield."

"No, but it's always felt more hers than mine for some reason," he said softly. "I figured you might feel that way, too."

His words broke my heart in half, its sharp edges scraping my ribs. "Daddy, of course it's her house. And those are her daffodils that she planted along the driveway. Those are the curtains she sewed that hang above the kitchen sink. But it's Granny's azalea in the front yard. And it's my great-grandmother's pecan trees in the backyard. And—" For a minute I wondered if I'd ever be able to say I'd added something to the house. "It's our house, too."

He reached across the table and squeezed my hand, his gnarled and callused hand easily swallowing my soft one. "Thank you, Rosemary. You're a good kid."

"Daddy, I only want you to be happy."

Tears threatened to fall from both of our eyes. I could see his and feel mine.

"Baby, that's exactly what I want for you."

The way his words hung in the kitchen, I could tell he was trying to tell me something in his crazy, stoic Satterfield sort of way. I just couldn't quite wrap my mind around it, and, like the best of the authors I'd studied, he sure as hell wasn't going to spell it out for me.

Julian

Romy had ruined me for tractor rides forever.

Considering how much time I was going to be spending on my tractor, the last thing I needed was to remember the feel of her sitting on my lap and the smell of her damned shampoo. Thanks to my thoughts of her I was making an unholy mess of the hay I was cutting on the Smith place.

Part of me wanted to leave my tractor right there in the field and run over to the Satterfield house and beg her to forget about Richard and take me back. That would be the stupid wussy part of me. The smarter part of me kept my ass glued in the tractor seat while I cut the last of the hay. Smart me knew that no matter how much I wanted her, she deserved better.

When I thought of all of those fights I'd been in back in high school, I cringed at the thought that she'd ever let me touch her at all. Back then I had been young and stupid. I'd thought I could overcome anything, including the infamous McElroy temper. Oh, it didn't matter that I'd beat up the bigger boys who'd thought they could pick on me because I was wearing Goodwill hand-me-downs instead of some Abercrombie bullshit.

No, that was different. I'd never beat up on Romy, I would tell myself. One fight in particular always came to mind when doubts began to surface. She'd agreed to meet me after football practice, but I was running late because I was talking to the newest member of the team, a transfer student from Chicago. We were in the middle of insulting each other's mamas when one of the offensive linemen, a burly Gates, picked Ben Little up by the collar and dragged him to the back of the cinder-block field house to "initiate him."

I'd endured such "initiation" myself, but a couple of high school seniors with a paddle had nothing on Curtis. In the end, they gave up because they couldn't make me yell. I told myself that Ben Little would survive it, too, and that I had a date with the prettiest girl in Yessum County. But something about his shriek made me run around the corner instead.

Ben Little was the only black guy in sight—odd for a team that was at least half and half—and they'd stripped him to his jockstrap rather than leaving his padded pants on. Instead of the old high school paddle that the team captain kept hidden, several of the guys had branches from the old peach tree across the street. Ben had angry welts all over, and they were calling him every name they could think of.

That's when I remembered the Gates boy's mama had been caught sleeping with a black man and that's supposedly why his daddy ran off and never came back. This wasn't their usual brand of cruelty. This was revenge for a crime Ben didn't commit.

I jumped into the middle of that circle, heard the whistle of the branches, and took more than one stinging blow without a flinch. "That's enough, Gates."

"Get out the way, McElroy. This has nothing to do with you."

"Beating someone isn't gonna make you feel any better." The words sounded good, but beating the hell out of me always brought a smile to my father's face.

"This ain't about you! Git out the way!"

"No."

One word and nothing but chaos after. There were four of them and just the two of us, but Ben had more in common with me than I'd thought. We might have beaten them, too, if Romy hadn't shown up wailing like a banshee for us to break it up. I heard her before I saw her, sensed her even. Fists were flying. I ducked and whirled at the tap on my shoulder, ready to knock the person who'd touched me into kingdom come.

But something held my fist back.

And for the rest of my high school days I pointed to that moment in that fight as proof I would never, ever hurt Romy. I had an irrational pride that I'd done something good. I'd defended the underdog. I'd managed not to punch my girlfriend in the process. Surely those weren't McElroy qualities. Surely that meant I could be someone different.

And then Graduation Day happened, and I knew I could never take the chance.

Because I could never be sure I was keeping her safe from Curtis. Or myself.

Just shut up, Julian. Don't think about it.

As I came to the end of the hay field, I remembered something: Romy's birthday was next week. At the very least, I'd finally have a good excuse to give her Beatrice. She didn't have to know the old nag was supposed to have been a wedding present.

Yeah, and that sums up the difference between you and Paris. He'd give her a Corvette. You'd give her a moon blind, swaybacked mare.

The last patch of hay cut, I went in search of the rake. If I could just keep myself busy enough, if I could just work the shit out of myself, maybe I'd be able to quit thinking about Romy.

Romy

After my little heart-to-heart with Daddy, I scooted out of the house in record time. We were Satterfields; we weren't supposed to be touchy-feely. Once I'd checked on the cows and fed little Star, I went to the garden, where I almost sighed in relief at the sight of so many butter beans to pick. Picking them gave me something to do then, and shelling them gave me something to do later.

Once I'd trudged back to the house with a couple of five-gallon buckets full of beans, we ate in silence then settled in on the front porch to shell the beans and watch the cars go by. It was unseasonably cool for a June evening, and we wanted to take advantage of being outside. Besides, now that Hank had aired his dirty laundry, the house seemed too cramped for the two of us.

"Damned idiots driving like it's the autobahn," Daddy muttered under his breath as someone in a souped-up Dodge whizzed past. Down the road, tires squealed and the car honked. It was probably one of Mr. Smith's lazy old hound dogs. They liked to lie in the middle of the road.

Once the car rumbled past, the night evened out into something peaceful. Frogs and locusts sang in a competitive chorus, and a couple of bobwhites called to each other. A few fireflies flickered as the sun faded from white to pink behind the old oak tree by the road. God, the air even smelled sweeter.

Well, aside from the tinge of manure from the pasture behind us. Come to think of it, I'd kinda missed that, too—sure beat the smells of car exhaust and wet city streets.

Daddy cleared his throat, and I wondered if he was as close to getting choked up as I was. We shelled in companionable silence, popping the pods open and letting the little flat beans hit the pan with a satisfying ping. Off in the distance I could barely make out the rumble of Julian's tractor, and my heart caught in my chest. This could've been my life.

But would it have made me happy?

I wanted to go to restaurants other than McDonald's and Taco Bell. I wanted to have a glass of wine with dinner, a glass of beer while watching the game. I would just about kill for an iced chai latte. Internet? Practically nonexistent. Bookstores? Might as well cozy up to Amazon and hope the mail carrier didn't leave a box on top of the mailbox in the rain.

And what about my kids? Sure, the school where I taught in Nashville had metal detectors and kids with a hard glint in their eyes that said they knew things no person should ever have to know, much less a teenager. But they were *my* kids. Who would take care of them?

"Hank!"

My head snapped to the McElroy edge of the yard. The person who'd yelped my father's name was nothing more than a shadow, a humped-over shadow with a limp. Still, I stood and put the old metal dishpan of beans in the lawn chair where I'd been sitting.

"Hank Satterfield!"

I looked at Daddy, and he nodded for me to go ahead. It would take him a minute to maneuver all of the buckets and chairs out of the way so he could get to the ramp. I ran down to the edge of the drive.

Debbie McElroy.

She stopped when she saw me and probably would've pushed me away, but she had to use her right arm to support her left. At the best she'd dislocated her shoulder. At worst, the stiffly awkward arm with the purple hand might be broken.

I stepped back, but she limped forward, looking even more like a zombie with her swollen eyes and cheeks. Blood from a busted lip outlined her teeth. She trudged past me as if I weren't there, stumbling as she walked up the slight hill to the gravel driveway to stand in front of Daddy.

"Hank, I need you to find Julian."

"Why, Debbie, I don't know where he is. Come inside and let's call nine-one-one."

"No!"

Hank had already started turning the wheelchair around, but looked over his shoulder to try to figure out why she felt so vehement on the subject.

"I just need Julian to take me to the emergency room. I'll wait for him here." She walked past the ramp and sat on the edge of the porch, rocking her injured arm.

"I know where he is," I said, but the voice came out as a whisper.

"Well, go get him then!" Hank waved his arm in the direction of the truck, and he started rolling over to where Mrs. McElroy sat. He grunted each time a wheel sank into a mole trail.

"Did you hear me, girl? Go!"

That got me in motion. I felt for the keys, which were blessedly still in my shorts pocket. I hopped into the truck and took off like a wild woman down to the Smith place. I swerved around the dog who was, indeed, napping in the middle of the road, and forced myself to slow down as I found the dirt road that led to Mr. Smith's fields, the ones he was letting Julian use for hay.

A couple of times my fear got the better of me, and I pressed the accelerator too much, only to hit a bump hard enough to bend the axle. Still, the old Ford kept going, no stranger to dirt roads or rough drivers. Finally, I made out the outline of the tractor through the veil of dusk. I'd forgotten to even turn on my lights, instead leaning forward and straining to see.

I ran over two rows of neatly raked hay before I realized what I'd done. Then, I yanked open the door and ran for Julian. He saw me just before I got there, cutting the motor and reaching for his shirt. His chest and upper arms glowed in the dark they were so white. I stopped short, shocked by the sight of the worst farmer's tan ever on the world's most vociferous opponent to the institution. But I put that information away in a different compartment, something to think about later.

"Julian, your mama's at the house and needs you to take her to the emergency room."

He scowled. "How bad?"

"Arm might be broken and her face is busted up, but she's still walking."

He exhaled, already jogging in the direction of the truck. I had to run to catch up with him. He climbed into the passenger side without a word to me, his lips pressed together in a stoic line. I knew his father sometimes beat up on his mother, but Julian refused to give many details. I'd never seen her in the immediate aftermath. This was something Julian had always had to live with?

"Switch on your lights," he murmured. No comments on how I'd ruined a couple of rows of hay, either.

"Julian, if you need me to—"

"I need you to drive," he snapped. He leaned his head against the back glass and closed his eyes. I concentrated on not pressing the accelerator down too much. It'd take us that much longer if I missed the dirt path that served as a road and got us hung up in a gully.

His eyes opened the minute I turned right on the pavement. "Did she have her purse this time?"

I swallowed hard, trying to remember if I saw a purse. "I don't think so."

He cursed, a new litany I'd never heard before. "Romy, I need you to take Mama to the emergency room. I'm going to have to get her purse."

Such harmless words, yet he said them with a grim determination.

"But—"

"He keeps her purse so she doesn't have the insurance card. That means I have to get her purse. From him."

"Okay," I whispered as I pulled into the driveway. "Anything you need, Julian."

"Thank you," he muttered, but he wouldn't meet my eyes as he shuffled out of the truck and turned to help his mama in.

"I'm not going anywhere with *that* girl." Mrs. McElroy fought him as best she could with only one good arm.

"Hey, now—" Daddy started, but I waved him off.

"Look, Mama. I'm going to get your purse. You're going with Romy to the emergency room. And that's that." Julian slammed the truck door for emphasis.

Since the truck didn't have automatic windows, I opened the driver's side door and stood to look over the top of the cab at Julian. "What do you want me to tell the doctors?"

His eyes bored through me, disgusted yet grateful I was willing to keep his family's not-so-secret secret. "Tell 'em any damn thing you want."

Julian

Damned if I hadn't known Curtis would pull a stunt like this.

You'll regret it, he'd said. That was one promise he always kept.

I trudged up the road, looking up one last time as Romy's taillights disappeared down the road that led to Jefferson. If I were smart I could've asked her for a ride to the house, but she needed to get Mama to the hospital.

And I needed a few minutes to calm down.

I walked around the house to the back door. I could see the orange tip of his cigarette long before he spoke. My hands instinctively curled into fists.

"I knew it wouldn't be long before you came dragging up here."

Don't answer him.

I reached for the screen door, but he was already blocking my path. "Son, it ain't happening this time. You—"

My fist connected with his ugly, red, pockmarked nose. A blow to the gut sent him sprawling to the ground. God, it felt good. It felt good. My foot was already back and ready to slam into his ribs, when I came to my senses despite the roar of hot McElroy blood in my ears.

I stepped over my bastard of a father and found my mother's purse hanging from the ladder-backed kitchen chair where she always left it. I felt around to make sure her billfold was there. Then I left before I could give in to the urge to beat my father as he'd never been beaten before.

My fists itched to pummel him. My feet twitched with the desire to kick his ribs with my steel-toed work boots. Maybe give him a taste of his own damned medicine.

But I didn't.

I stepped over him and walked as calmly as I could to the old Chevy truck beside the house. The beagle came out to greet me, but I ignored her.

Nothing I loved ever survived the wrath of Curtis, so I was going to have to quit loving.

Romy

Balancing the clipboard on my lap, I tried to block out the emergency room. A Hispanic man rocked in the corner with a blood-soaked towel wrapped around his hand. A skeletal elderly lady sat in another corner retching into a pan. Even worse, a young mother paced through the emergency room bouncing a curly-headed toddler. His screams curdled my blood.

But Mrs. McElroy sat in silence, stoically cradling her arm.

She'd answered my questions and allowed me to write the answers on the forms, but she'd closed off any hint of the vulnerability she'd shown at the edge of our driveway.

"Don't stare at me," she snapped through lips pinched thin and bloodless.

"Sorry. I can't bear to look at the baby," I whispered.

"Well, the baby doesn't want you to look at him, either. Look at the TV."

I looked up just in time to see a home video of a guy taking a crotch shot. Who in their right mind thought *America's Funniest Home Videos* would be good emergency-room entertainment?

My eyes almost traveled back to Mrs. McElroy again, but I stopped short to study my own print on the forms. Would it hurt the woman to show a little gratitude? I knew I wasn't her favorite person, but I'd never been able to figure out why. Other than each mother's belief that no woman would ever be good enough for her son.

"Don't jerk Julian around again," she said, her eyes never leaving the television, where a dog dressed as a bee went skidding into a swimming pool.

"What?" *Me? Jerk him around?* What kind of revisionist history was this?

"I told you not to hurt my boy. He's a good boy. Better than I deserve."

On that much we could agree. "Why do you hate me so much? I've never understood."

"You broke his heart. I don't want you breaking it again."

My heart leaped up to touch my tonsils. Something was very wrong here. I hadn't broken Julian's heart; he'd broken mine. "You told me he didn't want to see me ever again."

"If you'd really loved him, then you would've stayed anyway."

Had she been testing me? I couldn't understand this woman.

Julian appeared, still smelling of sweat and freshly cut fescue.

"Julian! Baby!" Mrs. McElroy's demeanor immediately became all sweetness and light except for the thin line between her brows. She masked her pain well.

The cuff of Julian's T-shirt folded up on his right arm, teasing me with another unexpected glimpse of white. Come to think of it, he'd been wearing long sleeves on the day of our infamous tractor lesson.

At some point over the years the world's most outspoken opponent of the farmer's tan had decided to sport the worst one I'd ever seen. Something wasn't adding up here. Even with my limited math skills, I was adding two and two and about to come up with—

"Romy." It was the louder tone of someone who'd already said my name at least once, and I jerked back to reality to take a look at Julian.

"You can go home now. I'll take it from here." His clear blue eyes held no humor, no sadness, no emotion whatsoever.

And I'm being dismissed? Just like that?

"Are you sure you don't need someone to wait with you, to help out?" I asked.

He smiled, but it didn't come close to reaching his eyes. "This is going to take two hours at least, and all you could do is sit and wait. You might as well do that at home."

His words were kinder, but he was giving off the same tone as his mother: *You are not welcome here.* This was their club, and I was an interloper, a dangerous person who might call the police and betray them.

I hadn't. And I already felt sick to my stomach for it.

I rose to my feet. "If you're sure."

He stood, placing a warm, callused hand on my shoulder. "I'm sure. And thank you."

That part he meant, and an unseen fist reached inside and squeezed my heart. There was my Julian.

Your Julian? He's not yours, and he never really has been. And he never will be as long as the two of you keep having these moments without sharing anything real.

I could feel Mrs. McElroy's hatred burning through my back. Apart from a certain semester at Vanderbilt that would live on in infamy, leaving when she told me to leave was the only time I'd ever failed. It was a shame I hadn't known I was being tested.

He had to have said something that made her think leaving was my idea. Nothing else made sense.

"Thanks, Julian, for throwing *me* under the bus," I muttered to myself as I made my way through the parking lot to find the old pickup. Even as I said it, I still couldn't believe Julian would betray me like that.

Yeah, and you didn't think he'd ever leave you high and dry at the old country store, either, now did you?

I slammed on my brakes right in the middle of Royal Street, and the person behind me lay on the horn and swerved around me on the wrong side of the road. Had Curtis ever beat Julian the way he'd just beat Mrs. McElroy?

I pulled over to explore this revelation in the parking lot of the

Bible store that had become a pawnshop. I scanned memories at least a decade old for some clue to what had happened. I could think of nothing. Julian's fights had always been after school with other teenagers. And I could count all of those on one hand because he wasn't one to look for a fight. Of course, he'd never been afraid to finish one, either.

Then why couldn't he finish us?

And then there was the image seared into my mind of Julian in the dim twilight, his chest and upper arms glowing in a white pseudo-undershirt. It made no sense unless he had something to hide. He'd said as much himself one lazy afternoon at the lake when we were seniors.

"You gonna get in the lake?"

I had been lounging underneath an oak tree, but I put my copy of Chopin's *The Awakening* down when he spoke. Water sluiced down Julian's chest, and I took a moment to admire the view before answering, "Never been one for swimming with snakes."

"You like to roll in the hay with them," he'd said as he toweled off. Behind him, on the imported sand locals liked to call a beach, two girls stared unabashedly at my boyfriend.

"Just have to parade around without your shirt on, don't you?"

"Well," he said as he lowered himself to the blanket, "when it gets this hot, the only reason to wear a shirt is if you have something to hide."

I traced his chest muscles and the hint of a six-pack underneath them. "You aren't hiding much."

He leaned over to kiss me, rolling me toward him. Lost in his sweet kisses, I didn't realize he was up to something. At least not until he snatched my top and raced for the edge of the lake shouting, "And neither are you!"

"I'll get you!" I hollered as I drew the blanket around me and fumbled for his discarded T-shirt. The two girls had stopped ogling him long enough to giggle and point at me as I struggled to get the shirt on without flashing the lake crowd.

In the end, he got what he wanted: me, in the lake, pressed up against him.

At least until I swam off with his trunks.

Of course, he walked up to the blanket, naked as the day he was born, to retrieve them.

Who was this Julian who shrugged into a T-shirt so I wouldn't see him? Who was this surly man, and what had he done with the boy I'd once loved?

The answer smacked me with enough force to take my breath away: his father.

His father had to have done something, something he didn't want me to see. Images flashed through my mind of Julian playing with me by the creek. More than once he'd had welts on the backs of his legs. More than once he'd said he didn't think he wanted to sit down. At the time he'd shrugged and said he'd been spanked, and I didn't think much of it because I'd been spanked, too.

But my parents never left a mark.

Then there was the last year we were together: a black eye he said came from horsing around with the guys or a bandage on his arm. What else had I missed?

I'd been so busy mourning my mother and trying to make my father proud with my schoolwork, I'd missed it all. I had been so naïve, so stupid. Julian had been fighting with his father the whole time, and he'd never once told me. No wonder he would only let me visit his mamaw and only when he was with me.

I had an irrational need to be home, and I pulled out of the parking lot, willing myself to drive at a safe speed. Finally, the headlights of the old pickup washed the porch with light, showing that Daddy had picked up all evidence of our bean shelling, despite the fact that it'd probably taken him forever while in the wheelchair. A sob escaped me as I fumbled with the front door, suddenly desperate to tell him in some way how glad I was God had seen fit to give me him as a father.

He snored soundly as I entered the room, not even stirring

when the door whined closed. I leaned forward to plant a kiss on his cheek.

He snorted awake. "What was that for?"

"Being my daddy."

He nodded in response, a tiny smile on his face, and I went on upstairs. All those times I thought our family had been irrevocably broken? No. We'd been wounded and scarred, but we weren't broken. We never had been.

I took the steps slowly. But the McElroys were broken. And Julian had been broken. Maybe whatever had broken Julian had also softened my father to him. Either way, I'd read enough Nancy Drew and Hercule Poirot to know I wouldn't rest until I'd ferreted out the truth. If Daddy wouldn't tell me, then it was time to take the question back to Julian.

From Rosemary Satterfield's
History of the Satterfield-McElroy Feud

When she was thirteen, your aunt Bonita did something despicable. She says she did it because she got sick just looking at Granny Satterfield's arms with their mottled white and misshapen skin. Your granny has always been a "turn the other cheek" kind of woman, though, so I know Bonita didn't get any of these ideas from her.

She accused R. C. McElroy of molesting her behind the County Line Methodist Church at a Decoration Day picnic. He said she'd told him she'd lost her puppy and wanted him to help her. Your granddaddy didn't believe her, but the sheriff at the time was not a fan of the McElroys. He had the county press charges anyway even after your granddaddy assured him that Bonita didn't even have a puppy.

Now R. C. was one of the few McElroys who never, so far as I know, did anything against the Satterfields. He was the first in several generations to start taking his family to church. He named each and every one of his kids after a person in the Bible. He was only forty-six when he died of what they said was a heart attack. I believe it was a broken heart.

Your granny always said R. C. was the only one who could do anything with his grandson Curtis. I have to wonder if things might have turned out differently if Bonita had kept her mouth shut and R. C. had lived a little longer.

Julian

By my reckoning, this was at least the seventeenth time I'd taken Mama to the emergency room. Before I could drive her, she would drop me off at Uncle Charlie's and drive herself. His wife understood a little too well.

That memory was one reason I decided to let Romy go. Maybe I'd held on for so long because I could be married to her without having to worry about hurting her. I couldn't reach her if she was in Nashville, but then she came back.

No way in hell would I let her go through this.

The minute I showed up, Mama had some extra paperwork—and it didn't have anything to do with her new insurance card, either. They called her up to the desk at least three times. I knew the drill: Sit tight and wait for them to be satisfied *I* wasn't the one who beat her. Hell, she was the only one delusional enough to believe she hadn't been beaten. She used to mutter something about deserving it, enduring those beatings as a penance for some unknown sin. I never knew where she went or how she did it, but she would disappear deep within herself, then emerge one day like a battered butterfly with a bad memory.

They finally called us back. Mama sat there through it all, neither moving nor crying out. A couple of tears ran down her cheeks when they set her arm, but she didn't say a word. The nurse on the other side muttered something about seeing people cry more when getting a plantar wart removed. The doctor, a stern older gentleman I'd seen a few times too many in my life, finished his work and grabbed my arm to take me outside. "Son, this has got to stop."

"I've tried," I said. "She refuses to press charges."

He closed his eyes and pinched the bridge of his nose. "I know I've seen your mother in here at least five times in the past two years. That's ridiculous."

"Preaching to the converted, doc."

His face turned dangerously red. "Maybe *you* need to press the charges."

"The last time I pressed charges, he got out on bail and beat her so badly she couldn't get out of bed for a week. If you think the police can keep her safe, then I'll press those charges. Otherwise, I'd like to keep her alive."

The doctor had been determined to stare me down, but he looked away. He didn't even know the part about how that time Curtis gave me such a whipping I couldn't sit down for a week. And I'd been two inches short of his height, a strapping football player at the junior high.

That's when I decided the only thing that would stop Curtis was to kill him.

"Guess I'll see you in another few months," the doctor spat. He pressed past me and left me out in the hall. I looked down at my hand and flexed my knuckles. My hand hurt like hell from hitting Curtis, but I'd never earned an ache like that one.

And the fact that I loved that aching bruise worried me most of all.

Romy

The next week I did a lot of wondering. I wondered how long Julian would avoid me. I wondered how long I could make myself wait before tracking him down. I even wondered if I was doing the right thing by staying put instead of going back to Nashville and Richard. The old Magic 8-Ball on my bedside table insisted "My sources say no," but my inner compass pointed in a different direction.

Well, that and I was pretty sure that old eight ball had only given one answer since I dropped it back in the early nineties.

The third time Richard called my cell, I told myself I had to answer it, especially since I was outside already.

He didn't even say hello, exhaling a relieved "I've missed you" instead.

I tried to say I'd missed him, but I hadn't. "You been doing okay?" I managed instead.

"Yeah, but it's been quiet."

The silence stretched between us, a gulf almost as wide as all of the gullies and hills and the Tennessee River that separated us. Had he really missed me that much, or had he missed the idea of me?

"So, I was thinking about coming up for your birthday later this week," he said.

My birthday. I'd totally forgotten about it.

"Richard, I don't think that's a good idea."

"Oh."

His single word sliced through me. I didn't want to cause him pain, but I wasn't being fair to him. A woman so obsessed with her estranged husband had no business being in the market for a new one. The one thing we could all agree on was that not getting an immediate divorce was the second stupidest thing I'd ever done.

The first was marrying Julian.

"Rosemary, are we going to be able to fix this?" With that vulnerable voice he wasn't Richard Paris, renowned Nashville attorney. No, he was Richard Paris, would-be fiancé.

I swallowed hard against the lump in my throat, and my vision blurred from my tears. I didn't want to lose him. But I didn't want to lose him because I'd never been on my own. I wasn't being fair to him, and he'd done nothing wrong. "I don't think so," I whispered.

"Rosemary, darling," he said. "Surely, there's something we can do."

And that was the problem. I'd been happy to let Richard "do." I'd been quite content to let him plan every date night, every vacation. On weeks I was too busy to shop, I'd even allowed him to pick out the dress I was going to wear to whatever charity event or fund-raiser was next on the calendar. I hadn't been living for myself or making my own choices—other than the deliberate choice to be with a man who was the exact opposite of Julian McElroy.

Shame burned hot on my cheeks. I swallowed and cleared my throat, attempting to gain control of my vocal cords even as hot tears streamed down my face. "I'm sorry, Richard. I didn't mean to."

"It's him, isn't it?"

I shook my head vehemently, not realizing I hadn't actually spoken my answer until Richard asked again in a voice half-hurt and half-angry, "Is it?"

"No!" I answered, too quickly this time, so quickly I couldn't even fool myself. "Yes."

I swiped at my tears and sat down hard on the front porch. "Richard, I tried so hard to just forget everything that happened, but I can't. I can't hide from my past. I'm gonna have to face it."

"Fair enough. And when you've faced it?"

God, how I hated it when he wouldn't let things go. "I don't know. I won't know."

"So you aren't coming back to Nashville in the fall?"

Badgering the witness had to be his specialty. "I don't know, Richard. I don't think so."

The last sentence came out on a sob, and I could feel rather than hear him relent. "This isn't a decision you should make over the phone."

What? "Richard, I can make a decision anywhere and anytime."

"You're emotional. You've been working too hard. We can talk about this when I come down for your birthday."

Anguish shifted to anger. My heart thumped a steady tribal drumbeat. "I've already told you I don't think that's a good idea. My mind is made up."

Maybe it hadn't been before, but now I knew Richard and I would never work, not if he thought he could pester me until I gave him what he wanted.

"Okay, okay. No need to get upset. I thought for sure you'd want your present, though."

Did he think I was six? Was he convinced I was only after his money? "Richard, you don't have to get me a present under these circumstances."

"Rosemary, darling. I had this idea months ago!"

Of course he had. Logical, practical Richard.

"Just don't come down. Please," I said.

Silence stretched between us, and I was afraid he would start arguing again. Finally, he spoke. "Okay. I understand."

Those last two words warmed my heart. Maybe he understood me after all. Maybe I only needed to understand why Julian had stood me up and then I would be able to move on with my life in one way or another.

We murmured our good-byes and I lay there, eyes closed, and tried to make sense of everything. I must have dozed off, but Hank woke me yelling out the screen door that Julian needed me to drive for him the next day when he hauled hay.

And that could be just the opportunity I needed to better figure out what Julian was hiding—aside from his farmer's tan.

I woke up to low, dark clouds the next morning, and I knew instantly why Julian had finally caved and asked for my help: Rain was coming.

Mom and I had always joked that we could be a month without rain and all Daddy had to do was cut hay to make those gray clouds form. He'd mutter under his breath, cursing his misfortune on those times he didn't manage to get his hay up before the rain got it. Those extra heavy bales would be among the last he fed to the cows, because the damp hay inside would mildew over the summer, thanks to the moisture that was baled inside with no way to evaporate out. The next winter the cows would snuff at the bale centers and bawl as if to ask why Hank Satterfield couldn't produce a better bale of hay. He'd shrug and tell them softly, "Look, it's all we've got."

Those were the moments when he was my daddy again. He'd look up at me with a hint of a smile and a twinkle in his eye, and the two of us could forget we were going it alone, having been left with one of life's moldy batches of hay. Thinking on such things put a spring in my step and got me to the back door ten minutes early.

Julian had his fist raised and was poised to knock when I got there. It did me good to surprise him.

"Ready?" he asked.

"As I'll ever be." I shoved the last of the granola bar into my mouth. He headed in the direction of his truck. "Oh, no. I'm not driving that damned Chevy."

"Well, maybe I don't want to haul hay in your damned Fix Or Repair Daily."

I lifted an eyebrow, staring him down in much the same way I would stare down one of my teenaged students. Finally, he spit out a "Fine" and started walking in the direction of Daddy's old truck.

"Did you run out of other options before you got to me?" I asked as I started the truck. Of course the carburetor chose that moment to flood so Julian could give me a pointed glance.

"Ben won't drive for me anymore, and the rain'll be here before I can get it done myself."

"And exactly how much hay have you tried to haul by yourself this week?" The question came out before I could stop it. Hauling square bales was a colossal pain if you had to move the truck a few feet, then get out and load up the closest bales, then drive the truck another few feet. . . .

"The Smith place and our field," he said with a shrug, his eyes straight ahead.

"You did the whole Smith place by yourself?" Was there no end to the lengths he would go to avoid me?

"Yes, I—"

"Julian, I swear! This wasn't what I had in mind at all. You shouldn't be doing all of this by yourself. And I bet you worked at the dealership this week, too."

"A couple of days."

"Dammit! Ask for help!"

Driving too fast because I was mad, I hit a gully and scraped the bottom of the truck.

"Glad we took your truck," he deadpanned.

I smacked his arm, and he gave me a crooked grin.

"This conversation isn't over," I said as I guided the truck to the end of the dirt road and looked out at a field full of perfect square bales, which were, ironically, more rectangular than square.

Julian's smile faded and he eased out of the truck. The slammed door was my answer.

Julian

It took Romy a good half hour to calm down enough to ease the truck down the row instead of jerking it forward. I'd wanted to finish it all myself, but meteorologist Dave Brown said it was going to rain. For once, I tended to agree with him.

I'd called Ben, but he'd told me in no uncertain terms that he hadn't gone to law school to drive some truck on some back forty and swat at mayflies. Sometimes Mama would drive for me in a pinch, but she still had her arm in a sling. Hank couldn't drive with his leg sticking straight out in a cast, and that left Romy.

I needed to get out more. Make some friends.

I stacked the bales neatly in the truck, crisscrossing them as I'd been taught to do. Back when I thought I was going to be able to buy out Curtis, I'd imagined buying a round baler—that would make this a whole helluva lot easier. Now I'd be lucky to keep the old square baler going. As it was, the machine was held together with twine, chewing gum, and McElroy gumption.

One thing I had to say for Romy: Normally she'd talk a guy into an early grave, but Hank'd taught her about hauling hay. She didn't say a word, only keeping an eye on the mirrors and making sure she pulled up just enough as I tossed up all of the loads of hay on either side of the truck. She knew just where to stop, and despite her drag race to get to the hay field, she maneuvered each load slowly back to the barn, making sure not to knock off the top tier.

Once we got to the barn, she started to stack the lower tiers, but I reminded her of her bum arm. At the end of each load, she used her good arm to slide bales down to the tailgate for me, and she did it all without complaining—not even when her stomach growled.

"Hungry?" I asked as we stacked the last bale of the fourth load.

"We've only got one more load to go, right?"

"Think so," I said, instinctively looking up when thunder rumbled nearby.

"Then let's finish this." Her green eyes burned through me, and I realized she hadn't forgotten a word of our previous discussion. No, she was biding her time. But even she had enough respect for the weather to know we needed to finish the job.

Fat drops hit the windshield not long after we started for the barn with the last load. By the time we got the hay safely under the cover of the barn, the bottom fell out, and the dry earth sighed with relief.

Romy stood beside me in the barn, watching the rain come down. "Man, that feels good. Thought the humidity was going to kill me this morning."

I could've wrung a bucket full of sweat from my shirt myself.

She closed her eyes and breathed in the rain and the sweet scent of freshly cut hay. A bead of sweat ran down her chest and disappeared underneath her tank top. When I looked up from where that sweat had gone, she was looking at me, her green eyes dark. "I think you've been working too hard this week. I think it's time you lived a little," she said as she grabbed my hand.

"C'mon, Julian, you owe me a dance!"

"That was high school. And it wasn't my fault I broke my leg right before the high school's first ever prom!" But it kinda was. If I'd listened to my coach and not played baseball that spring, I wouldn't have slid into second the wrong way trying to break up that double play. And I wouldn't have lost my football scholarship, either.

I took her hand and put mine at the small of her back, and we two-stepped into the rain like idiots. Rain pelted us, and still we danced until she threw back her head and laughed. I couldn't help but grin. This was the sort of silly shit we used to do back in high school.

"You know what?" She had to yell to be heard over the rain and the thunder.

"What?"

"I seem to remember a certain young man who claimed farmer's tans were for lazy jackasses who didn't work out."

She had my T-shirt half peeled off before I could push her back and grab the hem to yank it down. My breath caught, and we stood and stared at each other. Rain slid down her face, and thunder grumbled in the distance. How much could she have possibly seen in all the rain?

"Oh, Julian," she gasped.

Enough. I wouldn't have her pity. I turned and walked away.

"Don't you walk away from me!" she yelled.

The rain shifted sideways, stinging my cheeks. I didn't answer and didn't turn around.

She ran after me, but my legs were longer. I reached the truck first and climbed in, locking the power doors easily—that had to chap her hide. She ran to the front, banging on the hood with her fist so I couldn't pull forward to use the turnaround. So I backed up instead. Gravel flew as my truck squealed down the long driveway and into the blessedly empty road.

Romy

When he backed out of the driveway, I wilted in defeat.

The welts on Julian's back. I felt them more than saw them, but the thought of them and the pain he had endured turned my stomach. I fell to my knees to retch, but my stomach didn't have anything to give.

And he'd left me.

Again.

The hell if he'll leave me again before I'm done talking to him. Something snapped inside of me, something I hadn't known I was holding so tight. I jumped to my feet and stomped down the road the short distance to Julian's house. Lightning struck a tree on the other side of the road, but I walked on. Rain stung my face, but I walked on. Some idiot came flying down the road, splashing me in the dip between the houses, but I walked on.

No more. Julian was going to tell me the whole truth and nothing but the truth, so help me God. That thought carried me up the hill, past the sorry-ass trailer where he'd grown up, and up the steps to his mamaw's porch. I banged on the door.

He didn't answer.

I gave him a few minutes, and I banged again.

Nothing.

Fine. I'll walk around to the back door, which, unless you've fixed it, has a tendency to not shut all of the way.

Sure enough, the latch to the back door hadn't caught, and I opened it with ease. And there was Julian, with his scarred bare back to me, holding the tape boxers use. He looked over his shoulder, frozen.

When he turned around I couldn't help but stare at his chest. He'd always been lean, but now he was, as Shelley Jean had so eloquently put it, built. Only the white skin in the outline of his T-shirt made me frown. I was used to a golden brown, almost carefree Julian. This Julian was muscular—no doubt due in part to the boxing habit he'd taken up since I left—but he wasn't the Julian who'd brazenly walked up from the lake wearing nothing but a smile.

I stepped forward and he stepped backward. I almost laughed hysterically at the idea that we might be working on our foot-work.

"Julian."

"Don't. Don't look at me like that."

I forced my eyes to meet his. "Don't look at you like what?"

"Like I'm half the man I used to be."

What a ridiculous thing male pride is. But thinking it didn't keep tears from clouding my vision. My throat closed to the point I couldn't have formed words even if I'd been able to find the ones I wanted to say. Instead I reached out and gently traced a scar on his chest. It was a thin, tiny scar hidden beneath a generous dust-ing of blond hair. It was much smaller than the ones I'd seen be-fore. He flinched as though my fingers were on fire.

He backpedaled. "I'm serious, Romy. Stop it!"

Oh, the backing away. I was sick to death of having him back away. Anger flushed out anguish, and I took another step toward him. "Stop it, or you'll what?"

"Just stop." He hit the wall, and I stopped right in front of him. I reached for him again, but he grabbed my wrists, remind-ing me of the night outside The Fountain. That night, I'd been certain he was going to kiss me. That night, I'd been almost certain I was going to let him.

Today, kissing me didn't seem to be on his mind.

So I stood on tippy toes and kissed him. Determined to remain impassive, he didn't flinch when I brushed my lips across his. By the third pass, his breathing was shallow, and I was dizzy from the pull between us. As I leaned forward a fourth time, his lips caught mine savagely. I met him hungry kiss for hungry kiss, surprised to discover he'd released my wrists in favor of wrapping his arms around me and pulling me closer. Someone whimpered. It was me.

Parts of me I'd forgotten I even had ached, and the world spun as Julian kissed my cheek, my neck, and then my lips with all the fervor of a man who'd been given up for dead only to realize he was going to make it after all. "Julian, please. I'm begging you."

He froze and, with effort, pushed me to arm's length. "No. I can't."

Still dizzy. "You can't? Or you won't?"

"Both. Neither. You're engaged to someone else, and—"

"Not anymore I'm not."

"You're not engaged?" He held up my hand to see it had no ring, proof I'd made my decision the day before.

"Mostly not?" I said with a wince.

"What the hell does that mean?"

"I haven't given him his ring back, but I broke it off for good."

He closed his eyes, shaking his head slowly from right to left. When he finally spoke, his voice came out in a whisper. "Doesn't matter. I can't let anyone hurt you. Especially not me."

"What in the hell are you talking about?"

"I am not going to beat my wife." He said it louder because it obviously made sense to him.

"Why would you ever beat me?"

"I don't know!" And he exploded, jumping to the center of the porch, punching the bag that hung from the rafters then pacing anxiously. "I don't know how it works. All I know is when Curtis married my mama they were happy. I've seen the pictures. And then I came along, and he started beating her."

I swallowed in horror. "Julian, no."

"I told myself I was different. I thought I could control it, but then we beat the hell out of each other once, and I've wanted to kill him with my bare hands ever since." His nostrils flared. I wanted to kill Curtis McElroy for all of the pain he'd caused Julian, for all of the pain he'd caused us.

"Wanting to kill Curtis doesn't mean you'd ever want to hit me."

"But how do you know that? It feels awfully damn good to hit things, and that's not normal, Romy." He crossed his arms over his chest. "How do you know someday something won't snap inside me and make me beat you until you're the one sitting in that emergency room?"

"Because you wouldn't. You couldn't."

He ran a hand through his wet hair in frustration. "You have no idea what I'm capable of."

"But where do I fit in all of this? Tell me, Julian, why don't I get to have a say in this decision?"

"You don't understand."

"Because you won't tell me!"

"You're loyal. You'd stay. Just like Mama."

I snorted. "I am not your mama. Hit me once and see if you don't wake up with a pistol up each nostril."

He stepped forward, cupping my cheek with one hand. "Romy, I'm not going to risk the once."

"No, Julian, you don't get it." I poked his hard chest to punctuate each word. "I'm not leaving until you tell me exactly what the hell made you think you needed to protect me from you."

Julian

"All right. Fine." I started back into the house, but stopped to hold the porch door open for her so she'd know I was inviting her in. On my way to the kitchen I grabbed a clean shirt from the dryer. No way was I going to tell this story with those ugly-ass scars in plain view.

I pointed to one of the mismatched chairs and reached into the fridge to get a Coke for each of us, hoping she didn't see how my hands shook. Then I sat down, took a deep breath, and finally told Romy the truth.

"We'd come home from graduation, and I wanted to pack a few things before we left. At first I was too excited to catnap. Then Curtis started beating up on Mama. Again.

"I told myself not to get involved. I told myself she was a grown woman. She'd never once taken any of my offers for help. If she wanted me, she'd call for me. Then she cried out really loud, and I started to wonder what he might do to her when he found out I'd run off with you. He'd blame her for it. He blamed her for everything."

I closed my eyes against the memory of that night. I had been eighteen. I thought I knew it all.

"If I was smarter, maybe I would've called the police, let them handle the whole thing, but they weren't much help the time I did call them. Besides, I thought I could take him. I was younger, faster, smarter . . . sober. So I walked down the hall and hollered at him to stop. He only stopped long enough to yell, 'Go away, boy!'

"I barged in and found him sitting on her, slapping her face repeatedly like in *Chinatown*, so I pulled him off her. He hit both my ears so hard they were ringing. I only meant to hit him once, but once I started I couldn't stop. I think I wanted to take care of him forever since I knew I was leaving. But then Mama tried to pull me off him, and I pushed her back into a lamp. It crashed on the floor, and the bulb burst, leaving us in only the gray light from the kitchen.

"I looked at my bloody knuckles. I even had blood along the sides of my fingernails and underneath the edges. I'd only meant to stop him, but I'd hurt him. I'd hurt Mama. And I sure as hell didn't want to hurt you." I had to stop there. At least for a minute.

"But, what about your scars?" she asked. "Why couldn't you just come tell me this?"

"I'm getting there. You see, I was pacing in the yard, debating whether I would meet you or not. You were the only good thing in my life, and I didn't want to mess that up. Here, I thought I was able to keep a lid on my temper, but I'd just beat the shit out of my father and pushed my mother.

"I knew I had to tell you something, so I reached for my keys and headed to the truck. Only, I hadn't beaten Curtis enough because he came up behind me with a cast-iron skillet and whacked me in the back of the head.

"Yeah, I was younger and quicker, but Curtis was meaner. He never would've got the best of me if he hadn't banged on my ears until I was half-deaf and then hit me from behind. He'd already rolled me over on my stomach and got three licks in before I knew what was happening.

"He kept yelling, 'Boy, I'm gonna wear you out like I shoulda done every day of your damn life.' Then he unbuckled his wide leather belt. That belt whistled through the air, but I was still so stunned from the blow to the head that each stinging cut only began to hurt just before the next one hit.

"Every time I'd try to get to my feet, he kicked me in the ribs until I fell down and then he'd lash me some more. He kept yelling about how he didn't deserve to be saddled with me, about how I needed to learn my lesson. He'd probably still be beating on me today except Mama came in wailing like a banshee about how he'd promised he'd never do anything more than spank me. She kept pulling on his arm and crying, 'You promised!'

"He slapped her down, but she'd distracted him enough that he was done with me. He took out his flask and poured his rotgut liquor on my back. That's when I blacked out. When I came to, he was snoring on the back porch. Mama was still crouched on the back stoop, rocking and crying and wringing her hands. Somehow I managed to get to my feet and to trudge to the one place I knew he would never dare to look for me: your barn.

"I tried to tell you the other day when we climbed up to the loft, but I couldn't. How're you supposed to tell someone that your father beat you black-and-blue even after you were a grown man?

"I got lucky. Hank went looking around up there for something, and he found me. He wanted to take me to the emergency room, but I made him promise not to. Told him I'd drag my sorry carcass somewhere else before the ambulance got there, and I made him promise to never, ever tell you."

Romy swallowed hard, tears running down her cheeks. She did pity me, and, really, my sorry, scarred ass deserved nothing less. Still, she deserved the truth, so I continued.

"Hank called Dr. Winterbourne, who patched me up as best as a vet in a barn loft could. I finally told Hank he could call Ben, and the two of them kept watch over me until I was well enough to go home. But I didn't go back to Curtis's house. Instead I moved into Mamaw's old house.

"Dr. Winterbourne lost count of the stitches—both on my back and in my head. He bandaged up my broken ribs, too. He had to give me painkillers because I didn't know which way to lie down between the broken and bruised ribs and the sores on my back. I don't know how he managed to get antibiotics, but he did—probably damned horse pills. Ben changed out the bandages on my back despite the fact he gets faint at the sight of blood. I owe him more than I'll ever be able to repay him. Him, and Hank, too.

"At first, I didn't call you because I was too out of it to know where I was or what was going on. Dr. Winterbourne's pain pills worked a little too well those first few weeks. As I weaned myself off them, I had a lot of time to think. The more I thought about it, the more I thought about how smart you were and how much you deserved to go off to Vanderbilt instead of giving up that scholarship and staying here to be with me like we'd talked about after I broke my leg. I would've never forgiven myself for holding you back, and you wouldn't have forgiven me, either. I had a lot of time to think about the McElroys and how I didn't know of a one who wasn't a sorry bastard. Almost all of them have beaten their wives and drank too much. One uncle and at least two cousins were in jail right then.

"I didn't have anything to do but think, and I tried to think of any way I knew to stay married and be sure I would never hurt you the way Curtis hurt Mama or the way my uncles beat their wives. Or drink you out of house and home. Or leave you to fend for yourself when I finally had to serve a little time.

"I thought of the pictures of Mama and Curtis back when they were happy. They looked normal and in love. Sure, it was a shotgun wedding. Sure, I was one of those six-month miracle babies, but they looked so happy in all of their pictures right up until about the time I turned five.

"So I thought if I held back, you'd eventually send those papers in the mail. I wasn't going to go after you because I might end up staying. I never once thought you'd hold out this long."

I looked at her, willing her to understand. Even though I couldn't let her love me, I didn't want her to hate me anymore. "So that's why I've stayed away. There's something wrong with me, Romy. It's in my blood. Someday I might wake up and be just as evil as Curtis, and I'll be damned if I'm going to ruin your life over it."

Romy

"And you've put us both through ten years of hell because you're afraid you're some kind of genetic time bomb?"

"Only for your own good." He turned up his Coke and chugged at least half of it. Mine sat open but untouched with condensation beading up on the can.

Rage bubbled up inside me. "For my own good? Did I miss something? Is this the nineteenth century?"

"Of course not, it's not like that." He stood. "I think you should go now."

"I suppose that's *for my own good*, too? Oh, hell no. I'm not going anywhere." I stood to face him. "Do you have any idea what kind of hell I was in? Not knowing why you left me or why you weren't returning my calls? Or when your mother told me you didn't want to see me anymore? Or—"

"She did what?" To his credit, Julian looked honestly astonished.

"Did you really think I would just leave without trying to talk to you? When you wouldn't answer my calls, I walked up to your house and knocked on the door. Your mother told me you were indisposed. Then she told me you never wanted to see me again."

"And you believed that?" he roared.

"Well, how is that any different from your arbitrarily 'deciding' you needed to stay away from me?" I yelled back.

"I probably wasn't even conscious—"

"Well, I didn't know that at the time, and I wished I were dead!"

That ugly word hung between us, and his brow softened. "I'm sorry, Romy. I never meant to hurt you. I swear."

"Well, you did." And like that I was crying again.

Julian thumbed away my tears. "Please don't cry. There's nothing I hate more than seeing you cry."

I half laughed, half hiccupped. "Good thing you weren't around to see me the semester I almost flunked out of Vandy, then, wasn't it?"

His sharp intake of breath told me he couldn't believe in a world where Romy Satterfield even came close to flunking out. "And your scholarships?"

"I lost them, every one. But then I couldn't come home, now could I?" And I ached for what I'd missed. I thought I was just mad at Julian, but he'd stolen a part of my home from me. All those wistful weekends when I should've driven home to do my laundry for free, the summers I should've come home to help Daddy with the farm, and . . . no, that wasn't fair. I could've gone home. I could've faced my fears and my pain a long time ago. I was just as much a thief as he.

"Romy, I—"

When I looked up, he was still searching for the words, no doubt adding blame for those lost scholarships. I couldn't have that. If anyone were ever born with an Atlas complex, it was Julian McElroy.

"Stop taking the blame," I whispered as my hand traveled to his stubbly cheek. "It was my fault, too. God, how stupid was I to believe anything your mother said? I knew how much she hated me. How much she still does." I shivered, partly at the depth of Debbie McElroy's hatred for me and partly because my wet clothes and the air-conditioning were starting to get to me.

Julian gently took my hand from his cheek, grazing my knuckles with his lip. He sighed as he let my hand go. "You need to go on home and get out of those wet clothes."

I may have walked to the door like a good little girl, but when my hand touched the knob, I knew I didn't want to go home. Not yet. Not when things still weren't resolved between us. Instead, I turned to look at Julian. He stood up straighter, quickly erasing the anguished expression he'd allowed only because he knew I wasn't looking.

His white T-shirt reminded me of how his white skin had blinded me, and I ached all over again for all that he'd hidden from both the world and me. I thought of how he'd admitted to me that he hadn't slept with anyone since I'd left. "Julian, do you still love me?"

He weighed his words carefully, not exactly the response a girl could hope for. I could see him warring with the asinine notion he could best protect me from himself if he made me leave. Then he had to consider Richard and all the ways in which he thought he fell short, the things the world told him he needed like money and prestige.

Or was he thinking about how much he didn't like the idea of me with Richard? I couldn't help the pang of regret, but I wasn't going to let it rule me. I might have wasted time, but I wasn't going to let it waste me. Not anymore.

He still hadn't answered, so I walked back to him and repeated my question: "Tell me the truth. Do you still love me?"

"Remember that mess from *Romeo and Juliet* that you read to me back in tutoring? You would recite some shit about ancient grudges and fatal loins then laugh and call us star-crossed lovers? Well, it ain't a laughing matter. What if I do love you? It didn't end well for them, and I don't expect much better for us."

What if I do love you? And that question was my answer, the balm my soul needed to heal. "Do you really think I can walk away from you after you say something like that? There's nothing hotter for an English major than quoting Shakespeare."

"Dammit, Romy! I am *not* going to turn out like Curtis. I am *not* going to ruin your life." His fists clenched so tightly his knuckles turned white and his chest and arms flexed.

"What about your life? What if you ruin both of our lives by *not* letting me love you?" There was that heady pull between the two of us again. It robbed me of my next breath and left me dizzy. "What if *I* love you?"

"Don't." He almost choked on the word.

"Too late . . . husband." I advanced on him, and he quite predictably retreated again. A flash of lightning slashed through the house. Thunder rumbled directly overhead, signaling a new storm moving in. Still, I walked down the tiny hall between kitchen and bedroom. Still, Julian backed away from me. His back met the linen closet. The lights flickered and went out with a sizzle. I stopped short, shivering again in my damp clothes. He looked to his right for an escape route. I followed his eyes to the bedroom and straight to his unmade bed.

"Tell me you don't love me, and I'll leave. Right now."

"I don't love you," he said, his eyes on the floor.

I stood on tiptoe to kiss him, breaking away just as he gave in to me. "Tell me you don't love me, and I'll go. I swear it."

His breath hitched; his eyes closed. "I don't love you."

I reached up to kiss him again, but this time he met me halfway, bending down to kiss me. One hand knotted in my hair at the nape of my neck, and the other splayed across the small of my back as he pulled me to him. I felt at least one reason he might not want me to leave. "If you can look me in the eye and tell me you don't love me, then I'll go. Really, this time."

He dragged his eyes to mine, but all he could get out was an "I—I—"

"You are one piss-poor liar," I said before wrapping my arms around him and kissing his stuttering lips.

Julian

There were a million reasons I shouldn't give in to Romy, but I couldn't think of a damned one. Instead I dragged her body even closer to mine, giving up any hope of being able to tell her I didn't love her and mean it. Damned Satterfields were a pushy bunch, and the pushiest one of them all had her hand on my crotch.

Which reminded me of the upside of pushy Satterfields.

Once my spirit found its way back to my body, I kissed her in earnest. I could tell myself this was a one-time deal, couldn't I? After all, we weren't breaking any laws, nor any vows we'd made to each other or God. We might have to revisit those vows later, but for this moment, I wanted to pretend.

The most selfish part of me wanted her like I'd never needed her before. My fingers fumbled with her bra clasp, while she had lost the ability to unbutton my pants. We were more awkward than we had been as teenagers, but I tried to slow it down, to savor the moment.

"It's been ten years," she growled before pushing me back on the bed. Our mouths met again, teeth bumping at one point. I rolled her underneath, wanting to look down into those green eyes, searching them for any excuse to stop even though I knew I wouldn't.

"Julian," she said, her voice a plea as her fingernails dug into my arms. "For the love of God, get inside me."

So I did.

And it felt like home.

Afterward, we lay side by side, no longer needing a blanket nor feeling the chill of our wet flesh. Rain softly pinged against the old tin roof, and I should've felt sleepy. But I didn't. "There goes any chance you had for an annulment," I said, trying unsuccessfully to hold off on a grin.

She cupped my face, her thumbs rubbing against the stubble on my jawline. "Good thing I'm not interested in getting one."

"Romy—"

She moved that finger to my lips. "Not now, Julian."

She pulled me close, squeezing her chest against mine so she could trace each welt on my back with her fingers. I stiffened at her touch, at the memory of what I'd been hiding for so long. "Touching those scars won't make them go away, you know."

She kissed the tip of my nose and said, "I know." But she kept touching me anyway, and I finally started to heal.

Romy

"Julian?"

Debbie McElroy's voice brought me out of a deep, blissful sleep and straight into a panic. Julian, on the other hand, didn't seem to hear her at all. I had to shake him to get him to wake up.

"Your mother is in the house," I hissed as I tried to get under the covers.

He answered with a grunt, then rolled off the bed and looked for some boxers and a T-shirt. "Just a minute."

A similar scene from *Romeo and Juliet* came to mind, and I giggled. *Anon, nurse.* Or in this case, *extra-mean-and-nosy heifer.*

"There you are! I've been worried sick about you," she said from the hallway. "When you didn't show up for supper—"

And that gasp had to mean she saw my bra on the floor.

"Julian Eugene McElroy!"

"My house, Mama. You should knock before you barge in." He sounded so calm, and I could tell from the sound of his voice that he was backing her down the hall.

"It's her, isn't it? That Satterfield harlot who tricked you into marrying her. You know she's just going to leave you again."

My heart pounded against my chest. *Who uses the word* harlot *anymore?*

"That's enough. You need to go. Now."

"No. I want to talk to her."

Didn't see that one coming, and I was guessing from the pause that Julian didn't, either. I glanced around the room, but half my clothes were in the hallway.

"I don't think so. Now, hand me your key." His voice was reinforced steel. He'd been waiting to speak to make sure he didn't say anything he regretted. I didn't envy him the situation because what could he say? *Yep, it was a one-day stand, but we're hoping to make something more out of it.*

"I'm not leaving until that hussy comes out here so I can speak to her."

I've progressed to hussy. Nice.

"Yes, you are leaving. And you're handing me that key."

"Why? So you can give it to—?"

"My wife? I just might."

My wife. Just the sound of it made me dizzy.

"You're not saying a word about any of this to Curtis, either." The front door slammed, and I heard Julian's heavy, solid footfalls down the hall. He leaned in the doorway, drinking in every detail of having me in his bed as if he never wanted to forget a single thing. I reached my arm out to him, and he looked away.

"Oh, no. Don't you start that business."

"Romy, we've always been good together like this, but that doesn't mean we should stay together."

But you called me your wife!

"This is about *him*, isn't it?"

He was quiet for too long, long enough for a lump to form in my throat. Finally, he said, "Naw, I've pretty much made my peace with that."

"Then what is your issue?"

"What's good for me probably ain't that good for you."

I sat up, letting the sheet drop on purpose. "Why don't you let me decide what's good for me?"

He walked to the bed but stopped, as though still considering kicking me out on my ass. Then he slid in beside me. "God knows I should say no, but you have always been a persuasive woman."

I drew him closer, my hands wandering up his back. "That's because you always seem to be in need of persuasion, Mr. McElroy."

"Well then, Mrs. McElroy—"

"Oh, no. I'm keeping my last name. You McElroys aren't going to win that easily."

"Fine. Ms. Satterfield, it's a good thing I have you here to persuade me." He kissed me hard, surprising me because I was expecting more banter instead. When I went to pull him on top, he rolled over on his back and shifted me up top instead.

"But if we're going to try this, really try this, you have to promise me one thing," he said.

"Anything." My voice cracked on the word, and I meant it with every bit of my heart even if I had no idea what I was promising in that moment.

"You have to promise," he said as he guided me down on top of him and filled me up completely, "to leave me if I ever hit you even once."

My yes came out on a gasp.

He growled as I began to move, his hand reaching up to brush the hair out of my face. "I want to forget everything but you."

And I obliged him. Achingly slow and with every ounce of me held back over ten years, I made love to Julian while the world outside grew darker and the rain steadily pinged on the tin roof above us.

Julian

I half expected to wake up alone and find it had all been a dream, but no, Romy had burrowed into me, holding on for dear life. I watched her sleep—but not in that creepy, sparkly-ass vampire way. I grinned at the small smile she wore in her sleep. I hadn't seen enough of that smile since she came back to town.

And I was responsible for a lot of that unhappiness.

But you did it for her own good.

I wasn't going to admit it, but I felt so much better for having told her the truth and knowing she would gleefully shoot me if I ever beat her. That didn't solve the problem of what to do about Curtis or how she'd be better off with the Paris family and all of their fabulous wealth, but for this moment she was mine.

The phone rang, and I thought about not answering it, but something told me my time was up. I trotted to the old rotary phone in the kitchen, the only one I had. Sure enough, I answered the phone to a very pissed-off Hank Satterfield.

"Yes, she's here. . . . Yes, she's perfectly fine. . . . Yes, I'll get her—"

Romy appeared in the doorway, wearing nothing but one of

my T-shirts and a smile. That smile quickly faded when she heard her father's voice on the other end of the line.

"Yes, Daddy," she said as she turned three shades of red. "No, I'm sorry I didn't call you. Something came up."

I laughed at that, and she swatted at my chest.

"He did *what*?"

That didn't sound good.

"I'll be right there."

That sounded worse.

She hung up the phone and turned to me. "I have to go. Richard's up there."

I wanted to sink through the floor, down to the crawl space with the beagle and the snakes. This was it. She was going to change her mind and marry that sonuvabitch after all.

She brushed past me, gathering her clothes and dancing into them in a way that was almost as sexy as watching her shimmy out of them. *Hands off, Julian. She's probably going back to him.*

When she was as put together as she could be, she turned to face me. "Oh, Julian."

"What?"

"Enough with the stoic routine. I'm coming back to you." But after those confident words, the doubt seeped in. "Well, that is, if you still want me."

"I've never wanted anyone else." The truth of my own words knocked the wind out of me.

She grinned. I wanted to see that lopsided smile a whole helluva lot more. I owed her that much at the very least.

"Well, then. Happy birthday to me!"

My eyes bugged out. It *was* her birthday. "Can I bring your present by in just a little while?"

Her eyes narrowed. "Julian, you don't have to get me anything."

"I've had this present for a while." *A long, long while.*

"You, too?" she muttered. "Okay, but give me a minute to get rid of Richard and to smooth things over with Daddy."

Right.

I stood up and she wrapped her arms around me and kissed me soundly. I wanted to take her right back to bed, but I let her go. For the moment.

If she thought for one second I was going to hang back knowing her former fiancé was up the road, she was crazy.

Romy

As I did my trudge of shame up the driveway, I saw something even scarier than Richard: his mother.

The full weight of what I'd done twisted my stomach in knots, and I hadn't really had much to eat other than the omelet Julian made for me at two in the morning. Thinking of the omelet made me think of what came after.

Rosemary Jane, you are one despicable person.

Richard and his mother surveyed the little patch of land to the left of the house. At the moment, we were using that land as a vegetable garden, but I could guess Richard's mother had other ideas from the way she gesticulated. She, of course, was impeccably dressed in white capris and an expensive peasant blouse with matching jewelry. I wondered if there was any hope I could sneak into the house and shower before facing the music. Then I accidentally kicked a rock with my steel-toe boots, and Richard turned around.

To say he looked hurt and betrayed would be the understatement of the century.

"Rosemary, darling." His mother walked forward and air kissed just past each cheek as though it were the most natural thing in the world to have her son's would-be fiancé walk up the driveway in the nasty, sweaty clothes she probably wore yesterday after a night of wild sex.

"Good morning, Mrs. Paris."

"I was just telling your father that you really do have such a lovely farm. Richard had told me your father was a bit upset about the cathedral, and he needed me to help him drive your present, so I thought I'd take a look. This farmhouse is simply charming! Why, we could clear out this garden, lay down some sod, and have a very nice outdoor wedding right here, don't you think?"

Sod? Over the garden?

Wait. Drive my present?

I looked at the Leaning Locust Tree of Pisa and, sure enough, just beyond Richard's Porsche was a car with a bow on top just like Christmas commercials. I looked at Richard, but he looked away.

"Richard, you shouldn't have," I said.

He muttered something under his breath that sounded an awful lot like, "I know."

"Oh, silly me, rambling on about weddings when it's your birthday. Go on, Richard, show her!"

Something about her smug tone suggested showing me the car would remind me of just how unworthy of her son she thought I was—not that she would ever say such a thing out loud. Richard, who hated proving his mother right, wouldn't meet my eyes as he took me over to the car, a brand-new Mustang. A lump formed in my throat. "Richard, it's lovely, but I can't accept this."

"You need something other than that deathtrap truck," he said with a nod to the pickup. "Your Honda was a disgrace, and I knew you preferred Fords. And that you liked horses."

Such an over-the-top gesture when I'd done so much to hurt him brought tears that stung my eyes. "I'm so sorry. You're going to have to take it back."

He took the keys out of his pocket and pressed them into my hand. "You're going to need a car, and we both know this was chump change for me. I would've given you a more expensive car if I'd thought you'd take it."

His words hung between us, the only other sound the birds and the bugs and the occasional car going down the road. "I know you would have, but you deserve someone far better than me."

He studied me closely. "So this is it?"

I nodded because I couldn't answer.

"Rosemary, darling, do you think we could get the barn painted?" Mrs. Paris gestured to the barn across the street. "If it were red and white, that would be so . . . quaint, don't you think?"

"You didn't tell her, did you?"

Richard shrugged. "A man can hope, can't he?"

I swiped at the tears that streaked down my cheeks. I didn't want to marry Richard. I knew that. I also didn't want to hurt him, but it was too late for that. "Let me get your ring."

He nodded, and I raced inside.

"Rosemary Jane—" Hank started.

"Not now, Daddy," I said as I raced upstairs to get the ring.

I didn't even look at him as I trotted back outside. I handed the ring box back to Richard and he stuffed it into the pocket of his khaki pants. Then I tried to press the car keys into his hand, but he wouldn't have it.

"I meant it. You keep the car."

"Richard, this is ridiculous—"

A whinny from the corner of the yard made us both look. There was Julian leading the scraggliest palomino I'd ever seen.

And the hits keep coming.

Julian

It didn't take an idiot to see what was going on at the Satterfield place.

Richard had bought Romy a shiny red Mustang, complete with a damn bow on top. That made me stop in my tracks. I was bringing her Beatrice, who was old, blind, and swaybacked.

Good call, Julian. He really did buy her a car. He gets her a brand-new Mustang, and you get her an ancient palomino.

Richard stuffed a box in his pants pocket and made straight for me. That's when I noticed the nicely dressed woman fanning herself under the oak. She had the same dark hair, so I could only assume she was his mother.

Romy looked as though she might follow him, but she didn't.

He reared back to throw a punch as he reached me, but I easily caught his fist in my hand. "I know I deserve that, but you're not punching me today."

"You deserve a lot worse," he hissed, his pride stinging from how easily I'd kept him from hitting me. "You couldn't leave her alone, could you?"

"She's a grown woman. For the record, I told her she'd be better off with you." I nodded at the car to make my meaning clear: *She'd be better off* financially *with you.*

At that point my eyes went to the jewelry-box-sized lump in his pocket. My soul got lighter.

"I'm going to guess an annulment is a moot point now?" He stared through me.

"You could say that."

He sighed and pinched the space on top of his nose. Just when I thought he was more upset about losing the girl than losing to me, he looked up with eyes blazing. "You know what? Do what you need to do. It won't take her long to figure out she's better off with me."

"You think she's going back to you?"

His hand arced dismissively to encompass the farm around him. "This? You? She has to get that out of her system, but she's too intelligent and too educated to ever be happy here in the boondocks. And you? Please."

"What about me?"

"I looked up your records," he said with a smug smile. "Did a credit search. You almost didn't pass high school and don't have a dime to your name."

My left hand curled into a fist, but I saw what he was doing. I forced a smile. "That's all true, but I do have . . . other things."

He laughed this ugly bitter laugh, and I thought for a minute I'd got the best of him. Then he started recounting all the places and all the ways he'd had my wife. Blood rushed through my ears, and I had a flashback to Pete Gates's diatribe in The Fountain.

Only this time, everything Richard said was probably true.

"You're gonna shut up now," I said as I stepped closer to him, now nose to nose with clenched fists at my side.

"Yeah, but you're going to remember every word I said." He stared me down for a moment, but then he smiled and walked away, straightening the cuffs of his suit as he went. He knew what he'd said was far more painful than a punch.

Romy

I was so intent on Julian and Richard's conversation that I didn't notice Mrs. Paris had sidled over. "I see what's going on here."

I met her gaze. "I'm really sorry, Mrs. Paris. I never meant to hurt Richard; you have to believe that."

"Oh, I believe it. And that young man *is* a tall drink of water," she said as her gaze went out to Julian. "I tried to warn Richard that you were a money-grubbing country bumpkin."

The hell? "I don't need your money, and I'm not a bumpkin."

She shook her head in the direction of the Mustang with a simpering "Mmm-hmm."

The keys to the new car bit into my hand from how I was clutching them. Now I pressed them on her, and she raised her hands to her chest in a show of mock terror. "No, no, I couldn't!" before leaning down and saying in a stage whisper, "*That's* how it's done."

I gaped at her through a mixture of shock and fury.

"Mother! We're going." Richard stalked to the car, but the smile on his face was both grim and evil. As he walked past me, I tried once more to hand him the keys.

"No means no," he snapped as he opened the door. "Title's in the glove compartment."

He peeled out of the driveway, and the horse Julian led

danced around uncomfortably. I walked toward Julian to see what this was all about. He looked positively green. I could guess some of the things that Richard had told him. Just a few weeks before, I might've told Julian myself in order to inflict upon him the same kind of hurt he'd inflicted on me. But now . . .

"So what's this, Julian?"

He wouldn't meet my eyes, reaching over to rub the mare's nose instead. She was a gorgeous palomino, but her eyes were filmed over.

"This is Beatrice."

I remembered the other day when he'd said he had to go back and get his horse, Benedick. My chest got tighter.

"You always wanted a horse, so I got Beatrice here for a wedding gift, but I never got to give her to you, so happy birthday instead."

Tears came yet again, and I swiped at them. Dammit. Why hadn't I come back from Vandy at least one more time? I was fortune's fool.

Julian mistook my tears. "I know she ain't much to look at, up in years, and moon blind on top of that. I should've put her down, but I couldn't bear to part with her. Not when I got her for you."

"She's perfect." And I was not despite all those years of trying.

"And you named your horse Benedick?" I tentatively reached forward to rub the mare's long nose. She sighed, her eyes half-closed.

He nodded. "That play's your favorite, isn't it? I finally saw the movie."

He had remembered.

I tried to imagine Julian watching *Much Ado About Nothing*, but I couldn't. He wouldn't have passed a single test on any of Shakespeare's plays if I hadn't read them to him, often translating Shakespeare's English to a more . . . country version.

He scuffed his boot across the grass. "I can take her back if you don't want her. Maybe get you a better horse—"

Beatrice flicked her ears forward and snorted at him. I tended to agree with her. I rubbed her long nose with more confidence this time. "No, you won't. I love her just the way she is. Thank you."

He smiled, finally meeting my gaze.

"I don't know the first thing about horses."

"'Course you do. I'll teach you the rest."

I'll teach you the rest. Thank God. He wasn't going to run away again.

"If you give her some apple pieces, she'll love you forever."

"I can do that."

"Think Hank would mind if I patched up the old stables in the barn?"

Another sign Julian wasn't going to bail. Maybe.

"Probably, but you go ahead. He'll just have to get used to my money-pit-horse-that-only-an-idiot-would-buy."

We stared at each other until a lump took up residence in my throat. "Julian, about Richard—"

"I ain't talking about that right now."

Not right now wasn't never, but still. I opened my mouth to ask him if we were okay, but my father chose that moment to yell for me out the back door.

"You'd best go talk to him."

I nodded. So far this hadn't exactly been the birthday I'd had in mind.

Julian

As I watched Romy go, I asked myself if I wanted her to come back. I couldn't blame her because I hadn't done a damn thing to tell her I was still in love with her. I'd actually done anything and everything to discourage her. Then there was the fact I'd come awfully close to sleeping with Shelley Jean myself. But knowing facts was a sight different from overcoming feelings, and her asshole ex had put some pretty vivid pictures in my mind, pictures designed to remind me of how much money he had as well as how he'd had my girl.

Yeah, but in the end she chose you on both counts.

And I knew she wouldn't have left me in the first place if I hadn't made her.

But, sonuvabitch, I didn't want to touch her right then or even look at her. I sure as hell didn't want to *talk*.

It'd be best if I got to work, so I might as well show Beatrice her new digs.

"Beatrice, old gal, I've got someone I'd like for you to meet." She stomped and unloaded right there in the middle of the front yard.

"Beggars can't be choosers," I continued as I led her to the barn. "I should've sent you to the glue factory already."

She tossed her head at that.

"I know. I'm a sappy sonuvabitch. Ain't you lucky I am?"

About the time we came up even with the little pen, Star poked her nose through the slats in the gate to bawl at the horse. Beatrice whinnied back at her. She actually started to stamp and rock a little as I opened the gate, and I wondered why I hadn't thought of this sooner. Horses and cows weren't known for getting along, but it could still work. I'd heard of horses keeping a cow from eating or getting water, but Beatrice couldn't see where the water was. I'd seen a calf chew off a chunk of horse tail once, but little Star was desperate for companionship. As with people, we'd just see if the two of them could get along—at least while I finished the broken-down stalls inside the barn.

Walking inside to survey the damage, I saw where a couple of crude stalls had been. Faded fragments of flowery wallpaper curled on the wall, left over from when the barn had been a house. Putting my hands on a couple of the boards and testing them, I decided a trip to town would be in order. Those rotten boards wouldn't hold in a drunken llama.

Beatrice nickered and Star bawled in response. I almost tripped myself getting to the edge of the pen to make sure the twosome weren't hurting each other. Nope. They were playing. Then the calf did the damnedest thing: She led Beatrice to the trough full of water.

"Well, well. I guess you can lead a horse to water *and* make her drink," I murmured as Beatrice gulped up water. "You two behave now, and when I get back I'll see if I can open this pen into the barn a little more so you can both get into the shade."

As I walked down the side of the yard and toward the road, I looked back to the house and wondered how things were going between Romy and Hank.

Romy

When I walked into the kitchen, I could feel Daddy's anger. If he'd been a teakettle, he would've whistled. "Rosemary Jane, we need to have a talk."

I crossed to the Keurig and turned it on. *Coffee, sweet coffee.* "So, talk."

"What in the hell are you thinking? When I—"

"I'm thinking that I belong here. I don't belong in Nashville. And I don't belong with Richard, always feeling uncomfortable at his soirées, always wondering if I've dressed well enough or if I'm eating with the right fork. I don't have to teach in an inner-city school to do good when my own alma mater has a significant free-and-reduced-lunch percentage. I want to teach English here, to introduce Shakespeare to kids who live in trailers or drafty farmhouses and who think they'll never get any farther in life. I want to come home. And I don't give a damn if he has more money than Julian or not."

There. I'd said it. And I didn't even know for sure I had a relationship with Julian. I wasn't going to make any more decisions about where to live or work based on men. Not even my father.

I popped the cartridge into the machine and put a cup underneath. It was a black coffee kind of morning. Coffee in hand, I finally faced my father.

"You finished?" Daddy's eyes had narrowed dangerously, and his ears were bright, bright red. I hadn't seen him this mad since I was six and put the ladder against the tin roof of the barn and climbed up top. That was one of the three times he'd tanned my hide.

I swallowed hard. He wasn't going to spank me, but his disappointment weighed much heavier than it had when I was six. "I'm done."

"I could give a rat's ass about whether you marry Richard or not. And if you want to move here permanently, I'm all for it, but the next time you stay out all afternoon and all night and don't answer your phone, I'm calling the police."

I blanched, instinctively reaching for my phone, but it wasn't in my back pocket. "Daddy, I'm sorry. I didn't mean to worry you. My phone must've slid out of my pocket in the truck when we were hauling hay."

"Don't do it again." His voice cracked, and tears threatened. I might be twenty-eight years old, but I'd scared the shit out of my father.

"Really, Daddy, I'm sorry. I was finally getting Julian to talk, and I let time get away from me."

"I'm sure 'talking' is all you were doing, too," he harrumphed.

My whole face burned. Then I remembered something. "Yeah, just like you were 'talking' with Delilah the other afternoon."

He had the good grace to clear his throat and turn a little pink himself. "Fair enough."

I took my cup of coffee and popped in another cartridge for him. "Thank you for taking care of Julian. Back then."

"Hardest thing I've ever done was not telling you what happened," he said. " 'Course I didn't even find him up there until you bolted out of here so fast. I thought you were sure enough ready to get rid of me."

My heart squeezed in on itself. "Oh, Daddy, I'm so, so sorry," I said. "I never thought beyond how much Julian had hurt me by standing me up."

"I can see that now," he said as he reached across the table and patted my hand. "But you'd better let me know where you are. I can't be worried you're off somewhere on the back forty getting eaten by coyotes."

"I'll go find my phone and charge it now," I said.

As I walked past him he grabbed my arm. "I should've told you."

Yeah, I really wish you had. "So I guess I'd better go see if there's a job opening in town, huh?"

Then Daddy grinned wide enough for me to see the gap just before his molars. "Damn straight you should!"

He shook my hand, pressing in who knew how many twenty-dollar bills, just like he always did. "And happy birthday, Rosemary."

He let go of my hand when Mercutio came out of nowhere to land in his lap.

"Thanks, Daddy." I shook my head at the two of them. If anyone had told me a month before that I'd be living in Yessum County and that my father would have both a cat and a girlfriend, I would've laughed in her face.

And then there was the question of Julian.

All I could think of was Tennyson's suggestion that it was better to have loved and lost than to have never loved at all. I'd recited those words at my mother's funeral, and I'd hoped to never have to repeat them.

I still had that hope.

From Rosemary Satterfield's
History of the Satterfield-McElroy Feud

Romy, this is the part of the book that you're going to have to hold on to until most of my generation is dead and gone because the next chapter of the feud is much more personal, much closer to home.

None of us knows for sure if he started acting up before his granddaddy's death, but Curtis was definitely acting up by the time he was ten. Your granny caught him trying to set fire to the old home place that day. She grabbed him by his ear and dragged him up the road to the McElroy place. By that time, Matthew, Julian's grandfather, had taken over the farm. He said he didn't believe his boy would do such a thing, but your granny said the glint in his eye suggested he did.

Julian's grandmother, on the other hand, started spanking Curtis before your granny got halfway down the driveway. Even knowing that, your granny could never sleep well after that. She was too scared Curtis would come back and set fire to the house while they were all asleep.

So far as your granny knew, that was the only time Curtis tried to set fire to the house, although part of a barn burned down in the late sixties. Even more disturbing, she'd find squirrels shot out of trees and left lying around the yard. Some of the Satterfields' favorite pets mysteriously disappeared, too.

And then there's what I know about Curtis McElroy.

Julian

I'd been to town and back and was working as hard as I could on the stable for Beatrice. She and Star were getting along famously, but I had to work the next day and needed to get everyone squared away before then.

When I heard the rustle of grass behind me, I surprised myself with the hope that it was Romy, but then I heard the creak of a wheel.

"Afternoon, Hank," I said without even looking over my shoulder.

"Afternoon, Julian."

I paused hammering long enough to say, "Hope you don't mind I'm fixing up a couple of stalls here for the horse I gave Romy."

He snorted and muttered something under his breath about idiots and horses. "I reckon it's your lumber. You go right ahead."

I turned around to face him, wiping sweat from my brow as I did. "Then what can I do for you?"

He crossed his arms over his chest, managing to look ominous in spite of sitting well below me. Kinda reminded me of Patrick Stewart as Professor X.

"Well, seems you and my daughter have rekindled your romance."

242 *Sally Kilpatrick*

"Yessir." *Well, maybe, sir.*

"And you remember how I wasn't too keen on the idea to start with?"

"Yessir."

"And you remember how I was right and it all went to shit?"

"Yessir."

"Don't fuck up again."

"Yessir." He could've added an "or else" to the end of that threat, but leaving it wide-open seemed worse.

Hank took out his pocketknife and a piece of wood and started to whittle. "You see, when you did your little thing, she high-tailed it to Nashville and left me out in the cold, too. I'm getting old, Julian. I want to spend time with my daughter, maybe even play with some grandbabies one of these days."

"Perfectly reasonable, sir."

His eyes met mine as he flicked the pocketknife closed. "But that doesn't mean I want to see any grandbabies before the two of you work out whatever it is you still have to work out."

"Yessir."

He muttered under his breath about all the "yessir bullshit," then turned his wheelchair with a grunt and rolled off.

The minute his wheelchair was out of earshot, I grabbed a nearby five-gallon bucket and turned it over to make a seat. Plopping down, I reached for the Coke I'd bought in town.

Don't fuck up again.

Yeah, I'd fucked up. When a man had *been* fucked up, it stood to reason he *would* fuck up. Ironically, Hank's little talk cheered me up. He hadn't told me to stay away from his daughter. In fact, didn't his warning mean he cared? Don't fuck up again was as close to getting Hank's blessing as I'd ever come. Now, how sad was that?

Not too sad.

And Hank had reminded me of something: If I'd fucked up, Romy had kinda fucked up. I mean, not really, but still. Didn't that make us pretty even? *Except for the part where you didn't run after her like you should have, sure.* But she could've come after me, too.

Aw, hell. We both messed up. Like people do. Wasn't what we did from this point forward more important than anything we'd done before?

Both Beatrice and Star ambled over to the fence to see what I was doing. Star peered at me through the slats, and Beatrice sniffed in my general direction. Already thick as thieves.

"What are you two looking at?"

I knew she was speaking horse, but it sounded all the world to me like Beatrice said, "One happy sonuvabitch."

And I'll be damned if I wasn't smiling.

Romy

That night I rushed Hank through supper and through the dishes. He hollered, "What's your hurry?" but there was enough of a twinkle in his eye that I knew he was only feigning irritation. I'd given Julian about all the time I could stand to give him. I needed to know where we stood. The last day or two had been too full of ups and downs.

Slow down, Romy, slow down.

After grabbing a little something I'd picked up for Julian in town, I tripped out the front door into the pink dusk, frowning at the Mustang I had yet to move.

No, it was still my birthday, and I wasn't going to think about that today. Like Scarlett, I could just think about that tomorrow.

I was huffing by the time I reached Julian's door—not because I was out of shape, but because I'd run up the road in the heavy steel-toed boots he'd given me. A pretty beagle with a wagging tail appeared almost out of nowhere and jumped up on me. I scratched behind her ears while I waited for Julian to come to the door.

I'd meant to give him his gift first, but, when he opened the door, I melted into his arms instead. He crushed me to his chest.

I started crying in spite of myself.

He pulled me out to arm's length. "What the hell, Romy?"

"I guess I was afraid you'd kick me out," I sniffed. I was mad at myself for being so invested in him again, but there it was.

"After all the things I did to you? No way."

He drew me close again and rested his chin on top of my head. I could tell that peace he'd made was going to be a little harder than he'd first imagined, but I could feel it nonetheless.

I disentangled myself. "I brought you a present."

"But it's *your* birthday," he said as he drew me in and closed the door behind us. The beagle whined in protest at being left out on the porch.

"Yes, but it's my fault you lost the other one," I said as I drew the finely woven straw cowboy hat from behind my back and placed it on his head. He grinned, and it took my breath away.

"I'd lose that hat and a million more like it if it meant you'd come back to me," he said as he kissed me.

"I've got other good news, too," I said between kisses as he pulled me in the direction of the bedroom.

"Oh?"

"Yes, it's too soon to say for sure, but they may have a position open at the junior high, so I put in my application. It's not ideal, but it's a job. They promised they'd put me on the waiting list for the high school but that would probably take a few years. I'm officially moving home."

He groaned, which could've been from my good news but was more likely related to my hand squeezing his ass as we reached the end of the bed. There was no more talking from that point, and he'd managed to relieve me of both my shirt and my shoes with ample promise of service when we both heard the gunshot.

"The hell?" He ran for the door as I struggled into my T-shirt. By the time I got to the living room, the front door was open and he had crouched down beside his little beagle. Blood covered her front, but she was still whimpering. Julian reached for her, and she snapped at him.

"Get me a towel!" Julian growled.

I ran to the back closet and tossed out linens, trying to find the oldest ones then giving up and bringing a stack. When I got back,

Julian held her mouth closed with one hand and had the other pressed just above her front leg.

"I'm gonna hold her, and you're going to drive," he said. "Keys are by the door."

I grabbed the keys, stealing glances over at a now blood-soaked Julian, who'd let the beagle's mouth open but was still pressing the towel into the wound and murmuring to her. I called the vet while I drove, and he said he'd meet us there even if he wasn't all that happy about it. We were over halfway to Dr. Winterbourne's when I realized something.

Julian wouldn't meet my gaze.

Julian

All I could think while watching Dr. Winterbourne work on Little Ann was that it could've been Romy. If Curtis would shoot an innocent dog just for being mine, what would he do to Romy? Hell, we were probably lucky Curtis couldn't see because he'd probably been aiming for heart or head. As it was, Little Ann would have to stay with Dr. Winterbourne and would probably lose a leg.

When we finally made it back to the house, I showered. Blood rolled off my arms and chest and disappeared down the drain. Romy sat waiting for me on the edge of the bed, and I had to force myself to look at her.

If I were smart, I would've pushed her away.

If I were stronger, I would've pushed her away.

Instead, I pulled her close, and we had sex born of worry and sadness. Afterward, I rolled over on my back and she laid her head on my chest.

"I don't want you to get hurt," I said.

"I'm a big girl," she said sleepily.

"Seriously, Romy," I said as I stroked her head. "This is the sort of shit I've been afraid of. Even if you're right about me, I can't always be around to protect you from him."

She lifted herself on one elbow. "Julian, there's a huge difference between shooting a dog and shooting a person. Not even Curtis would stoop to murder."

Unless he thought he could get away with it.

I didn't say that out loud, though. Maybe because I didn't want to believe it. I pointed to a manila envelope on my dresser. "We can still get divorced. Ben drew up the papers and everything."

She smacked me repeatedly. "Julian McElroy, don't you even joke about it!"

"Hey, now! You're the one who asked me."

"Well, I can take care of those papers," she said as she tried to wriggle out of bed. Instead I clamped her to me and kissed her soundly.

"I don't want to get rid of you," I said. "I never want to be rid of you."

"That's good because I'm planning to, as Elvis would say, stick like glue," she said with a grin. She knew I'd been known to sing a Presley song or two on karaoke night when three sheets to the wind.

I frowned. "But you know he's dangerous, right?"

"Elvis? Is he still alive?"

I tickled her for being a smart-ass, but we both sobered when I stopped. "You know what I mean. Curtis. He's dangerous."

She shivered, no doubt thinking about poor Little Ann. "He has a few screws loose."

"Promise me you won't go traipsing around the farm by yourself." *Where did that come from?*

"What?"

"Promise me you won't be out alone," I said. I had that bad feeling in my gut like Curtis wouldn't be content with shooting the sweet dog I'd been trying so hard to ignore. People like him must've been the reason God first said an eye for an eye. He'd lost two dogs. I'd lost one. That wasn't going to be enough for him.

"What is up with you men today? I'm a grown woman."

She tried to wiggle away, but I wouldn't let her. "Promise me."

She sighed deeply. "You and your promises. Fine. I promise I won't go *traipsing* around alone. I'll have a lady's maid with me *at all times* since my father has also made me promise to apprise him of my whereabouts *at all times* and to have my phone on *at all times*. There. Are all of the men in my life satisfied I'm not sneaking off to some kind of female supremacy meeting?"

"Totally," I said as I cupped her breast. Her ragged breath gratified me beyond belief. "I can't get enough of you."

"Feeling's mutual," she said as she grabbed a little lower.

And that was enough to forget Curtis for at least a little while.

Romy

This time Hank didn't say a word when I came through the back door with the day's first rays of sunlight. For a fleeting moment I wondered if he'd subject me to having Delilah sleep over or insist I drive him over to her house for the evening. I pushed that thought from my mind and vowed to spend the rest of my nights at home. We might all be adults now, but he was still my daddy and I was still his little girl.

"Making up for lost time?" Daddy said from behind a safe curtain of newspaper.

"Maybe I am. Had breakfast yet?"

"Just a banana and some orange juice."

I took my spot at the stove to scramble eggs and toast some bread under the broiler. When I put a plate in front of him he grunted his thanks. "'Bout time to take this damned cast off," he said.

I looked over at the calendar to see the date circled in red really was only a couple of days away.

"Then what are you going to do?" I took a bite of toast, reveling in the homemade strawberry preserves, then wondering if Delilah had been the one to make them.

"Not a lot. Doc said the leg would still be weak," he said.

"But you're not going to sell the cows or the farm?"

"Naw. Called that Marsh fellow last night and told him the place wasn't for sale after all."

My fork stopped halfway to my mouth. I'd figured Julian's father was mad because he saw me go into Julian's house. What if he was really mad about losing the opportunity to sell the McElroy place?

"What's got you so green around the gills?"

"Curtis McElroy shot Julian's dog not long after I showed up last night."

"He. Did. What?" That got Hank Satterfield to sit up straighter. "You mean to tell me that crazy sonuvabitch was shooting at the porch of the house where my daughter was staying? I forbid you . . . well, I can't forbid you from doing anything, but I don't like it. I don't like it one bit. He's dangerous."

"That's what Julian said."

Daddy snorted. "For once that boy and I agree on something. Don't get tangled up with Curtis McElroy if he's about to go on one of his tears."

So we all had to wait for the other shoe to drop? "Well, dammit! If he's so dangerous, why hasn't someone done something to stop him?"

Daddy cleared his throat. "That wife of his refuses to press charges. Julian pressed charges once, and he like to have beat them both to death when he got out on bail."

"Ridiculous," I muttered under my breath before saying out loud, "He's just a man. Someone needs to stand up to him."

Daddy put his fork down. "Well, it ain't your job. Let me assure you of that."

Out the door I went to finish my chores. When I exhaled deeply at finding both Beatrice and Star safely ensconced in the pen, I knew Curtis was getting to us all.

Julian

I must've changed the oil in about forty different cars, but I couldn't shake the mental image of poor Little Ann. Dr. Winterbourne had called to say he wasn't able to save the leg, but she'd made it through surgery. I was supposed to pick her up in a couple of days depending on how well she was healing.

I think my eyeballs sweated a bit at the thought of a tripod beagle, but the vet had assured me she'd adapt quickly.

Now you should get Romy out of harm's way, too.

I didn't like that particular line of thought. Now that Romy and I were close to patching things up, I couldn't imagine a world without her. At the thought of her three-a.m. good-bye, I couldn't help but grin like a jackass eating saw briers.

"McElroy! Somebody here to see you."

"Be there in a second, Leroy." I grunted as I tightened the oil filter in place then patted the antique Silverado on the side for good measure. A quick look at the clock told me I only had an hour to go.

Just beyond the mesh-and-glass window of the door I saw my dear old dad. And my uncle Charlie.

"You've got a lot of nerve coming here," I said as I entered the tiny waiting room while wiping grease off my hands with a rag.

Curtis hitched his thumbs behind his overalls. "Deal with Marsh fell through. Hope you're happy."

Actually, I was.

"So, I need five thousand for the dogs you took off. Now."

"No." I turned to go back to work.

Curtis put a beefy paw on my shoulder and wheeled me around. "You'll get me that money. You owe me."

"I don't owe you shit."

"Be a shame if something happened to your *wife*, now, wouldn't it."

Anger flashed behind my eyes. There had to be a hint of fear, too, but I wasn't going to let him see that. Instead, I slapped his hand away and got right into his business. "Don't lay a hand on me or anything else that's mine."

"Or you'll what?"

"I'll enjoy knowing that farm's waiting for me when I get out of prison, that's what."

His eyes widened. He needed to be scared. He'd sent his message. Now I'd sent mine.

"Charlie, maybe this isn't the best place to conduct business after all," he said.

"Believe I told you that from the get-go," Uncle Charlie griped.

I watched the two of them waddle off. Someone in the corner began to slow clap. That's when I turned to see Goat Cheese. He leaned back and began moving his fingers one over the other as if wishing for a cigarette. " 'Bout done with my truck?"

"Yes, sir," I said. "Sorry 'bout that."

"Gave me a chance to catch up on my *People* magazine," he said with a shrug and some new juicy gossip to spread. The last thing I needed was for Romy to hear about Curtis threatening me.

"Don't suppose I could ask you to forget that conversation that just took place?"

"What conversation?" he said. "Unless, of course, you ever

need me to remember such a conversation in a court of law," he added, his beady eyes crinkled underneath his ball cap.

Goat Cheese was going to keep a secret? I'd believe that just as soon as I saw it.

Or didn't hear it.

Letting Len know that Curtis had threatened Romy wouldn't be the worst idea. It'd be a fine line, since hauling him in for a restraining order would probably spark retaliation. Still, it'd be good to have something on the record.

And to brush up on my target practice. Maybe make sure Romy had brushed up on hers.

I smiled at Ellery's unlikeliest gossip. If Goat Cheese was willing to keep something to himself, then you knew you were in the right. "You're all right, Go—Mr. Ledbetter."

"Don't you forget it! Now finish up with my truck. I've got things to do today."

Dismissed, I went back to retrieve the Chevy. As I lowered the truck, I frowned at the thought of Curtis and Charlie barging in on me. Hank must have officially backed out of selling his place, which meant Curtis was left high and dry.

And desperate.

Romy

"Still not wearing the rock, huh?"

Genie's question brought me back down to earth and the Calais Café where we'd spent the previous half hour going through the last of my part of the reunion plans: reservations, attendees, and the money they had paid.

"I gave it back," I said, not able to contain the blush creeping up on my cheekbones.

Genie's mouth hung open, then stretched into a grin. "I know that look! You and Julian are back together!"

"Shh! Not so loud. I don't want to jinx it."

"Oh, please. That boy's mad about you," Genie said. "I've never seen anything like it. Ben was telling me the other day that he tried for years to get Julian to do something other than watch movies, drink beer, and mope."

Again, the sadness of almost ten wasted years sucked a little life out of me. The stupid things we'd both done out of misunderstanding or fear. Even now we had yet to talk about the future.

"Hey! You and Julian have actually been married the longest!" Genie's squeal jarred me back to reality. "I'm going to have to change that award and everything! Boy, isn't Lacey Bolton going to be beside herself. But that's what she gets for waiting until June to get married."

"She's still married to Chad Anderson?"

"Mmm-hmm," Genie said as she twirled her straw in her Diet Coke. "I can't believe it, either, but to each their own."

"And how are things with Ben?"

Her face lit up like an overstrung Christmas tree. "He is so incredible. We went out once in high school, you know."

"Really?" No, I had not known that. It was hard to picture, too.

"Of course, then we weren't who we are now. He was still trying to fit in with his cousins, and I was still a mousy girl in a trailer. We wouldn't have been able to make it work back then. At least not until we figured out who we really were."

Her logic held some merit, but, really, what had changed between Julian and me? Even as I asked myself the question, I knew a lot of the answers. He'd been overconfident, often to the point of cocky. I'd been smug and overly sure of my intelligence to the point of disdain for my humble roots. My desire to be with him had warred with my desire to be a rich lawyer and show the world how smart I was. Now I knew money couldn't buy me happiness and that I wasn't half as smart as I'd once thought I was. Did we have to go through what we had in order to live happily with each other without wondering about what the future might've held? After all, the downfall of Romeo and Juliet had been the impatience and impulsiveness of youth.

"You're daydreaming again," Genie said.

"Oh, sorry. What did you say?"

"I said being a farm girl agrees with you. At first I thought I liked you better with the fancy hair and clothes, but I don't think so. I think you look better now."

I didn't want to think about my hair. Just as Delilah had suggested, I'd given up on the flat iron weeks ago. My nails were neatly clipped but not entirely back to normal. I had to admit the cutoff denim shorts and the Vanderbilt T-shirt were far more comfortable than the linen capris and button-down blouses Richard preferred.

"You need more coffee?" Genie grabbed her purse. "Despite your sparkling conversation, I'm off to work!"

I slapped a hand on the bill as she slid out of the booth. "Nope, this one's on me. I'm pretty sure I'll have a job teaching English at the junior high just as soon as they finish the paperwork, and I owe you one for being so distracted."

Genie started to say something but thought better of it when she saw someone at the door.

Shelley Jean.

Genie slid back into the booth and hid behind the menu.

"What are you doing?" I hissed.

"Hoping she'll sit down before she sees me so I can make my getaway," Genie said between gritted teeth while studying the menu intently.

Shelley Jean took a seat across the restaurant, but Ben Little chose that unfortunate moment to walk in. He surveyed the room and gave Genie a dazzling grin the minute he saw her. All conversation at the farmers' lunch counter stopped as he walked confidently to the booth and slid in beside her. "I was hoping I'd catch you before you left."

She leaned into the kiss he planted on her cheek, her expression half-thrilled at seeing him and half-resigned that Shelley Jean would see her, too. Sure enough, my cousin and nemesis stomped across the diner.

"There you are, Genie *Dix*." Shelley Jean put her hands on her hips as she emphasized Genie's maiden name. I resisted the urge to point out that being unmarried was better than having had three unsuccessful marriages. Then again, Shelley Jean had always been a proponent of "It's better to have loved and lost" and "Quantity over quality."

"Hi, Shelley Jean. I was just on my way out." Genie wasn't that convincing. Especially not with Ben sitting on the edge and hemming her in.

"I didn't know you were going out with Ben." Shelley Jean batted her eyes. I rolled mine.

"Do you still need committee members?" she asked sweetly.

"I think we have it covered." Genie's reply was laced with syrup even though she'd put me through my paces, and I knew she'd done twice as much work as I had.

Shelley Jean put a hand with red claws on Ben's shoulder. He flinched enough to answer my age-old question of whether or not he'd succumbed to Shelley Jean's advances back in her cheerleading days. That answer would be yes, but he wasn't proud of it.

"This man bothering you?" asked our uncle Liston, even though it was clear to anyone with at least one eyeball that Shelley Jean was the one who'd put her hands on Ben. Still, Uncle Liston was from a generation that remembered when there were two water fountains in the courthouse. He chose to forget the "Colored" fountain had always been broken.

Shelley Jean didn't answer fast enough, and the other farmers gathered around Uncle Liston. Ben's eyes met mine, and I knew he was thinking about the afternoon Julian and I came up on all the football players beating him. We never told anyone, and the football players didn't, either. Mainly because they didn't want to admit they'd almost had their asses handed to them by Julian and Ben fighting alone.

"Shelley Jean is fine, and I think she said she was leaving," I said with a clear voice.

Uncle Liston, my aunt Sandra's husband, wasn't a fan of his brother-in-law nor me by extension. The feeling was mutual.

"Ain't he friends with the McElroys?" he asked with narrowed eyes.

I'd planned to stare him down, but Shelley Jean decided to jump into the fray. "Oh, Uncle Liston, this is Ben Little. He is Julian McElroy's *best* friend. They played football together, remember? Ben made All-State that year Alan almost did."

She just had to go there, didn't she? Alan was another of our cousins who'd been the second-string running back when we were in high school. Half the Satterfields were convinced Alan would've made All-State—or at least got a scholarship for college ball—if he hadn't been forced to sit out while Ben Little played.

"That so?"

"You know, I think we should all be going," I said with a tight smile, since Ben was obviously clamping his lips tight to keep from saying what he really felt.

"And I heard you have a McElroy as your second string," Uncle Liston said. The rest of the overall-clad men behind him laughed.

"He's first string, actually," I said as I pushed my way past them to get to the cash register. I pretended not to see as Uncle Liston stepped into Ben's way to bump him intentionally. Then I was ashamed for not speaking up for the both of us.

"Those bastards are going to hold that stupid grudge forever," Ben muttered under his breath.

"The worst part is that Alan sucked anyway," I said.

Ben's eyes met mine. That wasn't the worst part, and we both knew it.

Genie let out the breath she'd been holding. "Okay. No more meetings at the Calais Café. The reunion committee might have ninety-nine problems, but a bitch ain't gonna be one."

Both Ben and I grinned at that.

"I'm sorry, Ben," I said. "They may be family, but they're a bunch of assholes. I'd disown them if I could."

"It's all right." He clapped my shoulder as he walked past, seemingly resigned. Genie waved then went to take his arm.

As she looked up at him with clear devotion, I wondered if they would be able to make it work. Would loving each other be enough to make up for the stupid things that sometimes happened in the world? Julian and I had almost been torn apart by such stupidity.

And we weren't out of the woods yet.

Julian

I wanted to be at home with a cold one. Instead I spent the evening in the Satterfield barn putting the finishing touches on the stalls I'd made for both Beatrice and Star. The two of them were still getting along quite well—except for the short-lived experiment in which Star attempted to nurse from Beatrice. Moon blind and decrepit or not, the mare had made short work of letting the calf know that well had run dry.

"Now, take a look at this, Beatrice." I led the horse into her new stall and coaxed her nose to the bin where I'd put some hay and a few oats. She swished her tail as she ate.

The calf wobbled around the corner and I showed her the stall next to Beatrice's. I'd put her trough down a little lower and poured in some sweet feed for her. She sniffed at the trough and tentatively licked it but gave a strangled moo that suggested she'd rather have a bottle, thank you very much.

At a shrill whistle, she turned and bolted for the gate. Romy stood on the middle slat of the gate and leaned over to hold out a bottle. One look at her took my breath away. Her wild hair hung just above her shoulders, and she giggled as she struggled to hold the huge bottle in place against Star's anxious head butts.

Now the calf swished her tail ferociously. She polished off one bottle, and Romy reached down to pick up a second one while the calf danced and bucked. "Aren't we impatient?"

Yes, yes we are. There was no way on God's green earth I was ever going to get that woman out of my system. That thought sobered me up. How stupid had I been? I'd only made her promise to leave if I hit her. I hadn't thought long enough about Curtis.

Send her back now. While you still can.

As if she'd listen to me! Now that she knew the truth, she'd never let up. I absently patted Beatrice on the rump while Star killed the second giant bottle.

"Hey, Julian, when are you going to let me ride?" Romy called.

"When do you want to go?" I asked, waggling my eyebrows.

"I'm not talking about *that*. I'm talking about saddling up poor Beatrice here. I bet she misses her Benedick."

Considering Benedick had been a downright asshole the last time I'd left the two of them alone, I doubted it. But it was gratifying to see her mind was just as much in the gutter as mine.

"I've got the day off tomorrow. Maybe after I cut some more hay?"

She rolled her eyes. "I swear all you West Tennessee men ever talk about is cutting hay."

I walked up to the gate she hung over. Star playfully butted my leg but then trotted off to run circles in the pen.

I had a flash of her with Richard, and I couldn't help but say, "Would you prefer I talk about golf or law or stock tips?"

She leaned in closer. "Absolutely not."

"Then you have to learn to get turned on by my hay talk. And baling and hauling. Putting wormer on the cows and tilling the garden."

"Mmm, talk dirty to me."

She might have been kidding, but the purr to her voice made me forget all about hay, cows, or the garden. I leaned in to kiss her, and she met me halfway—but the gate still hung between us.

We stopped for oxygen, our foreheads still touching. "Does this mean it's going to turn *you* on when I talk about canning tomatoes and freezing peaches?" she asked.

At the word *peaches*, my hands traveled to her breasts. They couldn't help themselves.

She grinned. "What if I send you to the store for lids and mason jars?"

"Honey, if you use that tone of voice, you could get me excited about mucking stables. With a toothbrush." I kissed her again, the gate rocking between us. The two slats she stood on made her just a little taller than me, and having her in control of the kiss was heady, better than two chugged beers on a hot day after skipping lunch then mowing the lawn.

We paused, our foreheads touching again. "I was thinking," she said, "what if we did this right this time? You know, got married in the church and built us a little house over there on that flat piece of land."

Anything you want. No! Not anything you want! "Romy, I don't know about right now. Curtis—"

"Screw Curtis." She jumped backward off the gate. "I'm talking about us. Or are you still too chickenshit for there to be an us?"

I had to open the gate to follow her and almost forgot to put the chain back in place I was in such a hurry. "I'm trying to tell you that he's up to something. If he'd shoot a dog on my front porch, what do you think he'd do to you?"

She whirled around and pounded at my chest. "I. Am. So. Sick. And. Tired. Of letting. That. Asshole. Rule. Our. Lives."

I grabbed her wrists. "Name the date and the time. I will be at County Line church in a suit and with a smile."

She crossed her arms and studied me. "What about The Fountain instead? I took the liberty of signing you up for the class reunion since you hadn't bothered to do it yourself."

"You know I don't want to get into that mess. I didn't like most of those people the first time around."

"But you owe me a dance," she said softly.

"We danced in the rain the other day. I'll dance right now."

"A *slow* dance." She stared through me, and I knew I was about to lose the argument.

"Fine."

"Really?" The smile on her face almost made it worth it.

"Yes." *Against my better judgment.*

She wrapped her arms around my neck, her body flat against mine. When she kissed me, one of her green work boots lifted just like in one of those old black-and-white movies.

"You'd better not stand me up this time," she whispered. "Or break anything."

Romy

I'd convinced Julian to come with me to the reunion. Thank God!

The next day I floated through the rest of my chores. Who would've thought I'd owe my happiness to Daddy's broken leg?

At the thought of Richard, I felt that familiar twinge of guilt. *Rosemary, you can't make everyone happy.* He would find someone, someone better suited to his political aspirations than me.

Then I thought of Julian and how I wished there'd never been a Richard, but I couldn't beat myself up over it. It was done. Over. Finished. No more.

I needed to be thinking of my own career aspirations since school started in a few weeks. But for now? Checking on Beatrice and little Star. Beatrice knocked about restlessly in her stall. I tried to rub her nose but she shook me off with a guttural horse noise that seemed to say, "You're not Julian. I still don't know who the hell you are."

"A fine birthday present you are! I finally get a horse and you won't have anything to do with me." She shook her head then kicked backward. I closed my eyes in anticipation of the crash of hooves splintering wood, but it never came. I peered around the horse and saw daylight. Lots of daylight, because she'd taken a chunk of wood out of the back of her stall and an even larger chunk of the neighboring one.

I looked over into Star's stall, but she was nowhere to be found. I turned on the horse. "You didn't."

She stamped about nervously, and now I understood. This wasn't about me; she'd lost her friend.

Don't panic. The last time she got out she went and joined Julian's cows. Maybe this time she went to visit ours. If not, she's gone back to Julian's side. Don't panic.

Hard not to panic when I already knew Curtis had no qualms about shooting a dog. The calf wouldn't mean anything more to him.

But by the time I walked around the little pen, I had panicked. Julian was off cutting hay only God knew where. Daddy was still wearing a cast. I could drive around our land, but if she'd gone back to the McElroy land, then I'd have to go past Mr. and Mrs. McElroy to search for her.

And I'd told Julian I wouldn't do that.

Squaring my shoulders, I walked back up to the house. I tromped across the back porch and into the kitchen only to be greeted by a rustle of newspaper and, "Hey! Take those nasty boots off before you walk in here."

"Sorry, Daddy." I kicked them back to the porch and raced upstairs for my cell.

"What's got your panties in a twist?"

I met Daddy's eyes and saw a concern that didn't match the irritation in his voice. "Star's got out again. I'm hoping she didn't go over the creek because I don't know where Julian is."

I dialed his number and held the phone up to my ear.

"Calf's been nothing but trouble," Daddy muttered as he picked up another section of paper. "Deserves to be eaten by the damned coyotes."

Coyotes? "I was more worried about Curtis."

He unfolded the paper and hid behind it, but he was worried, too. Mercutio wound his way around a table leg and sprang into

Daddy's lap, causing a rustling ruckus just as I was forced to leave Julian a message.

"Why do you people never carry a phone!" I shouted to my father as I ended the call and slid mine back into my pocket. "You would think you'd want one while on a tractor back in the middle of God only knows where."

"Ain't no reception. And you can't scare off a copperhead with a phone, so what's the point?"

"Whatever. If Julian calls here instead of my phone, tell him I'm going to drive over our land first and then go over to his side—"

"The hell you are! Don't go anywhere near that man."

"Daddy." My hands naturally gravitated to my hips. "He's not going to shoot me in broad daylight."

"Ha! He's a bona fide McElroy idiot, isn't he?" my father said with the righteous prejudice of several decades. "If you're going in the truck, let me come with you."

Tempting, but as I looked at the full leg cast, I knew I couldn't. "Daddy, if I pull the seat forward enough to reach the pedals, there's going to be no room for your cast. What are you going to do, ride in the back like an old hound dog?"

He made a face. "I've probably got the fleas. Possibly a tapeworm."

I shook my head and went over to give him a kiss on the cheek. "You stay here. I'll go get Star."

He slapped down the paper and rolled after me. "And just how are you going to get her in the truck?"

I hadn't thought about that. The last time Julian and I had put her in the cab, she'd been considerably lighter. The answer was to the side of the sink in the form of the huge bottles I'd cleaned earlier. "I'm mixing a bottle. If she went through their fence, she can just go back through it," I said as I bustled around the sink with some formula.

"At least take a gun with you," Daddy grunted.

"C'mon, you know I didn't finish the gun-safety class, so I'd probably shoot myself in the foot. I'll stay in the truck."

He pointed at me. "I don't like it. You'd better answer your phone the first time I call, or I'm calling the police. Just so you know."

"Fair enough. Julian will call."

He muttered something under his breath about how I was grown up and he couldn't do anything about the stupid shit I did.

"Love you, too, Daddy," I said as I yanked the door closed behind me.

From Rosemary Satterfield's
History of the Satterfield-McElroy Feud

For some reason that I can't quite figure out, Curtis McElroy was smitten with me. It was almost as though he knew Hank and I were destined to fall in love, and he was desperate to keep us apart.

I met Curtis at one of the high school football games. I was a senior, and he was there to see a cousin play ball. He looked younger than his age back then, and he was so charming I agreed to go to the fair with him.

That night he was the perfect gentleman, but there was still something about him that bothered me, even though I couldn't put my finger on it, so I declined his invitation for a second date. A couple of years later, I met your daddy at the diner. It was love at first sight. Two dates and we knew we wanted to get married.

Suddenly, Curtis McElroy popped out of the woodwork. When he asked me out again, I told him I was dating Hank now. I can still remember how red his face got at the mention of Hank's name. One night I'd worked late at the library. When I went to get into my car, Curtis was there. He'd been drinking. He shoved me against the brick wall of the library and demanded to know why I'd go out with Hank Satterfield but not him.

Thank the good Lord a police car cruised by about

that time. The officer asked if I wanted to press charges, but what could I say? This man pinned me against the side of a building? I was still too stunned to know it would've been worth the hassle, and the policeman took Curtis to jail for public drunkenness, so I thought it was all over.

The next week I went home with Hank to meet his parents. Since my family was fairly new to Ellery, I hadn't realized one crucial fact: The McElroys lived next door.

Julian

About the fourth time my ass vibrated I realized it was my phone instead of the movement of the tractor seat. I killed the engine and looked up at the gray clouds above me. It was a little field, so I still had time to get everything done before the rain moved in. Then I looked down at my missed calls.

Shit.

Why hadn't I considered the possibility that my phone might be ringing? Had I really been alone so long that I thought no one wanted to call me? Hell, Romy was lucky I had my phone at all because I often left it on the kitchen table, afraid it would fall out of my pocket and get lost in a field.

I listened to Romy's rambling message about the calf getting out again and how she was headed up to our place to go through our pasture if she didn't find Star in hers.

My blood ran cold. Had she not heard a word I'd said about never going out alone? She might be worried Curtis would do something to Star, but I was more worried about what he might do to her.

She'd only left one message, but it had been forty-five minutes ago. She'd had plenty of time to look around the Satterfield place then go up to the trailer. I started the tractor, gunning it as I traveled homeward as quickly as I could.

You just had to tick him off at the dealership yesterday, didn't you? You couldn't just swallow your pride one more time and at least tell him you'd give him some of the money. Again. Damn you, Julian, damn you.

I rolled into the barn, jumping off the tractor before the engine had completely cut off. I ran for the house, ignoring my stiff leg, the one that didn't run as well as it used to. By the time I reached the screen door, I was out of breath.

"Good Lord, Julian, where's the fire?" Mama asked.

"Romy. Did she come through here?"

"I don't know. Your daddy was at the door talking to someone. Then he left and took his gun with him."

"Talking to *someone*."

"Fine. He was talking to that Satterfield girl. Something about a lost calf."

"And you let him take his gun and go after her?"

"I don't *let* him do anything," she said, but her eyes wouldn't meet mine.

"How long?"

Mama shrugged her good shoulder. "'Bout ten minutes? Maybe?"

"If anything happens to her, I'm blaming you."

"Nothing will—"

"You know damn well he aims to hurt her. Just like he hurts you." I turned to go, but she grabbed my arm.

"He's just doing what he thinks he needs to do."

She believed it, too.

"Well, he's wrong. She doesn't deserve it, and neither do you."

"But you don't know what I did."

"Mama, it doesn't matter what you did." I shook free of her grasp and went after Romy.

When I glanced over my shoulder, she was wringing her hands.

Romy

I'd gone over all of our land, knowing as I did that I wouldn't find Star there. Crazy little thing seemed to sense she belonged just as much to the cows next door as she did to us, maybe more, since her mama had rejected her.

Getting into the McElroy pasture hadn't been as bad as I'd thought. Julian's daddy seemed drunk to the point of incapacitated and waved me on even as Mrs. McElroy shot daggers through me. I hadn't been able to quite reclasp the strand of electric fence behind me, but I figured the gate would hold the cows in until I got back.

After the fourth call I'd given up on Julian. He must've left the phone at the house. He and I were going to have to have a little chat when he got done with the hay. I'd already told him that all his talk of tilling gardens and cutting hay was hot, but being country didn't mean we had to forgo modern conveniences. Like cell phones.

I cruised three-quarters of the McElroy pasture, seeing neither Star nor the rest of the cows. I'd have to walk the last part of the pasture by foot since trees lined the fence and extended into a thicket I couldn't drive through. I parked, grabbed the bottle, and picked my way through the brush to the fence and our creek on just the other side. I hadn't walked a quarter of a mile before

I came upon the Hereford herd, and there was Star playing with some of her half siblings, little calves that could've been her twin except for their being mostly red and her being mostly black.

"There you are! You scared me half to death!"

At the sound of my voice, Star stopped her playing and galloped in my direction. At the sight of almost a hundred pounds of speeding calf, I threw up my hands. "Whoa!"

She skidded to a stop in front of me, though, and latched on to the bottle. I pulled it away, and she followed me toward the fence. She'd gotten older and tugged harder, not really wanting to work for her bottle.

Then I tripped on a tree root and fell backward, holding on to the bottle by some miracle. By the time I got to my feet, crazy little thing had sucked all the milk down.

Now what, genius?

I took my phone from my back pocket, but held it out to the side, hesitating. Should I even bother calling Julian again?

"He ain't gonna answer that phone."

At the sound of Curtis McElroy's voice, I froze from the inside out. Polite. I would be very, very polite. I would forget he beat Julian and ruined our lives.

For now.

Forcing myself to smile, I turned to face him. "Well, it's lucky you're here then, isn't it? I just realized there's no way I'm going to be able to lift this calf up in the truck, not after all she's grown these past few weeks. Maybe you could give me a hand?"

He stared through me. "Don't reckon I will. Calf looks more mine than yours."

I stiffened. Of course, he'd see the calf was half-Hereford and want to keep it. That's how the whole mess had started in the first place: a misplaced calf and a greedy McElroy. He held his rifle bent in the crook of his arm. I tried not to look at it. "Seems your bull decided to visit our pasture. A regular Don Juan, that one."

My reference and my smile were lost on him.

"Well, the little bitch is in my pasture now, and I reckon that's where she's going to stay."

Was he talking about the calf or me? I could leave the calf. Julian would fetch her for me. Why, oh, why hadn't I just let him look for her in the first place? *Because you were afraid she was off somewhere on her own and that she'd run into some coyotes. Or something worse.*

Curtis took the rifle from the crook of his arm and snapped it together.

Like Curtis with a gun.

"Maybe you have a point," I said, my smile tight from forcing it to stay in place. "She seems content here, so I'll leave her with you."

For now.

I forced myself to slowly put one foot in front of the other, in spite of the fact that I had the irrational feeling that something or someone was chasing me, that same fight or flight that causes a child to dash for the safety of bed after turning off the light. I stepped as far to the side of Curtis as I dared without tipping him off. "Thanks for coming to help out, Mr. McElroy," I said as I was level with him.

He nodded so I took a step in the direction of the truck.

He chose that moment to slam the butt of the rifle into the back of my head and send me sprawling.

I think I screamed.

Julian

I drove the old pickup so fast, she bucked like a bronco over the rough pasture. It didn't take long for me to see two trucks at the edge of the woods. One was Romy's old Ford. The other was a beat-up S-10 that Curtis shouldn't have been driving.

I pulled up to the two trucks and ran out into the woods. Now what? Surely they weren't far, but were they to the right or the left? Had he already found her?

She screamed, and my feet were already heading in her direction before my stomach bottomed out around my toes.

Romy

The back of my head was on fire. I gasped for breath, finally realizing I couldn't breathe because I had a knee on my chest.

"Nice of you to wake up." He pushed all of his weight on his knee into my chest as he stood. I gasped for air that just wouldn't come.

"Yeah, I'm getting old. Can't get up and down like I used to," he said nonchalantly.

I struggled to get to my feet, but his boot came down on my wrist. Something snapped, causing the world to go black for a second.

"I just want to know what it's going to take to make you go away."

He picked up the rifle and placed the muzzle at the spot just between my eyes. "I'm wondering if I'm going to have to kill you to get you to leave my boy alone."

He's going to kill me no matter what I say.

"Answer me, you Satterfield bitch!" He kicked me in the ribs, and I rolled over and coughed, cradling my broken wrist. Somehow I pushed myself to standing.

"Since you won't stay gone, am I going to have to kill you?"

"I reckon you are." The West Tennessee accent came out loud and proud behind the wheezing. Somehow I'd made the choice to die right here rather than pretend I would run away to something I was not.

Knowing he meant to kill me no matter what might've fueled my ill-advised bravado, too.

He put the rifle down, glaring at me with his crazy eyes. I didn't see the fist coming, but I tasted the blood and felt a back molar come loose. I landed on all fours then collapsed when I accidentally put weight on my bad wrist. Hitting my stomach knocked the wind from me.

"If that's the way you want it, but it seems a waste to kill such a pretty thing. Even if she is a Satterfield."

He unbuckled his belt, and terror sliced through me. I stumbled to my feet, but I only took one step before the belt whistled through the air and sliced open my back, sending me back to my knees.

"Your mama wouldn't have anything to do with me," he sneered as he brought down the belt with all the force he had. "No, no. She had to rub salt in my wound and marry that Satterfield bastard. She knew how much I hated him!"

Another blow and the world spun around me, but I felt it when Curtis McElroy fell to the ground on his knees. The earth seemed to tremble for me then stilled, and I heard each tooth of his zipper open despite the ringing in my ears and the wheezing of my breath. The air smelled of honeysuckle but tasted of blood.

"Maybe I should take what your mama wouldn't give me. Maybe I should figure out why ol' Julian can't seem to let you alone."

He undid my shorts and yanked them down then smacked my stomach. "Might oughta lay off the fried okra, though."

I gasped for air and found it. The hell if he was going to win.

When he sat back to push down his pants, I kicked him in the crotch as hard as I could and started scooting backward.

And the hell if I'm giving up fried okra, either.

Julian

The last thing I remembered before the rage set in was look-ing at the scraggly, naked ass of Curtis as he groaned in the fetal position, then seeing Romy as she tried to button her shorts while scooting backward. What came next were flashes, scraps of violence as I Hulked out on the meanest sonuvabitch I'd ever met.

Somewhere in the back of my mind I heard Romy's voice call-ing me, but my mind put that information somewhere else be-cause she didn't belong here. Not in the middle of all this ugliness.

Someone touched my shoulder, and I instinctively punched as I whirled, caught the flash of Romy and tried desperately to stop my fist as I had so long ago in the field house fight.

But this time I wasn't quick enough. My fist hit her belly, and she gave a soft "oomph" as she fell backward. I watched her fall in slow motion, her face contorted in pain, surprise, and betrayal. Like a sports clip of a nasty hit, I knew I'd replay that moment over and over again.

"Finally . . . like . . . a . . . McElroy," Curtis half wheezed and half coughed from where he lay.

I looked down at my bloodied hands and at Curtis's bloodied face. I'd finally hit that pockmarked nose, all right.

"Got 'er good, son," he rasped with a sneer that showed tobacco-stained teeth with bloody outlines.

"Romy?" I called.

"I'm fine," Romy grunted.

Not believing her, I stood. That's when I finally felt hundreds of fiery ant bites on my shins from where they'd crawled up my legs. Cursing, I took a minute to roll Curtis over. The ants had had a field day with his naked ass so I dragged him even farther away from the anthill and left him on his stomach so he wouldn't choke on his own blood. We both knew it wasn't far enough to keep all of the ants away. I mainly didn't want to look at his junk.

He'd been about to rape Romy.

Even I hadn't thought he would stoop that low.

I kicked him for good measure.

Romy grunted again, and I turned to see her struggling to button her shorts while sitting, her left arm cradling her ribs. Tears streaked down her dusty, bloody cheeks. I couldn't look at her face, but I scooted over to help her. She tried to raise up with only her right hand to hold her, but her arm buckled and she fell. I noticed the bandage had come undone from the dog bite that had been healing so nicely. Now that wound was angry and covered in dirt, too. I gently raised her up, buttoning her shorts. She collapsed into my arms, crying and wheezing.

He'd broken her wrist.

He'd broken *her*.

And I'd let him.

"We gotta get you to the hospital, baby," I finally said. "I think you've got a broken wrist."

She coughed, making strangled choking noises before spitting out a mouthful of blood. "He knocked a tooth loose, Julian. Who does that?"

Cold fury sliced through me. My eyes darted to the rifle and then to his hairy ass full of angry red welts from the repeated stings of the fire ants.

I *could* put a bullet in his brain.

My eyes went back to the rifle, and I took a step in his direction before Romy grabbed my arm. "Don't. He's not worth you going to jail."

I guess I could leave him for the ants and vultures. I looked at her. "C'mon, can you walk?"

She leaned into me, panting, and we only got a couple of steps before I realized she'd somehow hurt her ankle, too. I swept her up into my arms, and she cried out—no doubt from the ribs.

"What about the gun?"

I turned toward the rifle, but I'd have to put her down in order to pick it up. I sure as hell couldn't leave it where Curtis would find it.

"I'll take care of the gun. You go on."

I almost gave myself whiplash. "Mama?"

She held the gun trained on Curtis, but her hands shook. "I said git."

I moved toward the truck, not sure what I'd just seen or why.

"What about *him?*" Romy asked.

"Don't know. Don't care," I said, but in the distance I could hear sirens.

Romy

True to his word, Daddy had called the police when I didn't answer my phone.

When Len arrived on the scene, he wanted to put me in the ambulance, but I talked him into letting Julian drive me to the doctor. They'd need the ambulance for Curtis, and I wasn't about to ride with him. Julian called Daddy to tell him what had happened. That conversation didn't go well.

Finally, we sat in the emergency room. Again. This time he held my good hand, but he wasn't saying anything. That bothered me. I wanted to say something to him, but my jaw hurt like hell from where Curtis had punched me. My back stung, my ribs burned, and my wrist ached. My head had a lump and did some pounding of its own. How did Debbie McElroy put up with this? And why?

I thought of how she'd looked as she trained the rifle on Julian's daddy. Looked like she might be done taking it, after all.

I squirmed in my seat, and Julian pulled me as close as the uncomfortable chairs with their metal arms would allow. He pressed his lips to the top of my head and whispered he was sorry for what had to be the hundredth time. I wanted to be mad at him for not doing something, for not stopping his father, but I knew he'd tried more than once.

You were the idiot who went out there for a cow. You could've waited. You should've waited.

The welts on my back made me think of Curtis pouring alcohol on Julian's back, and I wished him dead. There was no way Julian would be with me as long as Curtis was living—not unless I could convince him to move to Siberia, and that would be highly unlikely.

"Rosemary Satterfield?"

Julian went back with me, and I noticed the suspicious looks from the doctors. They thought *he* had been the one to do this to me. I could tell by how they kept asking the same question over and over, trying to stump me. Julian withdrew even further into himself.

Finally, they decided to spend more time fixing me up than questioning me: a brace for my wrist and an appointment with an orthopedist, wraps for my ribs, which were blessedly bruised rather than broken, salve for my back, the number of a cosmetic dentist, an ice pack for my head.

I could feel the guilt suffocating Julian as they added one treatment after the other. If I didn't get him out of the hospital soon, I'd never get another word out of him. Finally, they let us go with a novel's worth of instructions. I was already thinking about what I would say to Julian once we reached the safety of his truck when we walked back into the waiting room and Len stood.

"Julian McElroy, you are under arrest for the murder of Curtis McElroy. Anything you say—"

"The hell, Len?" My speech was so garbled, I couldn't even understand myself.

"Curtis McElroy was dead on arrival and appears to have been beaten to death. I'm thinking you didn't have enough strength to do it," Len said, pointing at the brace on my wrist.

"He was alive when we left. I swear. He was taunting Julian, even!"

"Well, he's dead now." Len held up his cuffs, and Julian turned around, his eyes refusing to meet mine.

"Keys to the truck are in my pocket, if you think you can drive with one hand," Julian mumbled.

"Julian, what are you doing?" I asked as I reached in his pocket for the keys.

"What I have to," he said. Finally, his eyes held mine. "I'd do it all over again. Only difference I'd make would be getting there sooner."

"What does Mrs. McElroy say?" I asked.

"That's the damnedest thing," Len said as he picked up his hat to scratch his head. "She won't say anything at all."

Len and some deputy I didn't know led Julian away. The deputy gave Julian a hard shove, but he didn't stumble. He limped a little, but I only saw it because I knew to look for it.

"Julian, I'll be right there!"

Len turned to me. "No need, Romy. This is all going to take a while. Go patch yourself up."

Julian never looked back.

All I could think as I tried to drive over to the orthopedist was I'd gotten my wish, but it wasn't what I wanted at all.

Julian

It'd been ten years since I was last tossed into county lockup and that was an overnighter for a little drunk and disorderly. Nope. I'd kept my nose clean and avoided all of the major criminal acts until now.

That had to be some kind of McElroy record.

There I sat in a tiny iron-barred concrete hole that smelled like piss and sweat. Every time I closed my eyes, I saw myself punching Romy in the gut. Or her shocked look at the emergency room, her jaw swollen and already turning blue. I remembered the narrowed eyes and barbed questions of the emergency room nurse, who was certain that *this* time I really had done the deed.

Murder.

If I'd known I was going to jail for murder, I would've gone ahead and shot the bastard, but maybe kicked him in the ribs a few more times first.

"Hey, Julian, you've got a visitor."

"I didn't even make a phone call," I said.

The deputy snorted. "Well, someone called your lawyer for you."

Romy. She had called Ben.

Ben I would speak to. If he'd told me Romy was out there—

and I wouldn't put it past her—then I would've stayed put. Ben, on the other hand, had already seen me at my worst. I followed the deputy, some guy I didn't recognize with the last name March, down the hall to an interview room. Ben sat at the table. He was pretending to study some notes he'd written down, but his hands shook.

"Thirty minutes, you two," my new friend March said. He closed the door, but there was a two-way mirror on the other side so I was pretty sure we were still being watched.

"What the hell, Jay? Why didn't you call me?"

I'd never seen Ben so mad.

"I'm pretty much screwed, I think."

He slapped the table. "That's for me or another lawyer to decide. Please tell me you haven't admitted anything or signed anything."

"No."

"Thank God for small wonders," he muttered. "Have you given any kind of statement?"

"No."

He exhaled. "Dammit, Julian. This is a helluva mess. Romy's almost hysterical. I'm not feeling so good myself."

"I reckon I deserve it."

He grabbed the collar of my shirt and pulled me forward. "The hell you do! Listen here, you stupid fucker. No one deserves to go to prison and be someone's bitch for defending his *wife*, least of all you. So you are going to get your head out of your ass and quit playing the martyr. Got it?"

Well, hell. Ben the foul-mouthed badass usually didn't show up. Ben the educated lawyer almost always had things firmly under control. My eyes cut to the door, half expecting Len or Deputy March to come in, but apparently there was no rule against attorneys beating up their own clients. Ben's eyes followed mine to the door, and he released my shirt slowly then sat back and adjusted his tie.

"Preliminary autopsy reports should be in tomorrow. If they

show murder, then I have a friend from my Memphis days who can take your case. He's good, damned good."

"How's Romy?"

My question hung in the air. Ben stared holes through me. "You gonna ask me that question when you know she's at home resting while you're over here in deep shit?"

"Yep. That's all that matters."

He closed his eyes and pinched the bridge of his nose. "She's worried to death about you and would already be here if Hank hadn't stolen the keys to keep her home. Doc gave her a sedative to help her sleep, but I bet she'll be here tomorrow."

To see me here? Like this?

"Don't let her come."

"Ha! Haven't you learned yet that you can't make a woman do anything she doesn't want to do?"

"Speaking of women, where's Mama in all of this?"

Ben's expression screwed up as if he'd taken a bite of lemon. "She's making funeral arrangements with Anderson's. She didn't mention coming to see you."

Not surprising.

Ben sat up straighter, and his metal chair scraped across the floor. "You stop worrying about things you can't change and tell me exactly what happened so I can fill Byron in. Just in case."

I didn't want to tell him what Curtis had been about to do to Romy, and I didn't even remember too much of what happened after I started beating him—at least not until after I showed my true colors and hit her.

"Jay. What happened?" Ben held pen over legal pad.

I told Ben in a low voice, not yet wanting Len, March, or anyone else watching us to hear. I forced myself to tell him everything. When I finished, he exhaled deeply and looked at his notes with a frown. "We can work with this. What about your mama? Think she'd come in and make a statement?"

"She never had anything bad to say about Curtis while he was living, so I don't see why she would now."

"He's dead."

"I know that. I'm just saying we haven't been on the best of terms."

"She is your *mother*."

"Has a funny way of showing it."

"Whatever, cowboy. This is my territory," he said as he stood.

I had no doubt Ben and his friend would come up with a way to keep me out of prison or to give me the least amount of time they could. That didn't change the fact that I was still too dangerous to be with Romy—even now with Curtis gone. Jail might be the best place for me.

Romy

I would've already been by to see Julian except for two things: One, Daddy had to go to the doctor to get his cast off, and two, Ben had told me to wait until later in the day in the hopes the preliminary autopsy would show something to clear Julian. Even then Dr. Winterbourne called, and I had to talk him into keeping Julian's dog a little longer.

I still couldn't believe Curtis was dead. Julian had hit him— that much was true—but I couldn't see how the man went from taunting to dead that quickly. He was dead on arrival. That didn't make sense.

"Pay attention or you're going to miss your turn." Daddy grasped for the bar above the window, and I took the turn on two wheels.

"I'm driving home," he muttered.

"Look. I'm doing the best I can with one hand over here. Neither one's in great shape, you know."

"I know," he said softly, self-recrimination in his voice. He still blamed himself for the dog bite. Probably blamed himself for everything else, too. Both he and Julian seemed unwilling to accept the fact that I could make my own decisions and bear the brunt of their consequences. Sure, if I had it to do over again, I would've waited until Julian got home. I don't think any of us knew Curtis was quite *that* batshit crazy. All of the signs had been there, but we human beings seem predestined to make something out of nothing only to ignore the honest-to-God somethings right under our noses.

We parked outside the doctor's office, and I managed to wheel Daddy's chair out of the bed of the truck and get it opened and to the side door so he could scoot over. Both of us did a fair amount of grunting and cussing.

"We're a pair, aren't we?" I asked.

He grinned in spite of himself. "Yeah, I'd as soon skip all of these trips to the doctor for a while, though."

"I'm with you on that."

Getting the cast off wasn't anywhere near the ordeal I had thought it would be, although the smell inside was enough to make me wish I'd stayed in the waiting room.

"That leg is even whiter and skinnier than your other one," I mused before Daddy shooed me from the room to get his pants on.

Finally, he emerged, limping on his new leg but walking pretty well, all things considered. I thought about that hug I'd wanted earlier in the summer and I threw my good arm around him right there in the doctor's office hallway. He pulled me close then released me.

"I guess you're free to go now," he said. "You don't have to hang around and take care of this old fart anymore."

"Nah. Too late now. You're stuck with me," I said. "But you are going to have to teach me how to drive the tractor."

"I thought Julian did that," he said with a frown as we walked slowly out the door.

"He did. Kinda."

He arched a bushy eyebrow. I let him wonder. He'd defecate adobe if he knew I'd almost turned it over.

"You sure you don't want to run back to Nashville where all the important people are?"

Knowing I'd already taken a job here, he still couldn't believe

I was sticking around. He and Julian were more alike than either would care to admit.

"Know what, Daddy? I think all of my important people are right here."

He took my hand and squeezed, his own hand callused and warped with arthritis but warm and larger than life. "Guess I'd break my leg all over again to hear you say that."

"Please don't."

"I gotta get a new bull. Wonder if Julian would sell me his. I was thinking about some cross-breeding since I like the looks of that little calf of yours."

My heart caught in my throat at the mention of Julian. "I don't see why he wouldn't. Maybe we could even take the fence down and mix the herds together."

My father nodded noncommittally, not saying anything else until we finally reached the truck. "I'll take the keys."

I tossed the keys to him, reasserting the natural order of things, then I climbed up into the truck cab beside him.

"Aren't we out of them little coffee-cup doodads for your fancy machine?" he asked.

I grinned. Maybe things weren't quite what they'd always been.

"Stop by the store, and I'll run in and get some," I said.

"Get some of that candy bar creamer, too, if you don't mind."

"Anything for you, Daddy."

It was early afternoon by the time I got to the jail. I had been hoping the preliminary report Ben had talked about would've come in sooner rather than later, but Julian was still a prisoner of the state when I arrived.

I'd also thought we'd have to speak through glass, but Len had chuckled and told me not to believe everything I saw on television. I stood when Julian entered the room. Orange really wasn't his color, but he was still a sight for sore eyes to me.

"How are you doing?" I asked. I wanted to hug him, but I wasn't sure I could.

He cocked his head to one side, and I could tell he was going to be surly because he didn't want me there. It was almost as though the past few weeks had never happened. "All right."

"Did you get a lawyer?"

"Why? Gonna get your ex to defend me?"

His tone cut me to the core. Not that I was going to let him know that. "Stop being an ass."

"I am an ass. If it weren't for me, you wouldn't be hurt."

"If it weren't for you, I'd probably be dead!"

He finally looked me in the eye. "If it weren't for me, you never would've been in danger in the first place."

I bit back tears. "You don't know that."

"Pretty damn sure, actually."

"Seems to me I defended myself quite nicely."

"For the moment." Something about the tone of his voice made a shiver run down my spine. What would've happened if he hadn't shown up when he did?

He took a seat across from me, and I reached my hands across the table, but he wouldn't take them. He moved as if he would, but then he remembered they were cuffed.

"It doesn't matter now. He's gone."

"Romy, I don't know what's going to happen here, and—"

"You're going to get out of jail, that's what! I gave my statement to Len. You were defending me. They can't send you to jail for that."

"Manslaughter," he muttered.

"Maybe . . . maybe something else killed him." I was grasping at straws. We both knew it.

He snorted. "Let's face it. All of this has finally caught up with me. Now it's going to stop with me."

For a minute, hope fluttered in my stomach. Then I realized what he meant by that.

"Julian," I started in that voice of warning I often gave my students. "Don't do anything crazy."

"I'm not going to hang myself with my belt. But I did ask Ben to take you those divorce papers."

"No."

"No?"

"No."

He started to run a hand through his hair, but his hands were cuffed and he put them back in his lap. "You don't want a felon for a husband."

"Don't tell me what I want."

"Romy, I hurt you. I punched you."

I'd never seen Julian look at me with that much pain in his eyes. That's what this was about? He still felt guilty for punching me in the heat of the moment? "It was an accident!"

"And you promised me that if I ever hit you—"

Anger crackled behind my eyes. "You stop right there. I've had it. I can fight Curtis and dogs and my father, but I can't fight you. I don't know what else I have to do to explain to you how much I love you because, God help me, I do."

He leaned away from the table as though my words were a fierce wind blowing him back.

"One of two things is going to happen today: Either that report comes back and clears you or Ben posts bail. No matter what, you're going to be free to attend our class reunion on Friday, a place you promised you would go. If you show up, then we will stay married. If you don't show up . . ."

I blinked back tears because he couldn't see those. "If you don't show up, I am through. You gotta stop fighting me. There's nothing standing in the way of us being together now but you."

That pretty speech delivered, I turned on my heel and left.

Julian

"Don't leave town," Len Rogers said with narrowed eyes as he handed me my personal effects. The report Ben had been waiting for had come in, and it suggested I hadn't killed Curtis after all. No, it said the fire ants did him in. Ben used a lot of fancy words from the report, but the gist was so many bites in a certain sensitive region had caused a sort of allergic reaction that might have caused a heart attack or some kind of anaphy-shock thing. At any rate, Len was letting me go as long as I stuck around until the official report came in a few weeks later. Ben was outside calling off his lawyer friend.

"Told you the fire ants did it," I said as I worked my belt through the loops of my pants.

"Yeah, yeah," Len said. I got the feeling he was disappointed. He wanted to be in that *Clue* movie: *It was Julian in the pasture with his fists.*

"Come on, Jay. We've got other problems." Ben waved to me at the door, the phone still at his ear.

I followed him, not sure what was going on because he was talking about wills and estates, one of his actual law specialties.

Finally, about halfway home, he put down his phone. "You may need to find a new home for all your pets."

"What are you talking about?"

"Your uncle Charlie called, spitting mad. He's filing a petition for probate and said to tell you that you aren't getting a red cent."

"That so?"

"Seems your father left everything to him but the trailer. Your mama doesn't even get the land the trailer is sitting on."

"And Uncle Charlie called to tell you this?"

"At the time he couldn't call you, so I was the lucky one. He says he's going to make your life a living hell until you sell him what little of the property is yours."

"I've seen living hell. He ain't it." I leaned back into the seat.

"The good news is the whole thing will be tied up in probate for at least four months, probably longer. You'll have time to contest."

"Mm-hmm."

"You're not listening to me, are you?"

"I'm listening." But I didn't want to look at the swampy Harlowe Bottom or Wanamaker's store or to think about Romy's little do-or-die speech. I sure as hell didn't want to contest the will. Uncle Charlie could have the whole damn thing as far as I was concerned.

"What did you do now?"

I looked over at him. "What kind of friend are you anyway?"

"The kind who's going to steal a beer from your fridge in about five minutes, so you might as well tell me what you've done now."

"Romy—"

"Uh-huh," he said as he guided the car around the corner.

"She told me to show up at the reunion or we're over."

He snorted. "That's simple enough. Show your ass up."

"Ben—"

"Don't even tell me it's complicated because it's not. I know complicated. Your situation is no longer complicated." He pulled into the driveway and stopped just short of the porch. I caught myself looking for Curtis before remembering I wouldn't have to worry about him anymore.

"I hit her."

"Sure did. She tapped on your shoulder while you were in a righteous rage, and you accidentally punched her. Despite what you seem to think, only one person on this earth has ever put you in such a state, and his sorry ass is dead." Ben ended his sentence on the slamming of his car door.

I opened the front door, and he headed straight for the fridge, as good as his promise. "Know what your problem is, Jay?"

"Which one?"

"This big chip you have on your shoulder. So you had a hard time reading. So you grew up poor. So your father was an asshole. Not a one of those things is a good enough reason to deny yourself happiness. Get out there and make it happen, man. You've got a good woman who's been cheering you on from the beginning, and you're bitter because you couldn't do it by yourself? Well, that's stupid."

So many things I wanted to say to him, but my mouth was dry. I went for a beer instead.

"Aw, now he's mad at me," Ben said before he took a long pull from his bottle. "You just don't know who you are if you're not mad about something."

At the moment I knew who I was mad at. "Keep it up."

"There you are daring me," he said, his voice now soft instead of taunting. That meant he was really mad. He put his bottle down even though it was over half full. "I hope I see you on Friday night."

Then he walked out on me, too.

Since my beer didn't taste right all of a sudden, I went across the yard to check on Mama. At first I didn't see her, but she had to be in the living room since the TV was on. I did a double take at the shriveled woman in the monster recliner. I'd always thought getting rid of Curtis might bring her out of her shell. Instead, she seemed content to get his recliner out of the deal.

I sat in her seat, a stiff flowery chair across from the recliner. If I was expecting her to say she was happy to see me, I was apparently going to be waiting a long time. "What's going on with the will, Mama?"

She kept looking at the TV while she spoke. She had it on *I Love Lucy* reruns and Lucy and Ethel were gobbling up chocolates from an assembly line. "Seems your father left us both out in the cold."

"Why would he do that?"

She took a deep, ragged breath. "Because you're not his son."

"What?"

Her bleary eyes met mine. "You're my child, but you're not a McElroy. Not really."

"But Mamaw—"

"Your mamaw never knew, but your father found out when you were five."

When I was five? And I remembered my kindergarten teacher was the first person I told about Curtis. I'd always thought she was the first adult I'd trusted enough, but what if there'd never been anything to tell before then?

"Lester Ledbetter is your real father."

My father was a gossipy chain-smoker with aspirations of goat farming? "My father is Goat Cheese?"

My mind zeroed in on the last thing Curtis McElroy said to me: *Finally like a McElroy.*

Now I knew what he meant.

From the moment he found out his wife had hoodwinked him, he'd started his training. He'd treated me like those pit bulls, doing his damnedest to make me mean.

To make me a McElroy.

But why? If Curtis wasn't my real father then why in the blue hell had she married him?

"How?"

She shrugged. "Lester and I only went out that one time. By the time I figured out what had happened, he was practically engaged to Adelaide. So I walked up to the first man I saw and really poured on the charm."

My stomach churned. "And Curtis McElroy was the first man you saw?"

She smiled, and I saw a ghost of the pretty woman she had been before cigarettes and Curtis had each taken their toll. "Pregnant women who walk into bars soon find beggars can't be choosers—especially back then. Besides, your father could be quite charming when he wanted to be."

But not my father. "And when he started to beat you? You couldn't leave him then? Or at least send me to . . . Mr. Ledbetter?"

"But that was part of our deal, Julian."

"What deal? What are you talking about?"

"When Curtis found out that you weren't his, I begged him not to turn us out. I didn't have anywhere to go. I'd never even graduated from high school. Both of my parents were already dead. He beat the shit out of me. Then he told me I could stay as long as I didn't tell anyone."

"That's not a deal." I thought I was going to throw up.

"No, the deal was that he could hit me, but he could never do more than spank you. And only if you needed it."

My mind ran through all of my whippings. Up until my senior year, they had all been whippings. Even then he'd started with his belt. . . .

"But, Mama, why didn't you leave?"

She shrugged, but she could still only manage the movement on one side. "I tried once when you told your teacher. I thought maybe the good Lord had given me an opportunity to get out."

I swallowed hard. That was the worst beating Curtis ever gave her.

She looked over at the wall. "It didn't work out that way. And your father—Curtis—came back with apologies and flowers and chocolates. At the same time he reminded me I had no place to go and no job to support you. He said—"

Her voice broke, so I gave her a minute to move on.

"He said he would fight for you if I left him. He said no court would believe you weren't his. That scared me most of all, so I stayed."

She took in a shaking breath. "I almost shot him the other day."

I thought back to how I'd looked at the gun, how I probably would've picked it up and shot the bastard if I hadn't been carrying Romy. "Yeah. Me, too."

One thing kept bugging me. "Why'd you go out there, Mama?"

"Because you told me I didn't deserve it no matter what. I had been telling myself all these years that you hated me. I realized you didn't, but if something happened to her then you would."

I crossed the room and crouched down beside her recliner. Now I could hear the laugh track from *I Love Lucy*, a laugh track for the world's least funny conversation. I laid a hand on Mama's good arm. "Mama, I could never hate you."

She leaned over and kissed my forehead. "You could, but you don't. And I'm grateful for that."

Romy

Red dress? Check.

Fully stocked and awesomely decorated Fountain? Check.

Errant husband? Time would tell.

Genie and I stood on the threshold of The Fountain, dressed in our best and ready to start welcoming our classmates. By all rights, I should've been nervous, but I wasn't. I wanted Julian to show up, but I meant what I'd said. I couldn't fight him anymore. He would have to make the next move, and it would need to be the last one.

One thing I knew for sure: I wasn't moving back to Nashville. I belonged here in Ellery. No matter what happened with Julian, I wasn't going to let fear or guilt keep me from the farm where I'd grown up. I was actually excited at the prospect of teaching in the schools I'd once attended. Maybe I could inspire another little farm girl to go to Vanderbilt. Maybe she'd go be a lawyer.

"How do I look?" Genie had spent an inordinate amount of time primping. Between that and her hand wringing, I was beginning to wonder if there was trouble in paradise. Surely not.

"You look fantastic. That purple really suits you."

She grinned. "And you look like the Fourth of July with that red dress, blue cast, and white bandage."

"I wanted to be festive," I said with a shrug. "That and the red dress was the only one I could get on with the cast."

At that point, people started arriving, so we split up and acted as hostesses, directing people to the bar, the photographer, or the space Bill had cleared for a dance floor. I felt only a little twinge of jealousy when Ben arrived. He took a step back at the sight of Genie, then made her twirl for him before he drew her close for a kiss.

They headed for the dance floor, and I sneaked a peek at my phone. Julian had three hours left to show up. I took a ragged breath and forced a smile on my face before journeying into the crowd.

Julian

After spending most of the day cutting hay and getting Little Ann settled in on the back porch, I showered and sat in my favorite chair with a glass of water. I'd told myself I wasn't looking at the clock, but I'd sneaked a glance that told me it was two hours after the reunion started.

I flipped through the TV channels aimlessly. Reality shows. Spanish game show. Rose not scooting over to make room for Jack on the raft. The weather.

Once I'd studied the weather report enough to know I'd cut my hay too soon, I started flipping again, but I felt restless. A rerun of *Seinfeld*. The Cardinals game. The end of *When Harry Met Sally*.

Billy Crystal started running, and I put my water down on the end table. I was standing in front of the kitchen counter where my truck keys were before I knew what was happening. Mamaw's orange blossom ring sat beyond the keys, and I put that in my pocket, too.

Get out there and make it happen, man.

There's nothing standing in the way of us being together but you.

Out the door I went, not even bothering to turn off the TV. I slid into the truck and started backing down the driveway. I made it a few miles down the road when all the lights on the dash flashed and went black. The truck died. I managed to pull over to the side as it rolled, but I'd already seen the problem as the mileage flashed on the dashboard and then went out: seventy-four thousand nine hundred and ninety-nine miles.

The alternator. I'd never hear the end of that—assuming I got there in time for Romy to ever speak to me again.

I dug out my cell to call her. No bars in the dip where the truck had given out, and it would be dead by the time I got bars. I could expect to hear about that, too.

Dammit.

No taxi cabs in the country, so there was nothing left to do but start running.

Romy

My nerves had begun to fray in spite of my earlier resolve. We'd announced all of the awards, and Genie had been forced to give the one for Couple Married Longest to Lacey Bolton and her husband because I didn't have a husband there. It was beginning to look like I wouldn't be having a husband for much longer.

I'd mourned the possibility, then tried to hide from it. Now, the thought of losing Julian caused a bone-deep sadness, but I could still muster a smile. I would move on, if I had to; I, like the Gloria Gaynor song playing, would survive. I danced. I had a beer. I told myself not to stare when Genie and Ben shared a slow dance.

I checked my phone.

Thirty minutes left.

Julian

I ran up a hill on Bittersweet Creek Road, my sides aching and my feet hurting from my cowboy boots. As I reached the top, a truck came out of a hidden driveway, and I ran right into it.

Now a veteran of being hit by cars, I reached for my hat before it flew off.

"You all right?"

Goat Cheese? Are you kidding me?

"I'm okay, but could you maybe give me a lift to The Fountain?"

He squinted at me over the top of the driver's-side door. "Yeah. I reckon."

Once I joined him, Goat Cheese puttered along the road at an old man's pace, and I struggled to keep from slamming an imaginary accelerator into the floorboard in front of me. "Think we could go faster?"

"We could." The truck, however, did not speed up.

We passed the volunteer fire station and the Long place. I envisioned Romy waiting for me at the bar, her face sad.

"It's important."

"That so?"

"Yes."

Goat Cheese pushed down on the gas, accelerating from thirty miles an hour to a solid forty.

"Quit your finger tapping," Goat Cheese said around his cigarette. I hadn't even realized what I was doing.

"What do you think of Romy Satterfield?" Where had those words come from? It wasn't any of *his* business. *He* didn't know we were in the middle of a father-son talk.

He snorted. "A girl like that? I think you'd better go kiss the ground she walks on and hope she doesn't leave your sorry ass for that rich guy."

"Think I could do right by a girl like her?"

"Hell, you're the only McElroy I could ever stand. And I've known a lot of McElroys."

Goat Cheese pulled into The Fountain's parking lot, having to park at the edge because there were so many people. I jumped out before the truck stopped moving but knocked on the window. He fumbled for the control on the driver's-side door but eventually got it to roll down.

"I owe you one. Oh, and glad we could have this little chat, Dad," I said.

Goat Cheese's eyes went wide, and he almost choked on his cigarette. I left him to hack up a lung and puzzle it all out while I ran for The Fountain in the hopes I could make things right between Romy and me.

Romy

"Last call," Genie said into the microphone at the DJ's booth. "Bill's kicking us out in ten."

Good thing I'd only managed to snag one beer, since I was about to drive myself home. Alone.

Someone tapped me on the shoulder, and I pasted on a smile, steeling myself for whichever idiot had the audacity to disturb me when I clearly wanted to nurse a beer by myself.

My heart refused to function at the sight of Julian. I leaned forward from my stool ready to embrace him when the rational part of me remembered just how late he was. No way was I letting him off the hook that easily. "You're late."

He winced and mumbled something I couldn't hear over Prince's "1999." "What was that?"

"It was my damned alternator!" he shouted just as the song ended.

I spewed my beer, my heart hammering against my chest.

When I looked back at Julian, he had lowered himself to one knee and was holding out his mamaw's ring. "Rosemary Jane Satterfield, would you do me the honor of being my wife . . . again? The right way, this time?"

At this point the whole bar had stopped what they were doing to see what was going to happen next.

"I don't know," I said. "What's in it for me?"

"I figure at least ten years of me groveling and some toe-curling sex." He grinned. I found it hard to breathe.

"Are you going to get rid of that farmer's tan?"

"I guess." He hadn't expected that question.

"Will you marry me properly over at County Line with *my* minister?"

His grin faded to something more serious. "For you? I'd do anything."

"Like drive a truck with a reliable alternator? You know, a Ford?"

"Whoa! Let's not get carried away."

I fought the smile as best I could. "Julian McElroy, I'll keep you, Chevy and all."

He slipped the ring back on my index finger and stood to give me a kiss that brought whistles from our classmates. "I guess I'd better give you that dance before it's too late."

He led me to the center of the sawdust-strewn floor. The DJ had started a slow pop song, but he cut it off mid-lyric. I thought we were too late for our long-awaited dance, but then I saw Genie bend over to whisper in his ear. He fumbled with his laptop before going to the microphone. "Ladies and gents, here's our couple who's actually been married longest: Mr. and Mrs. McElroy!"

"You going to correct him about your name?" Julian whispered.

"Are you?"

"Not today, but how would you feel about being a Ledbetter?"

"What?"

"Long story." He pulled me close as the opening strains of "Islands in the Stream" began to play. Ben and Genie danced together not far away, but there was a hint of space between them. A crowd had gathered around Jim Price, who was giving money to Beulah. It wasn't even her class reunion, but I was glad to see her since I'd heard she was the only one to bet we were going to make it. Price looked up and yelled, "Hey, Romy, did you hit him on purpose the other day?"

"Nope."

Price swore and stomped his foot. More money exchanged hands.

Shelley Jean appeared at my side, dragging future husband number four to dance beside us. She leaned over to whisper, "Remember what I told you."

Julian flinched.

I stage-whispered back, "He doesn't have that problem with me."

She started to say something more, but her partner wisely guided her to another section of the tiny dance floor. Julian leaned in, his voice humming deliciously in my ear. "Are you about done?"

"What fun is a high school reunion if you can't cause a little trouble?"

He gave me that one-sided smirk, and I traced the thin white scar on the bottom of his chin before laying my head on his shoulder. Kenny and Dolly proclaimed they were islands in the stream, and I let myself think only of Julian as we swayed across the floor.

The song faded away and Julian muttered, "Finally!" under his breath.

"Wanna give them something to talk about?" he asked with a grin and a hint of the cocky teenage boy he'd once been.

I took the bait. "Why not?"

He cradled me into his arms so quickly I squeaked. And hoped my underwear wasn't showing. "Julian!"

"Hush, woman. We've got thresholds to cross!"

"My purse!"

Julian whirled me around. Genie handed me the small se-quined bag, and I wrapped my arms around his neck.

Over his shoulder, I saw her smile as Ben leaned over to kiss her cheek. As we went out the door, I heard Price calling for bets on how long we'd last this time, but there weren't any takers.

All these years I'd thought we were Romeo and Juliet while wishing we were Beatrice and Benedick. But Julian and I had never been neatly comedy or tragedy. As I twirled his mamaw's ring, it hit me: We were a problem play, more like *All's Well That Ends Well.*

And with all that bitter past, I couldn't help but look forward to the sweet.

Fried Okra

1 pound fresh okra
½ cup cornmeal
½ teaspoon onion powder
⅛ teaspoon black pepper
½ cup vegetable oil

Cut the stems off the okra and then cut each pod into pieces—
about a half inch. Mix cornmeal, onion powder, and black pepper
in a bowl that has a lid. Dump okra into the bowl, put the lid on,
and shake your groove thing—and the okra—until it's coated.
Heat vegetable oil in a skillet—cast iron is always best. Dump the
okra, but not the excess breading, into the oil and cook and stir it
on medium heat until golden brown, about ten minutes? Fifteen
minutes? As my father would say, "Until it's done." Fish okra out
of the oil and put it in a paper towel–lined bowl for serving.

*This isn't the super-pretty batter-covered okra you're used to seeing,
but it's tasty and quick.*

Tea Cakes

2 cups sifted self-rising flour
1 cup sugar
2 eggs
⅔ cup shortening (we usually use vegetable oil)
1½ teaspoons vanilla

Preheat the oven to 400 degrees Fahrenheit. Mix ingredients.
Work enough flour into dough to be able to roll it out. Cut with
cookie cutter or the rim of a glass. Bake on greased baking sheet
for 6–7 minutes. (I have a note that it took 8 in the electric oven.)

*This is my mother's recipe for tea cakes, and they are delightful. I would
love to share my granny's recipe in which they come out a little more like
shortbread, but she took that recipe with her to the grave. I'd be willing
to bet lard was involved.*

Acknowledgments

Time to round up the usual suspects! As always, thanks to my agent, Nikki Terpilowski, of Holloway Lit, and my editor, Peter Senftleben. I could not ask for better folks to take care of me. Thanks to Kensington for yet another gorgeous cover; and to Paula; and to Monique Vescia, for keeping me on my toes with the grammar and the time lines and all the things, really. Special thanks, too, to Alison Law, who helped me with book one and has helped me with many authorly things since.

Thanks and love to the entire Kilpatrick clan, but especially Ryan and the kids for letting me be more Jessica Fletcher than June Cleaver—well, without all the murders to solve. Thanks, kids, I promise to go lighter on the frozen pizza, rotisserie chicken, and sweet potatoes next time. Thanks to Ryan's parents, who are keeping the kids as we speak, and my parents, who will have a turn with the "babies" while I'm at a conference this summer. I wouldn't be able to do what I do without all of you or without your very generous support, and I love you! Oh, and Ryan? Thanks for being my Benedick.

I am also deeply indebted to all of the sharp sets of eyes that have read this story and all of the brilliant minds who have dissected it. Thanks, Tanya Michaels, for reading on even after I decided to make this story alternating first person. Sorry about all those head-desk incidents. Thanks to Romily Bernard and Jenni McQuiston, who, in addition to the usual writing advice, made sure I kept my cows and horses straight. Gratitude to Anna Steffl for many run-throughs and for helping me keep my characters true to their nature. Props to my beta readers: Mom, Janette, Gretchen, Ryan, and Cindy. I think that's everyone. If I missed you, then, in true Fountain tradition, I owe you a cold one.

I need to thank some folks for help with the research side of things. Per usual, if you spot a problem, it's all my fault and not theirs. It's possible I took some liberties for, er, narrative flow. Thanks, Daddy, for your knowledge of husbandry, i.e., answering all sorts of cow questions that you didn't want to hear. Hey, and thanks for giving me my own cow way back when. Rest in peace, Bambi, you were a sweetheart.

Thanks to Steven Salcedo, John Marchese, Jane Kurtz, and Heather Leonard, all of whom have tried their very best to teach me what I need to know about the law and lawyers. They have *tried*, y'all. My poor characters probably need a lawyer on retainer, someone permanently dedicated to their escapades. Alas, neither my characters nor I can afford it.

Thanks to Cinthia Hamer and Cheryl Perlmutter, who both talked me through protocol and treatment of dog bites. No dogs were permanently harmed in the making of this story. Well, except for the tripod beagle, but I'm happy to report she's up and around and perfectly happy.

Speaking of dogs, would it be a first if I thanked a character for taking care of a problem I absolutely agonized over? Thanks, Pete Gates, for taking on those poor, mistreated pit bulls. It wasn't their fault; Curtis made them do it. I feel much better knowing that you're going to rehabilitate them.

A hearty thank you to all of my English teachers and professors, especially those of you who taught me Shakespeare. Ms. Highers gave me *Romeo and Juliet*. Mr. Bryant introduced me to *Julius Caesar*, and Ms. Kelley gave us *Hamlet*. I'm not forgetting you, Ms. Keller. There's a hint of American romanticism, don't you think? I even threw in a little Thoreau reference.

As always, thanks to all my folks in Georgia Romance Writers and my other writer colleagues, too. Thanks also to Suja Kallickal for taking in Her Majesty as one of her own so I can get work sent to those colleagues!

All of my love to West Tennessee and little ol' Chester County. Read between the lines and sometimes on them to see all the things I love about where I grew up. Sure, I had to add some bad guys so we'd have a story, but there's no prettier place than home. And, no, none of these characters are based on real people, although I did borrow a few phrases from James Harvey for Hank.

Finally, but most importantly, thank you to anyone who's picked up one of my books and taken the time to read it. If your to-be-read pile looks anything like mine, I know you have a lot of books to choose from. It means a lot to me that you would choose one of mine. As Flannery O'Connor once said, "Success means being heard. . . . The act of writing is not complete in itself. It has its end in its audience."

So, my deepest gratitude to everyone in the audience.

BITTERSWEET CREEK

Sally Kilpatrick

ABOUT THIS GUIDE

The following discussion questions are
included to enhance your group's reading of
Bittersweet Creek.

Discussion Questions

1. *Bittersweet Creek* began as a sort of homage to *Romeo and Juliet*, with a dash of the Hatfields and the McCoys. How many references to Shakespeare did you run across? (Hint: Some are from other plays.)

2. The Satterfields and the McElroys are opposites in a lot of small ways (dogs versus cats, for example). How many little differences can you remember between the two families? Do those differences really mean a lot in the scheme of things?

3. Another theme of *Bittersweet Creek* is the idea that tradition is being passed over in favor of modernization. Richard sees no problem with selling the Satterfield farm. Romy has an unnatural attachment to her Keurig coffeemaker. Do you think the rural way of life is disappearing? Do you see it as a good or a bad thing?

4. Julian has watched a lot of movies in order to pass the time. How many allusions did you catch?

5. Why do you think Romy fell in love with Richard? In what ways do Richard and Julian represent city versus country life? Do you think she made the right choice?

6. In what ways is this a story of Romy finally overcoming the grief of losing her mother?

7. How would you describe Romy's relationship with her father? How was her relationship with her parents different from that of Julian and his parents?

8. Julian worries about his "McElroy blood," and *Bittersweet Creek* explores the idea of nature versus nurture. Which do you think plays the greater role in who we are and why?

9. Why do you think Debbie stuck with Curtis as long as she did? Should she have?

10. A lot of this book centers around animals. What does a person's treatment of animals say about him or her as a person? How do the attitudes of the characters who grew up with animals differ from those of characters who did not grow up around animals?

11. Which was your favorite flashback of when Romy and Julian were teenagers in love? Why?

12. Does *Bittersweet Creek* make you nostalgic for the country or does it make you want to run screaming for the city? Why?

13. Who's your favorite character? Least favorite?

14. "Islands in the Stream": Great duet, or . . . the *greatest* duet?